MOUNTING DESIRE

MOUNTING DESIRE

A Novel

Nina Killham

BLOOMSBURY

Published by Bloomsbury Publishing, New York and London

ISBN 1-58234-501-5

Printed in the United States of America

To my parents and their everlasting romance

Chapter One

I T'S NOT EASY being a virgin, Jack Carter thought as he leaned against the reception desk of the Venice Beach police station. His hair was matted against his neck, his shirt torn, his shoes muddied beyond recognition. For years women had been trying to seduce him. And for years they had failed, despite some truly heroic efforts. A few had even suffered injury. Muscle spasms, heart failure, drive-by shootings. Of course, no one had actually died before.

"Occupation?"

"Romance writer."

The police sergeant looked up, saw Jack wasn't kidding, and looked down again.

"Age?"

Jack paused. "Thirty-five."

"Relation to the deceased?"

"Date. It was our third date."

"Which is why she was naked?"

"Well, yes, I suppose so."

"Sign here."

Jack leaned forward and signed. He could feel the man staring at him. He knew he was the least likely character to be at a lurid scene like this. He should be slicking back his hair, a ladies' man with a nasty set of excuses, not your average Joe look-alike who lived his professional life under a woman's name.

The sergeant sucked his teeth. "We'll call you if we need anything else."

"Should I call her parents, or . . .?"

"We'll do the honors."

"Thank you."

The sergeant leaned back and eyed him.

"That was a pretty dangerous stunt she was trying to pull off."

"I thought it was charming."

Jack stepped out into the wet air. It was two in the morning, the end of September. The lights of Venice Beach shone bright against rain-slicked streets. He pulled his hood down low over his eyes, shoved his hands into his pockets, and walked off alone toward home. A foolhardy thing to do at this hour—but then, he wasn't thinking too clearly.

Because it had happened again. Expectations colliding like two atoms on the same track. And it wasn't as if he hadn't warned her. He had laid it on the table, as he did for all his dates, telling her his desire not to get involved, you know, sexually.

"You're kidding."

It seemed such an outrageous thing. No sex. He was a guy, for Christ's sake: He was supposed to fall to the ground, jackhammer ready, if a woman so much as glanced his way.

"But you look so normal."

It was true that Jack's dark brown hair, dove-gray eyes, and medium build did suggest generic branding. But underneath those winged eyebrows, he would argue, lay unplumbed depths.

"Are you religious or something?"

2

No. Religion had nothing to do with it.

"Well, what, then?"

Love, he'd say. True love. I'm waiting for true love.

"True love?"

Their eyes would crinkle, their mouths gape open, and he would usually have to remove their cappuccinos before they started banging their heads down on the table with mirth.

Jack always tried to smile and dismiss them with a wave of his hand. Destiny, he believed, was such a personal thing, and he knew his lay with one woman. A woman to whom sex meant something more emotional than a good scratch.

Because "Love 'em and leave 'em" seemed to be the motto of the day. He could not even remember the number of times he'd woken up after a passionate bout of lovemaking, during which he had offered the deepest part of himself, only to find his mate tiptoeing out of the house without a backward glance. Jack would lean on one elbow, sheets tangled around his hairy legs, sleep still in his eyes, and call out: "But when will I see you again?" And the reply would come back, cool and airy: "Give my secretary a call."

Then one night . . . it still hurt to remember . . . he met Serena. She was a friend of a friend and had possibilities. Nice job, funny. Not a great beauty, but in possession of a fabulous set. She was the most promising woman he had met since his crushing divorce a couple of years before. They met for a movie, brought home takeout, and talked until the moon moved to the edge of the sky. God, she was everything he wanted: lovely, kind, curious. And when she reached for him, he was already forming the memories to tell their children, making jokes about the Chinese food, remembering the exact color of the moon. He poured his soul into that moment, molding it for posterity. He gave her everything he had, fine-tuning his responses until she

3

was blind and shaking. And when they had cried out into each other's ear, he buried his face deep into her neck like a weather-beaten ship finally in safe harbor.

"Wow," she said when she had found her voice, "are you a good fuck."

Without a word, he disentangled himself, pulled on his clothes, and walked out the door. That night he became a born-again virgin. A bit extreme perhaps. But what was a man to do? He'd been nice, he'd been civilized, and he'd been thoroughly screwed.

So no more Wham, bam, thank you, sir. He was going to remain celibate until he discovered a woman who would keep her hands to herself until she committed to him. And only when they had grown to love and trust each other would they lie down together and allow their passion to combust into a raging physical blaze.

Of course, all this required that he get to know his dates. And, apparently, sometimes, their next of kin.

"She made mincemeat of your rhododendrons."

Jack looked up as he approached his house to find old Mr. Winston sitting on the front steps, drinking from a brown paper bag. Mr. Winston lived next door, in the top-floor apartment, and wasn't allowed to loiter in the garden below, so he spent a lot of time keeping Jack's steps warm. Jack didn't mind. It gave his house a lived-in look, and on those nights he didn't want to drink alone, he opened his door to an instant companion. Jack observed the tangled mash of purple blossoms where the body of his latest date had come to rest.

Mr. Winston eyed him. "You okay?"

"I feel bad for her family."

Mr. Winston nodded. "She looked like a nice lady."

4

"She was."

"Maybe you shouldn't have told her."

"Maybe," Jack said as he fished in his pocket for keys. But he didn't like to lie. How can you find true love if you begin a relationship under false pretenses? Which is why he was always truthful to his dates about what he did for a living.

"You're a what?" they'd say and he would have to nod and endure their stunned stares. Because whether they appreciated it or not, he liked women. He liked their flicker-ready smiles, their softness, the lightness with which even the heaviest woman took up the space around her. He liked their tenacity, their flexibility, their disarming willingness to laugh at themselves. And because he liked them, he had listened to them for years with a sympathetic ear, to their woes, their dreams, their fantasies. And with what he had learned he had turned himself into a small publishing wonder: a successful male romance writer.

So he'd list his latest titles (*The Rusty Rake, Withering Heights, Sweet and Sour Love*) his awards (the Rita, the Holt, and thirteen heady weeks on the *New York Times* best-seller list) his pseudonym (Celeste d' Arcy) and his mission statement (writing the skirts off any heroine and making it his business to have the results be as achingly satisfying as possible).

He filled his tales to order with raging literary alpha males who tantalized deserving females until they begged for mercy. These men had made Jack a very comfortable living. Shane Masters, plantation owner with a lurid past, paid for his house in Venice Beach. Gaston Drake, rogue trader with an appetite for virginal young brides, filled it with antiques. And Beau Honoré, pirate of the Indian seas, who reduced his female prey to emotional jelly, purchased the BMW Montauk motorcycle in front of it.

The trouble always began when his dates bought one of his

books. One skim through and they were salivating. Oh, the techniques he must know, they thought as they escorted him through the rituals of a few more dates—lunch, after-work drinks, dinner. Oh, the insatiable appetite he must have, they thrilled, biding their time until they were let into his secret chambers. He would watch them counting the minutes, running the paces, doing their utmost not to rush, not to be obvious. But then, slaves to their prehistoric selves, they would strike. It had become all too predictable. Sane women in tailored suits pulling out handcuffs and pointing to dog-eared pages from his book, their eyes clearly running the odds that his body would pretzel in a similar way.

But Mr. Winston was right. It all had to stop. Women were getting hurt. Janet, that nice if persistent entertainment lawyer, had strained a groin muscle trying to wow him, and required surgery. Antoinette, that cute financial advisor, took him for what she hoped would be a revving top-down cruise through her old neighborhood of Watts and got clipped in a turf war. Teresa, his English sub-agent, slipped on her marble foyer trying to get a satisfying grip and required twenty-four stitches.

And finally, Frederika, who had been so agreeable and sweet the first two dates but who arrived for date number three this evening with a battered copy of *The Earl and the Sex Slave* and a distinct lack of underwear. Flashes of the evening came back to him: the musk ox perfume, the bottle of blush wine that tasted like a pack of Chiclets, the purple scarf she had drawn from her pocket like a magician's assistant. Jack had tried to be amenable, tried to ignore the fact that the evening was quickly turning into a possible police report. The more frenzied she got, the more tired he became. Small yawns kept escaping from his lips until, possessed with the ambition of thrilling him, Frederika had climbed onto his bedroom balcony, her sails at full mast. The railings were slippery this time of the year, what with the rain they'd been having, but Jack never had a chance to tell her that.

Mr. Winston drained the last of his bottle and stood up unsteadily. "You shouldn't feel bad. It's a known fact. Women don't have our spatial acuity."

Jack opened his door. "Good night."

Mr. Winston headed for the gate. "Sleep tight. Don't let those ladybugs bite."

Jack watched to make sure Mr. Winston got to his door in one piece, then closed his own door and climbed up the stairs to his solitary bedroom. It never ceased to amaze him how the more he yearned for connection, the more the universe doubled up with laughter.

The next morning Jack was up at work as usual. Because nothing, not even an accidental fatality, stood in the way of his discipline. He stood in the bathroom, still wet from his shower, wielding his MACH3 turborazor. He then drew on his lucky silk robe, took a deep breath, and opened the door. He was ready.

His bedroom glowed from the flickering candles he had lit over his mantel. On the stereo, Ravel tortured himself sweetly in rising melodies. Jack sat down at his computer and arched his thick fingers over the keys like a pianist.

"Primrose, my love."

His lips reached down and enveloped Primrose in a fire of passion. Primrose clung to him like a rising tide as he searched her depths and she responded . . .

Jack wiped a drop of sweat from his brow. He plunged in again.

"Stop . . . stop," Primrose whimpered, pressed against his manhood. But Guy couldn't. He was beyond reason now. He loosened her pelisse . . .

"Oh, not the pelisse again."

Jack looked up. Primrose reclined on his chaise longue, her tender, bee-stung lips in a pout. "It's so early-nineteenth-century."

Jack stopped typing. "You *are* early-nineteenth-century."

"And it's hell on my sex life."

Jack regarded the imaginary vision before him. Primrose Dubois. His plucky firecracker of a governess, who was about to be consumed like an after-dinner mint by the man of the house. She was to be his greatest invention yet. He could already hear the reviews. Jane Eyre with sex appeal. Emma without restraint. Juliet with a happy ending. She would enter the lexicon of love, a legend in her own time. An unforgettable heroine. But unfortunately, as he'd come to learn over their acquaintance, she was the laziest creature he'd ever come across.

Primrose yawned and stretched like a cat. "Let's take a break."

"No, now, come on. I've got to get this first draft down."

Primrose sighed. "All right; where were we?"

"Let's see, you had your hand . . ."

"Like so?"

"Guy," she implored as she clung to him. "Don't, don't, do, do . . ."

"Stop, stop."

Jack stopped. "What now?"

Guy, immaculate in a spotless cravat over a plum brocade waistcoat, his skin-tight pantaloons outlining an impressive swelling where his manhood would have been if he were real, pinned Primrose to her seat.

"Do you know how many petticoats she's got on? How can I possibly ravish her if I've got about a half hour of unbuttoning before she feels remotely threatened?"

Jack scratched his chin and considered this. "Maybe you could surprise her while she's taking a bath."

"He'd have to slay several servants on his way up the stairs," Primrose pointed out.

"So what do you suggest?"

Guy unwound himself from Primrose's petticoats. "To tell you the truth," he said, "that's not even the real problem."

"What's the real problem?"

"Perky little Primrose. She's about as enticing as a broom."

Jack was stung. "She's strong, accomplished, and gorgeous!"

"And willowy, with big bazooms. Yes, I admit, if she splayed herself right out and it was easy access, I wouldn't say no, but I'm not gonna alternately pillage and grovel for two hundred pages."

Jack observed his creation coolly. Guy Courage: blazing blue eyes, tall, slim hips tapering into long muscular legs, a chest like molded armor, a jaw to crack a nut with . . . the ideal romantic hero. If a bit on the difficult side.

"My character wouldn't say that."

"Of course he would."

"Your research is shoddy."

"Oh, just shut up and get on with it."

Guy grinned and fell upon Primrose, who groaned with pleasure. Jack plunged in again. Cravats, laces, and buttons were flying when the phone rang. Jack glared at it.

"Hello?" he finally answered.

"Jack."

9

"Kate." He should have known. His older sister seemed to have a sixth sense in her knack for breaking his concentration.

"What are you doing?" she asked.

"I'm working."

"Did you get a job?"

"I'm writing."

"Oh, that. Melissa Adams says hello, she read another one of your . . . things."

"Books."

"I don't like the way she smiles when she talks about you."

"Maybe she liked it."

"Hmmm. Anyway, you've got to do something about Mom."

"She's just trying to make friends."

"She's going to get an STD."

"That's unlikely."

"That's what the manager said."

"Well, it's nobody's business."

"Of course it's our business. We can't have her screwing her way out of that retirement home. Do you want her to live with you?"

"All right. I'll talk to her."

"Good."

Jack hung up and looked at his keyboard. The "E" and "H" were wearing off. Were they the most used letters in the alphabet? He backtracked through his work, amazed at how "h" was hidden in all sorts of words: "that," "the," "there," "oh," "hung," "hard," "hot" . . . Jack sighed. It was no use. The magic was gone. He stood up.

Primrose groaned. "Oh, you're not giving up already?"

"I'm hungry."

"What about your deadline?"

"Okay, then, where were we?"

"Penetration."

"You wish," Jack said, and shut his computer.

"Couldn't you just do it?"

Jack's therapist, a small, rounded man named Simon, raised his hands to the heavens. "Do people have to die?"

Simon had spent weeks coaching Jack for his latest date, running him through the maze of options, helping him visualize the moment of impact.

"The police said it wasn't my fault. She slipped."

"Your virginity has a body count."

Jack held a can of lemon iced tea to his forehead. "I'm feeling attacked here. I'm feeling unsupported."

When Jack first started going to Simon, at his mother's insistence, Simon had been an earnest young man who wore corduroy suits. Now he was a single father of two boys who kept him up at night with their preschool studying.

At the initial consultation he had run Jack through every test and had frowned at the resulting reams of paper, which he said described Jack to a T. He then folded his hands over the notes and said, "Well . . . we have a lot of work to do." Three years later, Simon's book, *The Dark Side of Born-Again Virginity*, was published to great acclaim. It called Jack a repressive sexual psychotic with castration fears.

Jack still preferred the term "hopeless romantic."

"It just seemed premature," Jack finally said.

"We've talked about this before. The third date is what we call the window of opportunity. You wait too long, and then it's closed. Very hard to crack it open again."

"I did all the things you suggested. I breathed really slow. I took a long, sensuous bath, drank two big glasses of wine. But when she reached for me I just . . ." He trailed off.

"What?"

"Looked at her."

Simon tapped his pen. "And . . . ?"

"And saw . . ." Jack stopped.

"And saw?"

"Nothing."

"Nothing."

"She wasn't the one."

"How do you know?"

"I just know."

"Well, maybe she doesn't have to be the one. Maybe you just have to grit your teeth and do it."

Jack thought a second, taking it under advisement.

"Why?"

"Oh, God, Jack, we've been through this before. You're becoming a social deviant!"

"I just don't see what the big deal is."

"People just do it. Remember, sex is normal."

"Is it? Everyone is so weird about it. Last night I saw this ad for a car. It had all these women's butts waving in my face and this man crooning, 'Shake your ass, shake your ass.' Tell me, what does an ass have to do with a car?"

"Sex sells."

"Why does sex sell?"

"Because people want it?"

"Do they? My sister is obsessed because she has no libido. She doesn't want it and she's obsessed with the fact that she doesn't want it. Sometimes I want to yell at her: Relax. You don't want it. Your husband doesn't seem to want it. Looks like you've got it made. Why don't you build an empire with the time you've got left over? But no, she's read every book on the subject. She's popping ginseng pills like jelly beans."

"Well, that's a very different area."

"From what we're trying to do here, right?"

"Right."

"But I think it's exactly the same area. Wouldn't it be nice if everybody went about their business without sex screaming at them from every angle? Toothpaste will give you shinier, sexier teeth. Eat Super Cereal Plus for that sleek, sexy body. Drive that shake-your-ass car to work. Drink that Diet Coke on your coffee break and drool over the poor window cleaner. You know, I just saw an ad that showed this woman having an orgasm while she was using Drāno."

"It's what the market bears."

"I hate that phrase."

"Are you saying that your virginity is a political statement?"

"No. I'm saying who needs to have sex anymore? Who needs to see a female body anymore? Or a male one. We've got naked bodies draped all over the place. Everyone is grunting and groaning all around me. I just want everyone to shut up about it." He paused. "I want people to be a little more discreet."

"Jack, first it was an abstinence thing, then it was a men's-movement thing, and now it just seems to be a thing."

Jack shrugged.

Simon sat back and sighed deeply. "Are you really going to wait until you meet this true love of yours?"

"Yes."

"How will you know she's your true love? Is she going to have a secret handshake?"

"I'll just know."

13

"What if she never shows up?"

Jack swallowed uncomfortably. He stared balefully around the room he had been coming to for almost five years.

"So you think I should just do it."

"And put us out of our misery? Yes." Simon closed his notebook and stood up. "Jack, I'm afraid I'm going to have to call it quits."

"What? Why?"

"I don't have the insurance. When people start getting hurt I tend to draw the line."

Jack was speechless.

"I'm really sorry, Jack, but there's nothing I can do for you."

After his initial shock, Jack left his shrink's office calmly and made his way down Main Street in Santa Monica to his favorite bar for a drink. Because he remained optimistic. Defiant, in fact. He would show them. He would show them all. One day, he would find his woman. A woman who would appreciate his restraint. Surely there was a woman out there who still believed in restraint?

Chapter Two

"HI, MY NAME is Molly and I'm a sexaholic."

"Hi, Molly!" the whole room crooned.

"I've been sexually sober for"—Molly glanced at her watch—"approximately seventy-five minutes."

They nodded at her, impressed. After her spiel, Molly retreated to the back row of her weekly Sex and Love Addicts meeting. It was held every Thursday night, between Overeaters Anonymous and Web Design for Profit, at Our Lady of Sainted Palms. The meetings were court-mandated, so Molly had to show up. And show up she did, sitting with the others, fiddling with her foam cup, and listening to much more than she was prepared to hear. But that's what they were supposed to do. Talk and listen. For however long it took until the last sad case had his or her say.

Last time, one of the moderators had lectured about the difference between ejaculation and orgasm. He came in with charts and tapes of guys coming. Some of the men seemed to know what he was talking about, and by the end, they were so raring to pursue the big O that Molly wasn't sure the topic was such a wise idea. She could tell the moderator wasn't so sure either when the whole group exited, salivating, into the night. That was the problem with SLAs. They'd find any excuse.

Molly hunched down in the back row and tried to look inconspicuous. It had all been a misunderstanding. She was not like these people. These people had problems. Serious problems. Ever heard of an acrotomophiliac? Gets a hard-on at the sight of an amputee. What kind of sicko is that? No, Molly marked her problem down to enthusiasm. When she liked a man, she liked to offer body as well as soul. In fact, she usually insisted on it. And, okay, so she liked a lot of men. A couple a week, with great abandon. But was that a reason for her to be sitting here, unemployed at thirty, listening to Julio, three seats down, describe why Dunkin' Donuts really turned him on?

Her problems had started two weeks earlier, when she was fired. As much as she'd tried to blot it out, she could still dimly visualize her boss's flabby, smug face. And the security guards standing too close while she filled her cardboard box. And the secretaries with eyes bigger than golf balls. And all her former colleagues so suddenly preoccupied in their glass-walled offices.

After that, all she could recall from the day was the look on the liquor store man's face when she plunked down $100 for a chilled bottle of Dom and offered to share it and herself with him.

Well, she wasn't going to let it set her back. She just needed to get back out there. Call around. Get her name in circulation. She flicked open her Palm Pilot. Yahoo! had tried to recruit her two years before. They'd be her first call. News traveled fast, so she had to move faster. But she had to get her spin right. She stopped, stumped a moment. How do you spin sexual harassment?

Darryl the moderator looked up. "May I remind you to please pay attention while others are sharing. Molly?"

Molly sighed and put away her Palm Pilot. Darryl finally stood up, drawing one long and tortuous experience/fantasy to a close. "Tom, Tom, maybe next time you could cut back on the . . .

16

adjectives." He clapped his hands. "All right, people, I think we've heard from everyone. It's time for our Seventh Tradition. While we pass the basket, do we have any announcements from the secretary?"

"Gary is having a Halloween party next month. Come as your favorite lay. Kidding. Come as your favorite cartoon character. Same thing, right? Stop, I'm killing myself. But seriously, would anybody like to buy a raffle ticket for Bob's daughter's Shake Your Booty dance team?"

Molly glanced at her watch again. Five-thirty P.M. Ted Bodson from Amazon was usually in the office until eight. Had he heard already? The whole thing was ridiculous. He had to know that. After all, Adam had come on to her. Well, he hadn't said no, anyway. And this thing about her standing in the way of his advancement. The guy had just started, for heaven's sake. She couldn't possibly have promoted him already.

Darryl placed his clipboard back on the desk. "Now, Molly, perhaps you could lead us in the closing prayer?"

The twenty or so people in the room stood up, clasped well-used hands, and began.

"This is fabulous, darling."

Lucinda Burrows, Jack's editor, scanned the first pages of his new manuscript. She gasped. She turned the page. She gasped again. Jack smiled and heaved himself forward to reach for another petit four. He loved meetings with his editor, especially when she flew from New York and invited him to high tea at the Bel Air Hotel and told him how divine he was.

Lucinda pursed her lips. "That Primrose."

"Gorgeous?"

"Devastating."

Jack smiled as if just complimented on his wife's good looks. "I was just wondering, though . . ."

"Too feisty?"

"Well . . ."

"I'll tone her down."

"Maybe just a tad. Good wish fulfillment—pregnant princess bride and everything—but we do have to keep it within the realm."

"Gotcha."

"And Guy, oh, Guy. Be still, my heart."

Jack swiped the last chocolate roll. He knew he was an editor's dream, a writer with talent who could take criticism well. And, more important, take it constructively, actually act on it rather than agree sweetly the way some writers did and then passive-aggressively not change a damn thing. Jack was a professional; courteous, on time and, according to his publishers, a winner. Pity about his gender. Male romance writers just never did get the marketing push behind them. They were hidden behind beautiful pseudonyms and smoke-and-mirrors advertising. Jack had been after Lucinda a couple of years now to let him use his real name. It was a cherished goal: to see the name Jack Carter on the spine of his books. But she always said no:

"Women won't buy them."

"Why not?"

"Put it this way: Would you buy an action thriller by someone named Phyllis?"

Now she leaned back and tossed the manuscript on the table. "You've outdone yourself. It's just great. Definitely saga material."

"You think?"

"Oh, yes. We can fan out four or five."

Jack dunked the chocolate roll into his tea and gave it a good slurp. "Yeah, I was thinking mother, then aunt, then the aunt's aunt, everyone with a deep dark secret that makes her silky cheeks flame."

"Jack, you are just a natural. Who would think that a man would have such insight into our minds?"

Jack shook his head modestly.

"Such perception, such delicacy, such verve." She brushed his hand with hers. He stared down at it.

"Such magnetism." Her voice was thick.

He looked up. Behind Lucinda's chic black owl glasses lay two deep-violet eyes naked in their want. Her lips, frosted to an icy maroon, parted. Her notebook lay forgotten in her lap. Jack edged himself back. He had sensed the increasing interest with which she had started reading his material. Long intimate phone calls about the sexual needs of his heroines. Endless detailed notes about his heroes' secret desires. And this was the second trip to see him personally in as many months. Guy must have sent her over the edge.

Jack cleared his throat. "Lucinda . . ."

"Jack . . ." It came out in a low, soft moan.

Jack closed his eyes. Lucinda Burrows was no one's idea of a pinup, but every cell in his body was raring to go. His self-imposed fast had turned his body indiscriminate. He had the look of a starved man, his eyes often glazed over with need. His tongue stuck to the roof of his mouth as he watched her hand. Nothing like the vibrancy of the female touch: soft, inquisitive, so devastatingly accurate. Sweat sprang from his temples. His breath grew jagged and short. Bells started clanging in his brain as the fast train came pounding up the track. As her hand traveled slowly up his arm, his heart threw itself like a caged animal against his chest.

When her fingers curled around toward his chest, he grabbed her hand. "I don't think this is a good idea."

She looked at him with such disappointment, he winced.

She snatched back her notebook in one smooth move. "I'll expect a quick polish on this manuscript, say by . . . let's see . . . the twentieth? And get me a draft of the next book by . . . oh, let's say January?"

Jack nodded like a good boy.

She popped her notebook back into her bag and stood up on her kitten mules.

"Keep writing, Jack. I'm salivating for the next one."

Jack watched her walk briskly to the doors, which were opened by the doorman with a flourish. She folded herself into a taxi and disappeared. He sat back and grimaced. Every muscle ached, his head pounded, his bulging manhood threatened to explode. His body was thoroughly fed up with him. He tried to make peace with it, ordering it a dark frosty beer.

He'd never expected to do so well. By age thirty, he'd been struggling as a writer for five years with nothing to show but local magazine clippings and a video about how to live with incontinence. Then a woman in a screenwriting course he was taking left a romance novel on her seat. He'd picked it up and stared at the cover, mesmerized. "The Clutch," he later learned the image was called. A brute of a man clutching a semi-naked woman whose curves billowed and strained against his embrace, aching for release. He'd gawked at the cover for a good ten minutes, his body shifting, charged as it had never been charged before. That afternoon, he'd locked himself inside his apartment with the book and a six-pack and had come out feeling as relaxed as if he'd taken a sensible dose of heroin.

Here was a world where honor, love, and passion reigned. Where men thrust, women succumbed, and everyone got their rocks off. The closest word for the feeling he got was "safe." Reassured. Knowing that, in the end, these men and women would find each other, that love would prevail. It was a world where a man could let his guard down, because here was a woman who loved him and would love him for ever and ever.

He started checking out the books from the library. First one or two, hiding them underneath woodworking manuals and computer texts, joshing about the little wife who, in reality, no longer sat at home. Soon he was boldly filling his six-book limit. And when that wasn't enough, he started buying them secondhand on the Internet, searching fanatically for missing books in series. He spent a fortune on eBay tracking down every one of Leigh Greenwood's "Cowboy" books. He loved those. Men being lassoed in love by determined women. His purchases would arrive in plain brown boxes that filled his hall and overflowed into the emergency exit. The neighbors started complaining.

Then one night, after a really bad date, the kind where all that stood between him and a handful of silicone was a tiny trembling button, he came back and created the perfect woman. Naturally she was beautiful, small, almost breakable in her delicacy. But above all she was modest, thoughtful, and resourceful as she was repeatedly flung into circumstances beyond her control.

His first three manuscripts were rejected with tart notes tacked to the first page demanding "Give up, now!" But he persevered. He was editing his eleventh effort when the phone call came about his tenth.

"Celeste d'Arcy?"

Jack was silent, his heart bursting.

"Hello?"

"Yes," he finally managed, trying to keep his voice high.

Lucinda Burrows wasn't fooled. *"You're* Celeste d'Arcy?"

"I'm afraid so."

"I should have known you were a man."

"How could you tell?"

"The heroine has an insatiable interest in her own breasts."

"Will it be a problem?"

"No. No. You'll do. You have a real way with surrender and defeat."

"Thanks."

"Of course, the ending is complete rubbish, but we can fix that. When's the next one available?"

And so he had gone on from there, sliding right into category romances without a blip. He churned them out for a couple of years before making his way to longer single titles. And his readers loved him. They bought his books by the hundreds of thousands, making him a solid best-seller, because he remembered what all six-year-olds know: that all that counts is a happy ending. He plunged his readers deep into the abyss, then cinched them out of the pit of despair just in time. He remembered to make everyone beautiful, except for the bad guys of course. He remembered that the deeper the woods, the bigger the thrills, the meaner the stepmothers, the more saintly the stepdaughters. Most important, he remembered to wave his magic wand at the end and place his heroines triumphantly on the throne, cheeks red with sexual fulfillment.

Across the city of Los Angeles, in Tarzana, Jack's sister, Kate, sat back on the living room sofa, marking up her latest woman's magazine and feeling her heart sink with every scratch she made. She never passed these tests.

Are you and your husband having sex: (a) weekly; (b) monthly; or (c) yearly?

She hesitated between "b" and "c", wanting to put "b" but knowing the truth was closer to "c." She threw the magazine down and closed her eyes. Reading her score would be a mistake. It would tell her in light, flouncy language that if she didn't do something—buy a new negligee, cook oysters in grapefruit sauce, hang from the chandelier, *anything*, for godsakes—her marriage would explode into ice-cold fragments. Sex was paramount, the article would blare, and then list helpful suggestions on how to enliven the old libido, thought up by a twenty-year-old research assistant who was probably banging her two-timing boyfriend twice a day.

She'd tried everything to boost her interest in sex; pelvic squeezes, vitamin E, chanting. She'd even taken to going grocery shopping naked underneath her black shiny raincoat but nothing seemed to work. Her second chakra (the one that was supposedly wired directly to her genitals) remained deader than a lost cat on a four-lane highway.

Kate tossed aside the magazine and took a deep breath. It was time. She stood up with a groan and walked slowly up the stairs.

In her bedroom, her husband, Carl—his belly rising like a beluga whale from the depths of their bed—leafed through a mechanics magazine. Kate slid into bed with her socks on and tucked herself in.

Carl gazed at an ad for a Porsche 911, his eyes sliding along its long, sleek hood.

"Door locked?" he inquired.

"Yup."

"Killer of a day," he noted.

"Hmmm." Kate closed her eyes.

23

"You tired?"

Kate's eyes opened. There it was. The plea. "Please, please come out to play." All she had to do was make the move. Place a hand. Any hand. Anywhere. And the ball would be in play. But weariness enveloped her like a heavy wool blanket. She glanced at the clock. If she fell asleep now she'd have seven whole hours.

"A bit," she said.

Carl glanced at her. She stared straight ahead.

"Good night," he said.

"Good night," she said, leaning forward and flicking off the light.

Chapter Three

E VERY MORNING WHEN Jack opened the door, he had a fleeting thought that this would be the day when he met his special someone. The one who would complete him, who would yin to his yang, who would place her hand over his and give him a new identity. Every night as he went to bed, he did so slightly disappointed, but still firmly, resolutely optimistic that the next day could be his. That, if he only kept shaving and being a good person, his turn would come.

He believed that the unifying principle of mankind was the simple glue of romance. That the sound of heaven on earth was the steady beat of paired hearts. Which was why his greatest desire was to love and be loved. Forever. Oh, of course he wanted sex. He wanted it in every imaginable position. He wanted it hot, breathless, and peaking to a crescendo. But afterward, he wanted to fall asleep holding hands. He wanted to see the same crinkled face morning after morning over breakfast. He wanted His and Hers electric toothbrushes.

So each morning when he left his house, Jack set out to find a lady to be enamored of. For a knight-errant without a lady, as the great Don Quixote will tell you, is like a tree without leaves, or a body without a soul.

★   ★   ★

Rita Carter glared into her compact, examining the downy fuzz on her jaw.

"There's a man in room 3C," she said.

Jack rummaged through his mother's refrigerator out of habit. The pickings were slim. "A man? Really?"

"Of course he's eighty-five and practically deaf, but he has a fine head of hair and wears late model spectacles. He was ambassador to Liechtenstein."

Jack finally made do with a low-fat wheat germ yogurt and dug in. "Is there an ambassador to Liechtenstein?"

"Of course there's an ambassador to Liechtenstein." Rita primped at her scarlet curls until they swirled around her head like the last streaks of a sunset.

"So? Is he nice? Have you talked to him?"

Rita smiled as she snapped her compact shut. "Talk? Hmmm, no. Not a lot of talk going on."

Jack eyed her. "Where's Stella?"

His mother had been sharing an apartment in a continuing care community with Stella Stevenson, another widow, for six months. Already they grated like chalk on each other's nerves. They'd been bridge partners for five years. Having comported themselves civilly through tangled bids and failed makes, they had thought they'd be perfect roommates. But now the very sight of each other was enough to drive both of them into impotent, spitting rage. They couldn't even play bridge together anymore. And the management had proved to be no help at all. They had signed their leases. They were stuck with each other. The only thing they could do to release themselves was die. So they held their tongues as best they could and sought companionship elsewhere. Rita had her group and Stella had hers, the two gangs of Santa Monica Sweet Endings.

"She's at the beauty parlor. Fat good that will do her. It's ridiculous, primping at her age."

"Is that a new dress?"

Rita sucked in her belly. "Do you like it?"

"It's"—Jack's adjectives were well honed—"kicky."

"Yes, I thought so, too."

Jack relaxed back into an armchair and threw his leg over the other as informally as possible. "So. You settling in okay?"

Rita glanced at him warily. "It's all right."

"Meeting new friends?"

"Friends? No. People I can die with, yes."

"Oh, come on."

"It's what they are. Mrs. McKee goes up and down the elevator all day long just to talk to people. You get in and there's Mrs. McKee. She thinks she's the elevator girl. She even says, 'What floor?' But then you have to push the button anyway because she can't see so well."

"Have you met . . . men?"

"There's one for every ten women. What kind of ratio is that? It was better during the war."

"Kate got a call."

Rita's eyebrows triangulated in pique.

Jack pressed on. "They said that perhaps you were a bit too . . . active."

"Anything is active to you, Jack."

"They just asked that you . . . tone it down."

"And play bridge. Or needlepoint. Jerry Ebstein goes feeling up all the women in aquarobics and nobody makes a peep. I have some late-night drinks and it's the Salem witch trials."

"Now, it's not that bad."

Rita stood up. "I have all this time, I can't get pregnant, I've finally figured out what all the fuss is about, and they want me to knit booties. Well, I won't. And you, coming in here, being their messenger boy. Just because you deny yourself doesn't mean I have to follow. Frankly, Jack, I think you're a freak."

She stomped out of the room.

Jack sighed and made his own way out. He never could deal with drama from his mother. She had a habit of swinging freely from sunny to stormy and back again in a single conversation. So his tactic from early on had been to remain resolutely noncommittal. He held his sangfroid before him like a whip and chair.

"What floor?" demanded the small white-haired woman standing at the back of the elevator.

"Lobby," Jack said, and pushed the button himself.

"Where do you want me to put these?"

The aging repo man with a Willie Nelson beard stood at Molly's bedroom door, his arms filled with her collection of silk kimonos. Molly scratched her bed head. The repo men had come early. A professional trick, no doubt, designed to catch victims still comatose.

"Just dump them anywhere."

The guy raised an eyebrow and let them spill from his arms onto her now bare hardwood floor.

"Could you move?" The other one, younger, better built, stood behind her. He had a large baby bottle tattooed on his forearm. Molly gaped at it, mesmerized.

"Lady."

"All right, all right." She stepped aside. The two men lifted her three-month-old buttery leather couch and carried it out her door. She gazed down at the truck outside and thought that was the last time she spent so much at one store. It was too easy for them to just roll up and take it all away.

"Thanks for the coffee." Willie Nelson stood at her front door.

"No problem."

"You know, you make a payment you can get it all back."

She shook her head. "Nah, should never have bought it."

"Well . . ." he hesitated. Then, not finding anything else appropriate to say to the scantily clad woman in front of him, he left.

Molly gazed around at her empty apartment. Her empty life. It was like watching a painting in reverse. All those colors and textures, all that hard work, lifting off bit by bit until all that was left was a blank canvas.

"What's going on? What happened?" Nick, a former colleague, stood in the bathroom doorway, dripping from the shower. But if there was one thing Molly was not going to do it was admit that after three years of making over $100,000 a year (granted much of it only on paper), she was flat broke.

"I got robbed."

"That's . . . that's incredible. Last night?" He stared down at the rainbow of kimonos. "What are you doing to do?"

She locked eyes with him. "I'm going to need a place to stay."

He glanced at her and then blinked away. "Yeah?" He dipped back into the bathroom. She followed him. "A couple of weeks, so I can sort this out."

He shrugged on his clothes, concentrating fully on finding the right loop for his belt.

"A couple of weeks," she prompted.

"I don't know . . . the funny thing is I was going to talk to you about . . . things."

"Nick . . ."

"I was looking for . . . I don't know about you . . . but I was feeling a bit constrained . . ."

"We fuck on Fridays."

"I know. And it's been great, but . . ."

"Two weeks and I can get it all sorted."

"It's just that my coffee maker? It makes one cup. And the toaster is very temperamental. I can't have someone who doesn't know . . . and Mrs. S., down the hall? She'd flip. The lease expressly says no roommates."

"One week, Nick."

"The YMCA, I hear, is very clean. And so central."

Nick dashed out as if late for a bus. Molly sighed and leaned back against the bare wall. Well, that was Nick. She accepted his shortcomings. Sure, he was a bit self-centered, a tad on the emotional side, but he made a mean pasta carbonara and knew how to move just right when she was on the edge. She'd never expected much more from the men in her life. And they'd never disappointed.

Well, she'd have to figure something out. She gazed around her room and tried not to shiver. Crisis, she reminded herself, was the sign for opportunity as well as panic. But she'd better get going, she thought as she scooped up her kimonos, because she didn't have enough money to cover the next month's rent.

"My friend Molly needs a place," Kate called from her kitchen. "You remember Molly."

"No."

Jack sat in his sister's living room. The walls were painted sky blue trimmed with deep rose pink. A cow skull hung on the wall. BLESS THIS HOME pillows, needle-pointed by Kate in a fit of mid-nineties *This Old House* nostalgia, lay tossed on the couch. Jack examined the family photos, lined up like mug shots. They showed the progression of the family: Kate growing more pinched, her husband, Carl, growing more blank, and Leda, their fourteen-year-old daughter, elongating and morphing into a somewhat unfortunate combination of her parents.

Kate hurried in with coffee.

"You remember. I told you about her. I was her high school counselor—God, was it twelve years ago? She was caught screwing Mr. Hart, the chemistry teacher, her senior year."

She handed Jack his mug, the one with Carl's computerized face gaping out at him. "Well, she just got fired and evicted. I told her she could stay with you."

"You've always been generous with my stuff." One of Jack's first memories was of Kate passing out his baby pacifiers to her addicted kindergarten friends.

"It's just for a week. Two weeks, tops. You've got plenty of room. You won't notice she's there."

"Sure, I will."

"Come on, Jack. You're becoming the hunchback of Notre Dame in that place. You need to socialize more."

"I like space."

"Yeah, well, don't we all? And for God's sake, don't tell her about your thing. You'll scare her."

"My 'thing.'"

"Your celibacy."

"Ah, yes, my thing."

"By the way, are you getting anywhere? Finding your wo-man?"

"No. I'm thinking of getting a fish tank."

Kate set down her coffee and picked up a bowl of what looked like dark green shredded bark and started nibbling.

Jack wrinkled his nose. "What are you eating?"

"Seaweed."

"Why?"

"Aphrodite emerged from the sea."

Jack stared at her, uncomprehending.

"Aphrodite, sea, sex. Hello?"

"Oh."

"Then, of course, there is the similarity of human blood and semen to seawater. Sort of a part scientific, part mythological affinity with our primordial home."

"Right. Gotta go."

"I'll e-mail her your number," Kate called after him. "She'll take it from there."

Jack walked to the door and stopped.

"Whatever happened to Mr. Hart?"

"Mr. Hart?"

"The chemistry teacher. Did they end up together?"

Kate snorted. "No. I think he got divorced and moved to Atlanta. Why?"

"It's just sad. That's all."

"Jack, I say this as your sister, someone who loves you: I think you need to get out more."

When Jack's wife left him, stars shattered in the sky. He came home one day to find that she'd hired a van and cleared everything away, leaving only his large crate coffee table, their orthopedic mattress, and his cat, which she had shaved and hidden in the microwave. You bring out the worst in me, she used to say. She'd say this after a hard day, while he was rubbing her feet and trying to be supportive, keeping all the players in order, her manager at Save the Rhodesian Ridgeback, the manager's sidekick, the boss above her boss. They'd go out to dinner with her cohorts and she'd sit in the car on the way back, her arms crossed and forbidding, saying "You were about as exciting as a paperclip." She'd work, frenzied at the thought of not cutting it, staying up till all hours, making calls to breeders, surfing the Net, reading obscure manuals, looking for the edge. He'd bring her tea and ham sandwiches and close the door quietly and then pad to bed alone, dropping into a long, peaceful sleep until he woke to her tiptoeing in at dawn. And he'd open his arms and she'd curl into them, a small skinny child.

He didn't know what drove her. An unspoken need. But it melded well with his lack of ambition. Despite what his father had once said, the world was not his oyster. He remembered his father taking him out to the backyard long ago and pointing out the moon and saying, "Someday, you'll be up there." Men, he implied, reached the stars, and women looked on in wonder. But there was a distinct lack of looking on in the women he met. They were hell bent. On what, it varied. But they all had a purpose to which he never subscribed. An urgency. In college, his girlfriend bought blue interview suits and landed an entry position at a Big Eight firm before picking up her diploma. Jack graduated two years late and then made grande frappuccinos to order, fooling himself into believing that these experiences would gel into the novel that broke open the psyche of the American male.

When he first met Morgan, on the beach at the Fourth of July fireworks, she was with her friends on the next blanket trying to hit Jack with popping champagne corks. It was the early nineties and she had just returned from a year's travel in Africa. She was broke, wound tight, and abjectly thankful for any physical affection. They inhaled each other at night and then parted like strangers in the morning. He spent his days writing for the *City Paper*, exposing refuse collection mismanagement and the more suspect hobbies of their governor. He wrote, played hacky sack,

33

and surfed at Zuma Beach while Morgan toiled for a better canine world.

Marriage at age twenty-four might have seemed premature, but Jack was intent on showing it could work. Why wait, he'd reply to his head-shaking buddies, when he had found the perfect mate: a best friend and a lover. She mesmerized him to the core. At the wedding, she wore antique silk and a blue lace garter. He wore a secondhand suit, and he cried at the ceremony. They danced with such a frenzy that sweat poured down their faces and bathed their increasingly tactile well-wishers. That night was the happiest night of his life.

Three years later, it was all over. She shrugged him off like last season's fashion. Where did your love go? he asked her over and over in long, anguished letters to which she never replied. Her love had felt so infinite and robust. Like a massive, glorious wave he was happily drowning in. How could it disappear? Oh, he got on with life—he gently released his cat from the microwave and bought secondhand furniture—but still he wondered: Where does all the love go?

Chapter Four

MOLLY STOOD ON Jack's doorstep with two bulging duffel bags slumped next to her.

"Hi," she said.

Jack waved her in. Molly struggled past him with her bags and dumped them on the parquet floor. He stood quietly examining her. So this was Lincoln High's femme fatale. He'd been expecting a thick curtain of hair, an hourglass figure, and cleavage confident enough to shake your hand. But Molly's hair was cut short and twisted into what he could only describe as barbed wire. Her small breasts lay ineffectually behind a tight tank top. Her slightly plump belly was highlighted and punctuated by a gold navel ring.

"Well," he said.

He didn't know how to proceed. In his book, Primrose, who came to stay with her step-uncle on a cold and windy night, had been shown the ropes by the housekeeper and had only met the master of the house later, when she had been broken in, so to speak. Jack looked around and scratched the back of his head.

"You want some coffee?"

"No, thanks."

Jack smiled, relieved. He could get back to work.

"But I could sure use a drink," she said, heading for the living room.

He followed her, his eyes glued to her chunky hips, and watched her recline like an odalisque on his chaise longue. She lifted her chin like a grande dame. "Fancy furniture."

Jack nodded with approval. He'd spent a fortune on that particular piece, having engaged in a bidding war with a Russian oligarch and an Indonesian rock star. "That's a Grecian sofa. It's from the Regency period."

"Is that right?"

He handed her a scotch in a cut crystal tumbler. She raised it in a salute before drinking deeply, then smacked her lips and looked around the room. "God, this place is like a museum."

Jack smiled.

"It's like it's dead or something."

Jack frowned. He poured himself a drink. Molly had hopped up again and was sauntering around. Jack watched her progress, her hips swinging confidently, her shiny eyes catching everything. It was like having a leopard meandering around your living room. A fat one who'd just had lunch. She picked up one of his books from a corner table and flicked through it.

"Kate said you write about sex."

"I suppose so."

"That's funny."

Jack shook his head emphatically. "No. Sex is not funny."

"No?"

"No. Food is funny. You know, kumquats, bananas, baked Alaska. Those are funny."

"But sex . . . ?"

"No."

"I see." She peered at the stuffed bookcases. "Those all your books?"

"One in every translation. So far, twenty-four. Just sold the rights to the Faeroese. I'm pretty proud of that."

Molly's eyebrows raised in interest. "Lot of money in romances?"

"Fair to middlin'." Jack smiled magnanimously. "You like to read?"

"Yeah, I do. Don DeLillo. Jonathan Franzen."

"Oh. Them."

"Now, they're good."

"Personally, I don't get the big deal. They write a book every couple of years and we're supposed to fall over in admiration. I write five books a year."

"You know, I've always thought I had a book in me."

Jack sighed. Molly glanced at the small Regency writing desk in the corner.

"Maybe I'll write a little romance while I'm here," she said brightly.

Jack set down his drink. "Well, I have to get back to work. Your room's upstairs, second on the left. Here are your keys— these two are for the two bolts up top and this one is for the grille and that one is the latch in the middle."

She swung them around her finger. "All righty."

They stood in the hall, facing each other. She looked him up and down and grinned. "So, like, what percentage of your books is sex? Are they at it all the time?"

Jack crossed his arms. He'd heard every joke there was concerning his genre. So he had taken to reciting his publisher's guidelines. "My heroines wait until they have committed themselves fully before unleashing their physical selves."

Molly's mouth fell open. "You mean not until marriage?"

"Commitment leading to marriage. Yes."

Molly snorted with laughter.

"What's so funny?"

"What if they fall in love with someone they don't have good sex with?"

Jack stared at her mouth, at her lower lip which managed to be forbidding and provocative at the same time. "What do you define as good sex?"

"Oh, you know."

"No, tell me, what is it? Sparks? Screaming orgasms? Toe cramping?"

Molly grinned. "That's a good start."

"You guys are like lawn mowers."

"Excuse me?"

"You just plow through us. Leave us cut, bleeding on the lawn."

Molly laughed again. Her skin was smooth, Jack noted, and her hair, for all its razor's edge, still silky. "I hope you enjoy your stay," he said, stepping aside and waving her through like a bullfighter.

Leda, Jack's teenage niece, sat back in her Sexy Babe hot pants and clicked through the channels. There was nothing on. She flipped through the latest issue of her favorite magazine and glanced at the articles: "Hot, Sexy Bed Hair!"; "Sex Ed with Dr. Jude"; "4 Moves to an Amazing Butt"; "Do You Have HIV?" Leda yawned. God, she was bored. There was nothing to do. She'd spent all morning in chat rooms but kept getting pestered by some creep who called himself a twelve-year-old girl from Wisconsin but who couldn't stop talking about penis sizes. A sure tip-off. So lame. He called gel "hair spray." Hello? Flashing lights?

She padded out to the kitchen and popped open a Slim-Fast. It tasted like shit, but at least it kept her mouth busy. There was absolutely nothing for her to do. She'd spent her entire allowance on animal-print thongs yesterday. She'd seen a billboard at the mall of a girl, crouching over, her jeans low, showing off her thong. You could just see her nipples under her shirt. She looked so good. Everyone wanting her. Wouldn't that be perfection, everyone wanting you? So Leda had walked into the store and grabbed three thongs in every animal pattern: tiger, leopard, and zebra.

Now she shifted uncomfortably, trying to ignore the wedgy, and gazed around at the gleaming kitchen. It had recently been remodeled again. All the chrome appliances were lined up like robots: bread maker, ice cream maker, tortilla maker, sandwich griller, blender, super sundae churner.

"Hello, hello." Her mother came bustling in with shopping bags.

Leda gazed at her glumly. "Hi."

"Look, I got you this cute little top. Perfect for a pool party."

"Thanks." Leda let it dangle from her fingertip.

Kate raised her eyebrows. "What?"

"Nothing."

"Come on."

"I'm bored."

"Bored? How can you be bored? You've got every amusement known to mankind. Why don't you paint in the studio we set up for you? Or play with your Barbie chemistry set. Discover a cure for cancer."

"Can we make brownies?"

"Brownies? Are you trying to make me fat?"

"Oh, come on. We haven't done it in ages."

"Oh, I don't know. I just want to sit down. Relax." Kate took her magazines to the couch. "Get me an iced tea, will you?"

"How about a hot chocolate?"

"What has gotten into you?"

"It'll be fun. Hot chocolate. We could watch a video together."

"You watch. I'm reading."

Kate plunked herself down and flipped to the table of contents. "Better Sex," it read. She licked her finger and flipped to page 26.

Leda watched her mom a moment, then made her way upstairs.

"Jack, my man. It's been ages." Richard slapped Jack's shoulder when he walked into Lulu's. Richard already had two empty margaritas on the rocks displayed in front of him. Jack collapsed into the booth and ordered a shot. It was good to get out of the house and Richard, a friend from college, was always good for a few laughs.

Richard worked for a construction and development firm whose latest deal was buying the surrounding hills near Laguna Beach and turning them into one hundred town houses, an industrial park, and a Whole Foods. He himself lived in a high-rise apartment block overlooking the Sherman Oaks Mall. On Friday nights he began happy hour early, drinking three-for-one Sex on the Beach shots until he went howling into the suburban playland, a couple of high school girls teetering on his arm.

"You gotta come with us next time. Geez, these girls. Nobody knew any of this stuff when I was in high school. They're like robots, some of them."

Richard and Jack had played a lot of ball together, laughing one minute, smashing brutally into each other the next. Richard couldn't believe it when Jack finally started earning real money from his books. He'd been so used to Jack being a loser professionally that it had taken some time to adjust. But now they talked investments and tax dodges. Sometimes they didn't talk much at all, just popped open beers and collapsed in front of Sky Sports. When they did go out, Richard liked to use Jack as part of his pickup repertoire—"Hey, come over and meet my friend the virgin."

"So, you notice anything different?" Richard angled his face left and right.

"You've lost more hair?"

"Funny."

Jack peered. Richard's cheeks had swelled into two bronze plums.

"Did you run into something?"

"Nope. Just a little . . . reconstruction."

Jack's mouth fell open.

"A thousand bucks a cheek and worth every penny. I'm thinking next month, some pecs. It's a whole new attitude. It's about being true to myself. Presenting the best me. I've started eating better, getting lots of sleep. I've started getting myself professionally sprayed with tanning lotion. You should try it sometime."

"Right."

"Of course, first time was a disaster. Looked like I'd contracted a bizarre skin disorder. Turns out you're supposed to scrub off all your dead skin cells before spraying, otherwise your tan gets all patchy and obvious. So the next time, I tried a body scrub, and feel my skin, it's fantastic."

He held out a perfectly tanned, manicured hand. "Go on, feel."

Jack leaned back. "I'll pass."

Richard picked up his beer. "You know, you've been looking a little tired lately. And don't say you don't have the time. I use idle moments to tone my buttocks. I clench 'em in the elevator. I do deep knee-bends while I'm waiting for my car to be maximized . . ."

"Could we change the subject?"

"Okay." Richard let out a long, misty burp. "I'm getting married."

Jack was speechless. He had expected man to colonize the sun before Richard tied the knot.

"Can you be my best man?"

"Me?"

"I know I should probably ask Bill, but . . . he's such an asshole, you know?"

"Well, sure, I'd be . . . honored." Is just not the word, Jack thought.

"It's gonna be on the beach at sunset. And when he pronounces us man and wife, I want lots of doves let loose into the sky. Won't that be cool? And then after the party we're going to fly off in a hot-air balloon. How cool is that?"

"Way cool."

"All right." Richard rubbed his hands together.

"So Zara . . ."

"Maryann."

"Maryann? What happened to Zara?"

"She . . . well. I think I'd be better off with a bullet in my head. You know what I mean?"

The thing was, Jack did know what he meant. Zara was one of a kind.

"So, where did you meet her?"

"Church."

Jack laughed.

"No, really. Good place to meet nice ladies. You know, when you're ready. I mean, she's not much in the sack, but she'll be a good mom. I see her with peanut butter sandwiches and glue on her nose. Real sweet."

"Are you sure about this?"

"It's my time, bud."

Jack stared at him. "How did Zara take it?"

"I haven't told her yet."

Jack let out a low whistle.

Molly undressed for bed in Jack's extra bedroom, muttering. She'd been making phone calls all day, looking for work, and all day they had been laying it on thick. Everybody was appalled at her lack of judgment. How could she treat a vulnerable young man like that? On and on it went, until you'd think she'd strapped the guy down to her desk and had her merry way with him. Which was sort of what she did, but he certainly didn't protest. Well, not after she had secured him tightly.

What could she say, she was a woman who liked to work hard and play hard. It relaxed her. Made her forget about all her responsibilities. Of which she had a fair number. Her high-pressured job with its insane hours and bosses who couldn't understand how she knew so much. Her massive school loans. And then there was her younger sister—Molly had to help her out. Which was Molly's pleasure—it was what money was for. But it all led to stress, and sometimes she just needed a release.

Which was how she got tangled up with Adam, her strapping, gorgeous hunk of an assistant. When he walked into her office for the first time Molly didn't know whether to pass out or genuflect. His typing sucked, his phone manner offended, so she put him to work at the only thing he was good at. And things were fine, if a little unfiled, until he got grand ideas and wanted a promotion.

"You just got here."

"I'm thinking the management trainee program."

"You need an M.B.A."

"Maybe we can fudge it . . ."

"Adam, I don't think your future lies in high-risk web management."

He pulled away. "You don't think I can do it."

Molly paused. Adam was in the middle of some serious pleasuring and she didn't want to put him off.

"I'm sure you could do anything you put your mind to."

"Bullshit, I don't think you've ever respected me." He rolled off the hotel bed and shrugged his clothes back on. "Some of us have work to do," he said piously, and walked out.

When the manure hit the fan, Molly found that hell hath no fury like a man scorned. He rallied Human Resources behind him like a Roman battalion and recruited no fewer than three civil rights lawyers (all women, Molly noted) whose dour faces could not help but light up when they were talking about their client. The end came swiftly. Resignation and a lifetime membership to Sex and Love Addicts if she wanted any hope of being employed in the top firms again. Adam joined the management trainee program with a company-paid private tutor and all the Number 2 pencils he needed.

Molly climbed into bed and pulled the covers to her chin. She could hear Jack typing in the room next door. What a strange man. Though very cute, if you liked that absent-minded look— like he was thinking deep thoughts and got off at the wrong exit and was no longer sure what county he was in. Kate had been quite insistent that Molly stay with him. Molly had been all ready to check into a motel down on La Cienega, but Kate had begged her to spend the time at her brother's, practically offering to pay her.

"Why?"

"He could use the company. I think he's going through a hard time."

"What kind of hard time?"

"Controlling, subversive, antisocial. But I'm sure it's just a phase."

Well, she wasn't going to stay long. Just enough to get her back on her feet. She figured she needed a couple of weeks to secure a job and the deposit on another apartment. Molly clicked off the lamp and fell into a dark, heavy sleep.

In his room, Jack clicked his computer shut. He listened but couldn't hear anything next door. He couldn't believe it. A woman in his house. It was the last thing he needed. So close, so near, so female. Jack swallowed, then shook himself. Unlike his heroes, he had every intention of remaining a complete gentleman. He settled back into his bed, his arms clasped behind his head, and closed his eyes. But then he remembered: Tom, his cat, was in Molly's room. The cat liked to sleep in the spare bedroom but was terrified of closed doors. If he came upon a shut door he became completely unhinged and flew around the room, all claws and sharp teeth. In fact, he was probably trembling now, ready to explode into a vicious furball. Jack padded out to the hall.

At his knock he could see Molly's light click on. "Yes?" she said.

"Could I come in?"

"Now?"

"Tom wants to come out."

"Excuse me?"

"He gets agitated when he's by himself."

There was silence.

Jack cleared his throat. "I didn't want to disturb you but I don't want him to explode."

Molly opened the door and stared at him curiously. Jack brushed past her. At the bed he sank to his knees and pulled out a terrified sable-brown cat from underneath. The cat stared at Molly with blank yellow eyes.

She gawked at him. "That's a cat."

Jack gathered the cat in his arms and held it like a baby. "Tom."

Molly laughed with relief. "Hello, Tom." She reached out to pet it. Its paw flew out and scratched her.

"Ow!" She snatched her hand back.

Jack nuzzled the cat. "He's a little sensitive. He almost got his testicles cut off last month."

"What a pity."

"You, too? Why does everyone give him a hard time? My neighbors can't stand him. They say he's seducing the local cats, scattering his genes all over Venice."

"A real stud, is he?"

"They send me letters, make threatening phone calls. I tell them he's just exercising his reproductive freedom. But one night they caught him. I reached the clinic just in time. So he's still intact." He scratched the cat's stomach. "Aren't you, my friend?"

The cat closed his eyes and rumbled.

Molly eyed Jack warily. "You don't keep your mother upstairs in the attic, do you?"

"No, I put her in a home. She was scaring the mice."

"Good."

Jack's eyes swept over her—she was wearing a long T-shirt with the words "The Revolution Will Not Be Televised" across the front. "Good night," he said.

Chapter Five

WHEN JACK CAME down the next morning, dressed and ready, he was feeling good. He'd done his fifteen hundred words and charted out the plots for his next three novels. His heart was full of optimism, happy endings, and good people who triumphed. He rubbed his hands together. He had an active day ahead: tai chi, horseback riding, and then fencing. Part exercise, part research, it made him a well-rounded man. A Renaissance man. He stopped at the mirror and drew a finger across his freshly shaved face. He nodded with approval. There was, after all, he reminded himself, his head still filled with his work, a lady in the house.

"Morning!" Molly chirped when he walked into the kitchen. She leaned against the counter, munching Cheerios out of the box and wearing a very small camisole-and-panties set. Jack gawked at the vision before remembering his manners and averting his eyes. He set about fumbling for a bowl and spoon before realizing that Molly was standing in front of the cupboard containing his oatmeal. He decided to make do with bread and butter.

She watched him while he shredded the soft bread with cold butter.

"I read one of your books last night," she said.

He inclined his head modestly. He was used to praise.

"How do you write that stuff?" She warbled in falsetto. " 'Oh, my love, your wondrous eyes.' "

He stopped and stared at her.

She smiled back. Her teeth, he noted, were small and evenly spaced.

"One," he said, "they don't talk like that and two, what would you know about romance?"

Jack took his plate into the dining room, where he could keep an eye on Tom, who was in the garden. Molly followed him.

"They say women invented romance. And last time I checked I had a vagina."

"Which, from what I hear, you service daily." He shook his head at himself and took a deep breath. That was a cheap shot. Unworthy of a gentleman.

She grinned. "That would be if I was in a coma."

Jack chewed on his bread and stared straight ahead.

Molly dug into her Cheerios. "Did you know that three romance writers were recently killed by abusive husbands?"

"And your point is?"

"I'm just saying that it's not all airy-fairy, there's a strange destructive undercurrent."

"I think you're overanalyzing. People read my books for the happy endings. It's something they can have control over. At least they know that here in their hands is something that will work out all right."

"So they read all that just for the ending?"

"Yes."

Molly whistled. "What a waste of time."

Jack glared at her. "Ah, another fanatic in the antiromance brigade."

"Women have done more despicable things in the name of romance than pigs in the name of hunger."

Jack stopped chewing. "Like what?"

"Like letting men kill their own children."

"That was not romance, but fear."

"No, fear was afterward. Romance, that elusive hope that it will all work out, made them look the other way."

Jack didn't answer. Molly leaned closer.

"Do you really think that if men would just act like men and women would just be spunky but ultimately submissive, the world would turn a little easier?"

"I didn't say submissive."

"I see. Then how do you get two people, each with their own wants and desires, to live with each other? Doesn't one have to submit to the other?"

"Well, submitting isn't all bad, is it?"

"Aha, you just changed tactics."

Jack shrugged.

Molly shook her head. "Well, I can't believe these women are silly enough to waste their money on these books."

"Look." Jack sat up straight. "You have no idea what 'these women' are like. You don't know them. You don't know what they want. Most of them are saddled with drudgery and domestic service after all that talk of equality. Trying to prop up their men, raise kids, and more than half the time bring home the bacon, too. And then they shove their purchases in the closet to hide them, because their kids can have a million toys and their husbands a million gadgets, but God forbid they should shell out a couple of bucks on a book!"

Molly opened her eyes wide. "Wow, that was moving. I had no idea who you are. But now I do."

Jack nodded curtly.

"A middle-aged housewife," she said.

Jack scraped back his chair and stood. "Look, Harvard graduates are writing this stuff. And making millions."

Molly raised an impressed eyebrow. "Well, if you put it that way."

"But they've got something you haven't got," he added.

"And what's that?"

"A beating heart."

He gathered his pile of romance novels, all covered in brown paper—a man didn't invite needless grief—and walked out.

Rita kicked dutifully. She held on to the edge of the pool, her crimped hair wrapped in a cap, her shoulders weaving back and forth as she exerted herself.

"Keep kicking, ladies. I vant to see splash."

Heins, their Finnish swimming instructor, loomed over the line of women's heads. He wore a small European-style bathing suit that barely contained his genitals. The ladies tried to look past his dripping crotch but failed. Rita glanced over at Stella, whose face was pruned with disapproval, and winked. Stella lost her grip and disappeared under the highly chlorinated water.

And then he arrived, walking like a tiny emperor, his shorts to his knees, his belly sucked in, his legs white and roped with veins. The ambassador strode past the row of grasping hands and kicking feet and placed his eyeglasses carefully on the bench. He took a deep breath and made a passable dive into the swimming lane. All twelve heads turned to watch him perform a whale-flopping crawl to the other side. He climbed out of the pool, wheezing

slightly, picked up his glasses, and disappeared into the men's
room.

Rita kicked with renewed vigor.

The café was full by the time Jack arrived. He strode in and slung
his leg over the stool at the coffee bar.

"Jack, my man." Joe the barista saluted him and brought over
his usual. Jack slugged down his espresso and banged his cup back
on its tiny saucer.

"Gimme another one. A double."

Joe headed back to the machine.

Jack slumped in his seat. He was sick and tired of cynics. Sick of
those too intellectual for words. Here, he produced a simple tale
of passion and romance and you'd think he was offering his
customers dog excrement. All these new women who snubbed
romance. What a façade. *Someone* was buying the books.

The worst were those who thought they could write a
romance. "Hey, it's all formula. Just change the names, tack
on a happy ending, and you've got a new book." What horseshit.
Yes, of course, each book had to have that happy ending. If you
didn't, your readers would bring back the offending tome, fingers
holding it high as if it were a dead mouse. But did those big talkers
have any idea how hard romances were to write? Because you
had to make your readers forget the inevitable. So you threw
every obstacle you could think of between the lovers—physical,
mental, emotional. If that wasn't enough, you threw in a mother-
in-law or two. You whipped them, lashed them, drove them to
their knees. And only when you had taken away all hope could
you let them struggle up, weeping and stumbling toward each
other's ecstatic embrace. And that took artistry.

Jack swung around on the stool so his elbows were leaning

back on the bar. He glanced around the café. The usual crowd was there. His kindred spirits. Fellow artists. Writers, actors, comedians. Okay, so most were unemployed, but they had talent, drive, hope. He shot a finger at his pal Ron, who sat huddled with his agent. He jerked his head at Terry, who sat deep in conversation with a B list actor. He rolled his eyes in commiseration with Aaron, who sat in the corner staring glassily into thin air. Jack leaned back and sighed. This was his home away from home. These were his kind of people. A clan of high distinction. Men who took language and ideas and melded them into works of poetry. Like him, they dealt with the topics of the day. Like him, they tried to bring truth to the world. Like him, they were supplicants at the altar of good writing.

Because Jack had high hopes. High aspirations. He was going to be the greatest romantic novelist of all time. Laughable perhaps, but it was what got him up in the morning. A private goal he kept close to his chest, away from the guffaws and rolling eyes. Eventually he planned to come out from behind the mask of a female pseudonym and claim greatness again for men. After all, he would argue, didn't men invent the genre? Wasn't *Don Quixote* the greatest romantic novel of all time? Wasn't *Romeo and Juliet* the prototype? (If you could forgive that unfortunate ending.) He was thinking of the true greats. The originals: Shakespeare, Hugo, García Márquez. Oh, sure there were Jane and Emily, Charlotte on a good day. But who could ever forget the scent of bitter almonds?

Harry from the *Hollywood Reporter* sat down two stools away. Jack leaned forward. "Good column," he said.

Harry lifted his bloodshot eyes, regarded Jack, then returned to staring into space.

Jack reached over and patted him chummily on the shoulder. "Rough night?"

Harry shook off his hand and glared at him.

Jack chuckled. He was used to the old coot. "Ready?" he said cheerfully. He pushed himself off the stool and took a seat at a corner table.

Harry sighed and followed him. One by one, the others—Ron, Terry, and Aaron—moved toward his table. Jack sat at the head and dug deep into his satchel. He handed the men stacks of paper he had scribbled on. The men grabbed them and skimmed through.

"Good stuff here. Ron, some good dialogue. But remember, keep it simple. Keep it true. And Terry, for God's sake, use your spell check. Remember, though, it's the emotion we're looking for here. All right? Make 'em laugh, make 'em cry. Above all, make 'em hot. Okay, it's Harry's turn to read."

Harry looked around to see whether anyone else in the café was listening. He glanced at the group. He hesitated. Jack drummed his fingers on the table. "Come on. We're here for you. Gotham system: two positives, two areas for improvement. No one's looking to claw at your throat. Right, men?"

The others averted their eyes. They were still embarrassed about their need. Their need to write a romance. To express their deepest amorous desires. And to possibly make a quick million. They had been cool when Jack first divulged what he wrote, nodding curtly from their tables when he passed by, until the day Nora Roberts hit the best-seller list with three books at the same time. Then they had approached the table where he sat reading his brown-paper-covered books and asked him to tutor them. Jack had been more than happy to oblige. He took himself as a prophet of romance. The more converts, he felt, the better the world would be.

Harry took a rolled wad of papers from his shirt pocket. He

pushed his reading glasses back up his nose, then took them off again.

"Okay—this is where they finally come together for the first time. She's worried about her father, who's on his deathbed. And the hero has to tell her he's really an undercover agent come to spy on her father."

Jack sat back, his fingers together, and nodded. "Okay, excellent potential. Let's hear it."

Harry put on his glasses again and searched for the place where he'd left off. He cleared his throat and began to read. " 'With his knees, he pushed her legs apart and nudged his erection between her firm moist thighs . . .' "

Jack sat back and smiled. He closed his eyes and sunk into the story, sighing as the warm waters of good craftsmanship lapped against his skin.

Back in Jack's living room, Molly paced distractedly. She supposed she'd deserved that. That was what happened when you had an incorrigible habit of speaking your mind: Others spoke their minds back. But she'd never been one to smile benignly and let contrary thoughts bubble inside her. She believed in clear dialogue. She hated lies. She'd seen it happen too often, how lies, even white lies, led to heartache.

She shook her head ruefully. What was it about Jack that just made her want to bait him? And to run her fingers through his hair? She laughed. Look at her, having the hots for him. All right, all right, so who didn't she have the hots for? Well, quite a few, thanks very much. Why does the world think that if a woman likes men she likes every man who ever lived and would welcome them all to her bed? She was quite particular, in fact. They had to be kind, funny, inquisitive. Looks varied. She'd always liked the power of the short and stocky, that feeling of being drilled by a steady, squat machine. She also liked them plump and fleshy. There was something downright erotic about being consumed by a heavy man, feeling like that delicious first bite of an exquisite chocolate tart. But if she had to choose, which she didn't, she'd probably say that long and lean was her favorite. For example, Jack, if she was interested, which she was not, was exactly her type. But he was her host. Not to mention the fact that he was a fruit cake. Not that that ever stopped her before. But mainly, he was one of those men who took it all very seriously, and you didn't want to get involved with those.

She shook her head. How had she gotten on that? She had more important things to think about. Finding work, for example. Her sister had left a panicked message on her mobile, so Molly had dipped into the last of her savings. But she was going to have to wait until things cooled off, until memories had blurred, to approach her target companies for employment. In the meantime, she'd have to find something else. She looked around the room again. Her eyes fell on the Regency writing desk.

"Relax," the woman said

Kate, her eyes screwed closed, tried to shut down her mind, to exist solely through her immediate senses as the pamphlet had suggested. She took a deep breath and let the warm air in the cramped room gently caress her body. She listened hard to Joni Mitchell crooning in the background and took a big whiff of the frangipani-scented candles. She tried not to cringe in fear as the woman standing above her supine body slid hot stones across her navel. The woman, a trained stone mover with expertise in energy channeling, skimmed the stones down until they came to rest on Kate's pubis. Kate winced as the heat singed her skin.

"Be gone, queens of hell," the woman suddenly bellowed. "Leave now, you hags, you barren hags."

Kate flinched but remained calm. It was an exorcism after all. "Drive Out Marriage Frigidity Once and for All!!" She had picked up the flyer at her local health food store. It had promised that the procedure would release the evil spirits which had set up camp in her private parts like common squatters. Or her money back, guaranteed.

"Oh, spirit master," the stone mover intoned. "Free our sister here. Free her so that she may enjoy the sexuality of her husband. Free her so that she may climax her way back to paradise."

Kate cringed, knowing all that separated her from the waiting room full of women flipping through *Natural Life* and *Prevention* magazines was a thin rice paper shade. The harried receptionist had been curt, taking down her credit card details, then handing her a cotton robe and a lavender-scented towel.

"Free her from the repressive boredom that encircles her like chains."

Kate pursed her forehead, trying to visualize the repressive beasts loosening their grip on her labia and floating up into a weightless puff.

"In return, let her honor you with parted thighs . . ."

Kate's eyes popped open.

"Let her submit to your will . . ."

Kate glanced down her body to find the woman coming toward her with a large metal probe.

"Let her open her gates . . ."

Kate screamed and jumped off the table. She stood naked, shivering in the cold, backed against the humidifier. The practitioner set down the poker. She cupped her hand and yelled to the next room.

"Sherry! Did Mrs. Mandrell ask for the deluxe package or did she not?"

There was a pause, a rustle of paper, then a small "No."

"Damn it, Sherry, how many times do I have to ask you to write it down? You keep forgetting."

"Okay, okay!"

Kate glistened with sweat. The practitioner wiped her own forehead with a handkerchief.

"Well, I think we're done here today. Go home, grab a mirror, and explore your newfound glory. Get familiar with it, introduce yourself, make it your friend."

She fished in her pocket for a card and stamped it with a small vulva-shaped stamp. "Here you go. Come back for five more sessions and get the next one free."

When Jack got home from the café, he found Molly at the Regency writing desk, banging away on her laptop.

"What are you doing?" he said.

She held up a hand, staring into the air as if listening. Then she returned to typing, finished her sentence, and finally looked up.

"I'm writing," she said with the self-satisfaction of someone who had just met God on the street and been greeted by name. "A romance."

Jack laughed. "It's not something you can just pick up right away."

"I know. But I thought I'd give it a whirl."

"It takes years of practice, masses of rejection, determined hard work."

"Like anything."

"It could break your heart."

"Well, since according to you I don't have one, I've got nothing to lose."

Jack glared at her. It incensed him that she thought she could just sit down and whip up a romance like a Betty Crocker recipe.

"You'll never make it," he blurted.

"Ouch. I'd have thought you'd be more supportive."

He took a deep breath. She was right. Why was he being so negative? Why did it matter if she started what she would never be able to finish? Everyone started with high hopes, but soon broke down on the long, difficult road to publication. She, too, would end up in the gutter. She would fail so spectacularly that respect would finally shine from her eyes for the man who had made it to the other side.

He smiled indulgently. "You've got to start somewhere."

"I hope you don't mind my using this desk."

"Go ahead. It's just sitting there."

She ran her fingers around its rim. "It's just that I feel so inspired by it."

He understood her enthusiasm. He softened and smiled chummily. "I've got a lucky cup."

"You do? That's great."

"Yeah."

"I feel released, you know . . ."

"I know."

She walked over and gave him a hug. After a surprised second, he hugged her back. She released him and stretched to the ceiling. She rolled her head around her neck and let out a long sigh.

"God, what a day. I am so tense."

"Writing's not easy," he acknowledged.

She placed her hands on his chest. "Wanna screw?" she said.

He jumped back from her. "No!"

She cocked her head. "Why? You busy?"

"No. But no. God, no. No!"

She held up her hands. "All right. All right. A simple 'No, thank you' would have been enough."

She sauntered to the door. "I think I'll take a hot soak." She turned and grinned. "You do have a detachable shower head, right?"

Jack fell back against the couch and groaned.

Chapter Six

"YOU CAN'T GET rid of her, Jack. She has nowhere else to go."

"Doesn't she have parents?"

"They live in Florida," said Kate.

"Lovely state, sunny, full of fruits. I'm sure they'd love to see her."

"They have Alzheimer's."

"*Both* of them?"

"Yes, what are the chances of that?"

"God, I'm sorry."

"Oh, she looks on the bright side. She tells them she's married to a doctor and has 2.4 kids, and they believe her."

Jack was silent. He could hear Kate chewing at the other end of the phone. She finally swallowed.

"So, have you talked to Mom yet?" she asked.

"Yes. She seems very happy."

"Of course she's happy. She's acting like the cheerleader with the biggest pom-poms in there."

"And what's wrong with that?"

"At her age, with her heart?"

"Look, I've got to go."

"Missy Gilbert says you should stick to Harlequin Blaze. Says you're a little too randy for Temptations."

"Good-bye, Kate."

Jack hung up and sat morose in front of his computer, flexing his thumbs in anti–carpal tunnel syndrome exercises. Ever since Molly had moved in a week ago, his muse had flown the coop. He couldn't sleep, he couldn't work. He had been doing fine, top of the world, churning out five a year. But now every morning he stared at his screen in a cold sweat. In the next room, he could hear Molly whoop with delight. He had let her bring the Regency desk up to her room, and now he could hear her typing, her incessant typing. All morning he had to listen to her. The stifled laughs, the muffled guffaws. He closed his eyes. He visualized her committing hara-kiri with her mouse.

He slumped in front of his computer. He tried to concentrate. Think, he told himself, of the beauty of Primrose's soft cheek, of her bashful blue eyes, of her modest glance. But when he tried to visualize her all he could see was Molly's decisive jaw and Molly's piercing mud-brown eyes.

He finally logged onto the Internet. He glared at his Amazon ranking. This was the fourth time he'd checked it that morning and his latest book's ranking had still not budged from 30,453. He checked out his three main competitors and found with a sinking heart that they were at least 5000 more popular. He feared he'd passed his peak as a writer already, and all that lay before him and his books was the indignity of the remainder pile.

Then he heard Molly's door open, the creak of the hallway floorboards, and the inevitable knock at his door.

"Yeah?"

She stuck her head in, her eyes ringed black with unwashed mascara. "Making some coffee. Want some?"

"No."

"Sure?"

"Yes."

She walked in and scratched at her rounded belly. "I am zinging today. Hot, hot, hot. I mean, it's so intense. The way the characters just appear. Fully formed. It's like typing, isn't it?"

"No."

"It is for me. I can't type fast enough. And what they say, it's sooooo funny. I find myself laughing. And now I see what I want to do in the next chapter. I'm like a horse smelling water. Just trotting along."

Jack closed his eyes.

"How's yours going?" she asked.

"Oh, great. Just great."

"It's a hoot, isn't it?" She slapped the door. "I can't wait to get back to them. See ya!"

She closed the door. He gritted his teeth. There was nothing worse than the optimism of a beginning writer. He could hear her whistling down the stairs. He took a deep breath and closed his eyes. He tried to settle his mind, to return to writing mode. Again he tried to make the transfer from thinking like a man to thinking like a woman. What a leap it was. To where everything was porous and expandable. He constantly lost his way. He felt pummeled after a day in a woman's head. So much time spent willing to please, anxious to do her bit. With relationships of the utmost importance.

Which was one of the reasons he normally enjoyed writing his female characters. They worried about everything. Everything was drama. They couldn't walk into a room without turning the matter of whether So and So spoke to them into a masterpiece of high-tension spectacle. Their sense of the absurd was impeccable.

But today, silence reigned. Where pain, misery, and exquisite yearning should have danced before him, lay only a sullen empty screen. So by the end he was typing "Shoot me," "Shoot me" until the word count registered 1500 and he was free for breakfast.

Downstairs, Molly watched Jack walk in with a smile. She sat at the kitchen table, wearing a short apricot kimono, a notebook open in front of her. Jack set about whirring cold coffee, milk, maple syrup, and three raw eggs in the blender.

Molly leaned forward. "So let me ask you something."

Jack regarded her warily.

She tapped her notes with her pen. "My heroine is a fighter pilot. She's just come back from the war and she's having flashbacks about bombing a poor village. My hero is the military psychologist who's treating her."

"How novel."

"Ya think?"

"No."

"Well, I might change all that. Anyway, my question is this: How do I best express her yearning for the love of a real man? A man who will cherish her and support her in her chosen field and yet truly get her rocks off."

Jack tasted his concoction and whirred in more maple syrup. "You as a writer are going to have to work that out yourself."

"Yes, but you're the master at this. I read another of your books. You really are . . . a master."

Jack glanced at her. He perceived awe in her eyes.

"I've been writing a long time."

"It shows."

He divided his shake into one large glass and a small bowl and set the bowl outside the door. "Tom," he yelled, "breakfast!"

He returned and sat down at the table. Molly looked up, her pen poised for action.

"So?" she prompted.

He thought a moment. "I guess I'd have to say it's all in the timing."

Molly nodded vigorously. "Could you maybe suggest some positions that would express her independence and yet satisfy her sexual needs?"

Jack leaned back with his fingertips pressed together. "Well, first thing you need to do is add a few 'I need you's. To show the primal need on his part. He is to take her in the most basic way that fulfills his need, and by fulfilling his need he fulfills hers."

"God, that's great. Just great." Molly nodded enthusiastically and started scribbling.

"He needs to release himself within her," he continued.

"I like that."

"And she needs to take him in wholly without reservation."

"Oh, yeah."

He hesitated.

She looked up. "So what do you suggest?"

"I . . ." He stopped, staring at her flimsy kimono, her almond eyes, her plump bottom lip.

"Go on," she said.

He swallowed. "I often find doggy style appropriate."

She struck her head. "Brilliant." She finished writing her notes with a flourish. "*You* are the man," she said.

"Could you pass the jam, please?" he asked and shifted stiffly in his chair.

Rita examined herself in the mirror. Everything was decaying. What had happened to that gorgeous smile she'd once taken for granted, now all yellow and craggy? To her high, perky bosoms, now dreary pouches on her chest? To her legs, all etched with blue. Yes, she looked young for her age. Not a day over sixty. Well, lucky me, she thought ruefully. She dug into her pot of moisturizer and slapped it over her face, swirling upward. Always upward. Next cream blush—the better to paint two red circles with, she thought. Eyebrow pencils. The world could burn to ash tomorrow but she would wade off with the refugees clutching her eyebrow pencils. Last pat. She blinked at herself. Richard Milhouse Nixon in drag, she concluded, and threw open her closets.

She chose sunny yellow, matching it with her red-striped Nikes. A dreary day like this needed a bit of color. That ambassador in apartment 3C was proving elusive. A kiss-and-run driver, she called him. What nerve. He had ears the size of Hindenburgs. But he was one of nine men in a nursing home full of fifty-two women. Five of the men were still married and three were confined to wheelchairs, so that left Ol' Big Ears to rule the roost. He'd shuffle down the corridor and enter the activity room, and all hell would break loose in the hearts of the card-playing, bingo-hopping, needlepointing women clustered around the room like defiant weeds. He had a thing for blondes, naturally. He hadn't been in the place three weeks before the most requested look at the in-house beauty parlor was the Marilyn Monroe special. The hair lady poured L'Oréal's Champagne goo all over already raw scalps, teased the resulting straw and curled it back to cover as many bald patches as possible. The end result was hair-sprayed so much, the nursing home's lawyers were advocating that fire hazard warnings be stuck to the back of the women's heads. Refusing to bow, Rita continued her flame rinse as always. For she had one thing those women didn't have: eyebrows. She

66

used her eyebrows the way flamenco dancers used castanets; to punctuate every fleeting emotion that rippled through her body. She had kept two children, a husband, and many a hapless customer service manager in line with those eyebrows. An ambassador to Liechtenstein was small potatoes.

Rita took one last look at her ensemble, tweaked the collar to cover the back of her neck, popped a breath mint into her mouth, and opened her door. She could hear the ruckus already. The ambassador must have come down early.

The line of cars inched along the loop in front of Leda's junior high school, car doors opening and closing like an airport taxi dropoff. Kate blew her hair out of her face and stared out the front window at the car ahead of her. She sat slumped, her chin on her elbow, trying to visualize a ray of energizing light shining down into her vulva. But she was distracted and kept having to stop to add things to her grocery list. She opened her eyes to jot down bananas. She gasped as a young black man appeared from nowhere, holding a sharp set of pruning shears, and headed straight for the open window of the car ahead of hers. He dropped a small package into the car and then kept on sauntering.

"Happy holidays, Mrs. G.," he called.

"I'm sure they will be," the woman inside the car replied.

Leda jumped into the car. "Hi, Mom."

Kate held her hand to her racing heart. She nodded at the man who was now standing by the gate entrance, dangling the shears between thumb and forefinger and talking on his cell phone.

"Who's that?"

"Oh, that's Elroy. The school drug dealer. He poses as a gardener so he doesn't get hassled."

"Drug dealer? That's awful."

"He's pretty nice."

"Why was he talking to Betsy Green?"

"He gets Viagra for some of the moms."

Kate opened her mouth, then closed it. "God, Leda, the things you know."

Leda shrugged. Kate gazed at her daughter's unlined face and felt a pang. She reached over and touched Leda's long, thick hair. "So, how was school?"

"Mom, I want a boob job."

Kate's hand returned to the steering wheel. "Oh, don't start."

"It will help me get into the college of my choice."

"That's ridiculous."

"A magazine did a survey and they proved that people with big breasts are far more likely to succeed in their careers."

"Your breasts are fine."

"They're a generous B. But statistically, it's been shown that C and over receive the highest benefits."

"You are too young to have a boob job."

"Are you saying you want to hold me back from my potential?"

"Leda, I'm not having this conversation."

"Yeah, well, the magazine thought you might say that, so the article included this." Leda rummaged through her backpack and pulled out a sheet of paper. "It's my right," she read, "as a consumer to augment my satisfaction. A boob job will interface with my other purchases admirably." She waved the paper at her mom. "I'm to sign it and send it to my congressman."

Kate grabbed the paper and tossed it out of the window. She shoved the car into gear and screeched out of the school driveway.

"Watch it, Mom," Leda cried. "You're littering. They'll shoot you."

The bookshop owner rapped the table.

"We are very pleased to welcome Celeste D'Arcy!"

A smattering of applause. Jack stood up and strode to the podium. He was in his element at these book signings, reading from his work, talking about himself, taking insightful ("Where *do* you get your ideas from?") questions. He knew Lucinda preferred he refrained from revealing himself like this, but Lucinda, Jack felt, was wrong. Women could handle all this passion and love coming from a man. Oh, sure they always looked a little startled when they first arrived at his signings, but they got over it quickly, and by the end they seemed to think the package (sensitivity, sexual insight, and a third leg) more than acceptable.

His eyes roamed the shop, making quick calculations on numbers. Fifty or so people had shown up. Mostly middle-aged, they clasped his book tightly in their hands. He was always hoping for a younger group, a group to be nurtured and enslaved by his writing. But he smiled with indulgence. These women, with their sensible gray hair and oversize glasses, were his bread and butter. They were also the catalyst by which he planned to move from mere best-seller status to the exalted heights of super-stardom. Only ten or so in his field got that distinction—Nora Roberts, Linda Howard, Catherine Coulter, Virginia Henley, to a name a few. They were the ones who got the flashy promo-tional campaigns, the print, the TV, the radio. They got the special treatment because they passed the biggest test: even people who "didn't read romance" read their books. Jack wanted to join their ranks. He wanted to be the first openly male romance writer to do so.

In the corner, a beautiful young man preened. Jack had shelled out his own money for a cover model to pose while he read, hoping to draw patrons from behind the Business and Self-help aisles. The women eyed the young man, his long black hair pulled back in a ponytail, his taut legs encased in breeches.

As Jack began to read, he caught sight of a stray spike of brown hair poking from the other side of the Mystery section like the rigid back of a hedgehog. He continued to watch it with one eye as he read, tailing it through the bookstore as it weaved through every section but his.

When he had finished reading, the women's faces were red, their mouths open, their hands clasped against their breasts. They formed a line immediately. On and on they came, pressing Jack's book into his hands to sign. His cheeks had grown red with lipstick, his hair mussed with caressing fingers; his shirt had been plucked and pulled.

"Not bad."

He saw her hands first. The square, trimmed nails. She pushed his book at him. "I thought I'd support the cause."

He looked up into her eyes, noting for the first time there were flashes of brilliant gold in the mud.

"To Molly," he wrote. He paused. Should he write something more personal than "best regards"? After all she lived in his house. He looked down at the page. There were a couple of possibilities that came to mind immediately: "Please go away." "House on fire." He sighed and finally wrote, "Thanks for coming."

She smiled. "I'll see you later."

"Yup."

"Can I ask you a question?"

Oh, no. Here it came. "Wanna get a drink later?" "Can I get a

70

ride home?" He was going to have to tell her that their personal lives were to remain strictly separate.

"I suppose so."

She pointed at the model, who was holding court in the corner, a gaggle of women hanging on his every word. "What's that guy's name over there?"

"Ken."

"Ken. Great. Thanks. See ya."

She made a beeline for the man. Jack watched her step boldly up and touch his arm. Ken looked down from his great height and grinned.

When Jack was finished signing, Molly was gone. He experienced a momentary letdown. He had wanted her to tell him how his reading had gone. Okay, he admitted it, he was looking for a little pat on the back. It was funny, that. So many people were dying to know him, and yet he rode home alone to his house. But it had made him so tired, all the adulation, the fawning, the queries about influences ("How do you spell Evelyn Waugh and what's her Web site?"). On this evening, he found himself wanting the silence of his home and, strangely enough, a chat with Molly. Maybe she had some questions. Maybe they could have a good absorbing discussion about his work. If nothing else, he had been impressed by her dedication. Most aspiring writers fell apart after a few days. But she had been singleminded. No shirker she. She'd certainly put in the hours. He would show her his old *Punch* magazines, where he got his best historical details. He bet she'd like that. They could look at them together.

As he neared his house, he could hear the voices from inside.

"Oh, oh, oh!"

"Yes!"

"Oh, yes!"

"Yes."

"Yes."

Inside, he stood in the middle of the hallway and gazed up at the ceiling. The chandelier swayed back and forth.

"Oh, God, oh, God, oh God . . ."

"Yes . . ."

"Oh, yes, oh, yes!"

Jack turned off the lights and went to bed.

Chapter Seven

IN THE MORNING, Lucinda was on the phone. "I heard about your little soiree last night. I wish you wouldn't expose yourself like that. The fewer readers who know the truth, the better."

"I tell you, they can take it."

"Can they? Your last book didn't make the numbers we were expecting."

The walls suddenly seemed to loom in on him. Jack sat down abruptly. "Oh?" he finally managed.

"Now, don't panic. Just keep a low profile. I'm sure it will pick up. And this next book will be sure to turn the tide. How is it coming, by the way?"

"Oh, fine, fine. Great."

"Excellent."

He took a deep breath and expelled it shakily. "Actually, I'm having a little trouble . . . I'm thinking maybe I'm not sure about the character . . ."

"Oh, please don't think, Jack, just write."

"Fine!" He banged down the phone.

He stared at his screen, then deleted every last word, took a deep breath, and started again.

Her dress was white and pink and covered the essential parts of her anatomy.

Primrose laughed from her spot on his bed. "That's a sentence? That's a blot on the American school system."

Guy let out a ferocious yawn. "You need a break, my friend. Let's all get a bagel."

They were right. It was awful. Jack raked his hair with his fingers. Maybe he needed a new era. Maybe he was just burnt out on the 1800s. Maybe he should go medieval. Knights, armor, damsels in distress. Better yet, a hard, thrusting Viking to get them going. He could see it now: Elfew, a Viking wench with hair like a raven's and a heart to melt the iron pots and pans around her. Yes, that was it. Just a costume change, really. He looked up to where Primrose reclined, rouging her lips.

"Elfew!" he called.

"Bless you," she replied.

He blinked and there she was. Arms to crack nuts with. Breasts encased in . . . what did they call those things? He'd have to look it up. Her black hair flowed over her skirts. She gnawed on a deer haunch.

"You've got to be kidding me," she said.

He ignored her and began to type.

Helsgut the Viking strode in. Elfew raised an appreciative eyebrow. She tossed her deer haunch to the side and wiped her greasy fingers on her . . . [he'd have to look it up]. Helsgut grabbed her by the shoulders and bent her back. Her raven hair flowed like a midnight waterfall down her back.

Jack grinned. He liked that. "Flowed like a midnight waterfall . . ."

"Get on with it!" Elfew barked.

74

Helsgut ripped her . . . [he'd have to look it up]. *Elfew glared defiantly but did not budge an inch. His thick, firm lips encased her large, sturdy, bulbous breast and she closed her eyes against the desire that shot through her loins like a flame unleashed. She felt his hands slide up her muscled thighs and grab her buttocks. She moaned against her will. He was demanding, searching her depths with his majestic tongue and she responded like a she-wolf. She felt his desire beat against her stomach like a ramming rod. She was his slave and he was her master. Little did she know that she would crave all that he had in store for her.*

Jack stopped and wiped his brow. "Not bad."

"I'm holding a rod here . . ."

"All right, all right," he muttered, and plunged in again.

She unsheathed his rod and pointed it toward her love core.

"Love core?" Both Elfew and Helsgut looked up.

"It's got a certain ring."

He thrust like the great beast he was and she groaned. Mercy, mercy, she whispered urgently but he knew no control and together they touched the stars. The night sky blackened like Helsgut's eyes and Elfew knew that she was his forever.

Jack rested his head on the computer keys, spent. Helsgut's head fell back; he began snoring. Elfew leaned against the pillows and grinned at the ceiling.

When Molly came down the stairs an hour later, Jack lay on the hall floor, his hands over his face, tears streaming past his ears.

Molly stepped over him. "What's wrong?"

Jack shook his head violently.

She peered down at him. "Want a drink?"

"No." He sobbed into his hands.

"Oh, come on, it can't be that bad."

"Oh, it is. I need to do a series. They liked the first one, now I have to write a second one."

"So?"

He looked up at her. "Do you have any idea how *unreasonable* that is?"

"I thought that's what you wanted to do."

"I did. But it's horrible. I sit down and nothing comes. Or if it does, it's all wrong, but I don't know that yet and I type like an idiot. All morning I type their murmurings, thinking Yes, this is it. It's coming. And then when I stop and look back, I can hear them laughing. It's crap. It's all crap. And I've got nothing."

"It's just a bit of writer's block. You'll get over it."

"It's not writer's block! God! If only it were that easy. No, crap flows from me; it won't stop. Every morning it erupts from me like Mount Vesuvius. It rolls down my shoulders and makes puddles under my chair."

He reached up and grabbed her hand.

"Do you have any idea how deeply unromantic I am?"

He struggled to his knees and pulled her down toward him so that his face loomed two inches from hers. His eyes bored into her cinnamon lips.

"Do you have any idea how much I just want to . . . be with someone?"

He lifted his eyes to hers.

"Anyone," he whispered.

Molly took back her hand and stepped back, brushing out her skirt. A skirt, Jack thought. He'd never seen her in a skirt. It flowed from her waist and over her abundant thighs like a lake stream.

He wrapped his arms around those thighs. "You could help me." His voice was hoarse with want.

She put a hand on her hip.

"Don't you have an editor or something?"

"Oh, her." He collapsed back to the floor. "She's waiting, sitting there like a vulture, waiting for me to give up my spirit so she can swoop down and settle on my carcass and feed." He sighed. "She's not particularly helpful."

"Oh, gosh, I almost forgot." Molly rummaged in her bag and stuck a pile of papers under Jack's nose. "Check it out! Three chapters and a proposal."

"Of . . .?"

" 'The Well Hung Husband.' "

"Sounds inviting."

"Can you read it?"

"I'm a little busy."

Molly raised an eyebrow at his limp body on the floor.

Jack sighed. "All right, give it to me." He stared at the first page. "Molly Desire?"

"My pseudonym. What do you think?"

He shook his head.

She smiled. "And then I thought, if you like it you can give it to your editor."

"My editor?"

"Maybe she's looking for something like that."

Jack gaped at her. "You have no shame, do you?"

"What do you mean?"

"You just come in here, you eat my food and sleep in my bed, and now you want to take my editor."

"Surely there's a market for you and for me. What are there, a zillion different imprints? There's room for all of us." She patted him on the head. "Do you want me to pick up anything from the store?"

"A casket."

Kate sat in her car outside the school again waiting for Leda. She peered out the driver's window and spotted Elroy four cars down, chatting with Mabel Cunningham. Kate blanched. Mabel Cunningham, head of the PTA, with kilts to her shins and turtlenecks in every color of the rainbow. Kate looked around carefully before poking two fingers as unobtrusively as possible out her window. Elroy waved to Mabel and sauntered over. At Kate's window, he dropped to a squat.

"How's it hanging?" he asked.

"Fine. Thanks." She cleared her throat. "I was wondering . . ."

"Hey you!"

They both froze. The school's principal stood on the other side of the car. "Do you work here?" he demanded.

Elroy stood up, imaginary hat in hands. "Why, yes, sir. Yes, I do."

"Well, just look at those pansies. They're gasping."

"Yes, sir. I'll get right to it, sir."

The principal leaned down and peered into the car. "Mrs. Mandrell, is that you?"

Kate swallowed and waved. He gave her a sharp look and then walked away.

"And don't forget the clematis by the steps."

Elroy nodded. "Yes, sir." He dropped down again and rested his elbow on Kate's door.

"So, what can I do for you today? I got a special going on Retin A and Prozac."

Kate hesitated. He was young, eighteen or so, with burnished skin, high cheekbones, and eyes like golden corn syrup.

"Testosterone patches," she finally whispered.

"Testosterone patches? Never heard of them."

"They're new. I read about them in a magazine. But you need a prescription."

He leaned close. "Your man got no testosterone? Baby, that's too bad."

Kate noticed how his chest filled every inch of his T-shirt. She tore her eyes away. "They're for me, actually. I just need a little boost."

"You tried therapy?"

"Excuse me?"

"You know, sexual therapy. Worked good for me and my girlfriend. I was . . . you know, having trouble staying alive."

"I see."

"Took ten months but she set me straight."

"I was hoping for this weekend."

"All right, if you say so. But you know, it all takes time. You gotta give it time." He wrote down the order. "You want an order of Ecstasy with that?"

Jack read Molly's manuscript that night in bed, his eyes wide, his extra limb in a state of rigor mortis.

Then he nailed her . . .
Then she slithered up his . . .
Then she reached down and . . .

Jack shut the book over his extended maypole and stared wild eyed into the night. He shook his head. What on earth was he going to tell her? He couldn't lie. He owed it to her to be honest. Maybe he could write a note. He scrambled about, searching for blank paper, before finally lifting some from his printer and writing her a considered note. If he put it under her door now, he thought, she could digest it privately in the morning. He opened his door. Molly stood on the other side.

"So what d'ya think?" she asked.

Jack clutched his heart and fell back. "It was . . . mmm . . . fine," he panted.

"Fine?"

"Yes . . . fine."

"Honey, I don't get out of bed for fine."

"Excuse me?"

She strode into the room. " 'Fine' is a useless word. It means nothing. Neither good nor bad, happy nor sad. If you're going to critique me, I want 'great' or 'horrible.' 'Downright gruesome' is preferable to 'fine.' 'Fine' is forgettable, not worth the effort, a dull, watery gray. 'Fine' is"—she thought a moment—"hell."

Jack considered. "Okay, then. It was . . . unusual."

Molly grinned. "Good stuff, huh?"

He let out his breath. "Exhausting."

Molly held up her hand to high-five.

Jack shook his head. "I've never read a book so devoid of romance in my life."

She lowered her hand. "What do you mean?"

Jack deepened his voice. "Cyberspace cop Tess Muldoon, in order to avenge the murder of her husband, goes head to head with the dark forces of Rock Gage, who turns out to be a good guy after all, something she doesn't manage to notice for three quarters of the book, so busy is she catering to his every sexual need."

"What's wrong with that?"

"Where's the tenderness, the mystery? The love?"

Molly beheld her pages.

Jack tapped the manuscript. "They're banging each other senseless and they never once look into each other's souls."

"But they discover at the end that they're perfect for each other."

Jack shrugged. "I'm not convinced."

Molly stepped forward "It's . . . it's about identity, emancipation. The question of the twenty-first century."

Jack shook his head emphatically. "That's not the question of the twenty-first century."

"Oh, no? What is the question of the twenty-first century?"

"How not to die of loneliness."

They gazed at each other in silence. Molly's eyes darkened. She cleared her throat. "So, basically, you're saying you don't like my book."

"Basically, I'm saying it sucks."

He felt bad when she stalked off and slammed his door. He wasn't in the business of denigrating beginners. But she had a thing or two to learn about romance. Love was not sex. Love was not the best position. Love was not getting your rocks off simultaneously. Love was . . . endurance. Anyone could tell you that.

Chapter Eight

T HE WOMAN BEHIND the desk looked puzzled.

Jack cleared his throat. "You know, untouched. Um, virginal."

"Virginal?" Her eyebrows rose to the ceiling. She glanced down and eyed her panic button.

The dating agency had come highly recommended by Richard. Some of the best ass in town, he had promised. Others had stressed its exclusivity. Jack had finally come to the conclusion that if he was to find the proverbial needle in the haystack he must whittle down the quantity of hay. He glanced around at the peach interior, at the club chairs, at the black-and-white photos of naked bodies tastefully melding together, and leaned forward.

"I just want someone who is nice, who'll take things slow, who's willing to wait."

Her smile was dry. "Of course."

She tapped her keyboard. "Well, we do have one on the books. Let's see." She glanced at the photo. "Ah, here we go. Agnes Sykes." She hit Print and handed him the page.

A nun stared out at him. An old nun.

"I thought you had an age limit."

"We do."

"But she looks . . ."

"She states quite clearly she's thirty-one."

"She's a nun."

"Lapsed, I suspect. Shall I put you in touch?"

"Does she have an e-mail?"

"Yes, here we go. *AgnesofGod@yahoo.com.*"

He took the note and walked out. He was getting desperate. He had tried everything; chat rooms, personals, even mail order ("Virgins? We got virgins. This one she come in a box, never see man before. You be the first").

Outside, Jack sat on the steps and watched the world go by. His desperation was becoming obvious. He could feel people on the sidewalk giving him a wide berth. He gazed longingly at the couples sauntering by, their heads close, their arms entwined: How did they do that? How did they find each other? Why had the gods of romance smiled down on them and not on Jack? He sipped sullenly at his Big Gulp. His whole life now seemed to be about waiting for someone to slot herself into the crook of his arm. That empty space he wanted to fill with energy, love, heat. He ached for it.

Rita sat in her bedroom and listened to the chatter in the living room. Stella had her family visiting again, her two granddaughters and their snotty brood. They arrived every Friday at eleven and took over the living room, sprinkling cracker crumbs on the couch and dribbling stale milk on the carpet. Stella would sit smugly, perched in her armchair like a queen. She liked to leave the front door to the corridor open so that anybody walking by was sure to see her crowd. In this place, visitors were like poker chips, signs of wealth and worth.

Rita's family wasn't so attentive. Oh, Kate did her best,

between work and chauffeuring Leda around. And Jack did visit occasionally, when he could tear himself away from his Regency smut. But her one grandchild didn't come very often. And when she did drop by, they would sit staring at each other warily. Rita, bursting with love for this child, would rack her brains for conversational tidbits, asking about school subjects, knowing full well she hadn't come within a mile of Leda's real interests. Rita hadn't a clue as to what those were. She remembered not so long ago sending her a wedding veil for one of her dolls only to be told by the eleven-year-old that her dolls would never succumb to such a patriarchal system. She'd pronounced it "partridge system," but Rita got the idea.

Rita perked up her ears. Stella's family was making its endless noisy good-byes. She heaved herself off the bed. She was desperate for a cup of tea.

When she came out, Stella's mouth was puckered from the large canary she had just ingested. "I don't see why you coop yourself up in there. You could come out and be sociable, you know."

"I had some reading to do."

"What was it? The *Kama Sutra*?"

Rita rolled her eyes. Forget the tea. She was not going to spend the afternoon cooped up with Stella, their tongues clicking like cicadas. She headed for the door.

"Where are you going?"

"Bingo."

"You don't like bingo."

Rita shrugged.

"You just want to see who's there."

"Is that a crime?"

"Men don't like girls who chase."

"Do you want to come?"

"No, I'm going to read," Stella said piously, and picked up her magnifying glass.

As Rita closed the door, she again found herself wishing she could see more of Leda, her only granddaughter. What did the young girl think about? In the end, that was what Rita was dying to know. What did the new generation, her genetic footprint, think about?

Leda sat in the middle of her princess-pink four-poster bed and inched a condom over a large peeled banana. Her friends Tiffany and Armani watched.

"Easy," Tiffany barked.

The banana broke off at the base. Leda sat back, frustrated.

"Look, it's gotta be one smooth move, like this." Tiffany took another banana from the bunch on the nightstand and in two expert maneuvers had rolled the condom over. She presented it: a neat banana sausage.

Armani shook her head in admiration. "She's the condom queen."

Tiffany smiled smugly. "And that's just for starters."

Leda fell back on the bed and laughed. She couldn't remember ever being this happy before. Here she was having a sleepover with her best friends in the whole wide world. Well, she'd always wanted them to be her best friends. They'd been in school together since kindergarten, but Tiffany and Armani had always been too popular to let Leda into their group. Then suddenly last week they'd approached her in the hallway outside Mr. Peck's class and asked her to join them in a competition. It turned out that Tiffany and Armani were going up against three girls from a rival junior high and needed a third.

Tiffany handed Leda the wrapped banana. "Okay, now slowly . . ."

Leda opened her mouth and jutted her chin forward.

"Easy," said Tiffany. "It's not a hot fudge brownie!"

Armani slapped Tiffany high-five and they all began hooting. Leda fell over again in convulsions. When they managed to pull themselves together, they began the lesson again.

"Keep a rhythm," instructed Tiffany. "You got to count in your head. One one thousand, two one thousand, three . . . good. Good. Hey, look at that. I think she's got it."

"Ooh, ooh, ooh," Armani wailed, and fell back on the bed laughing. Leda cracked up again and slithered to the floor.

"Come on, you guys," Tiffany huffed. "This is serious. Stephanie's team is gonna kick our asses if we don't get it right."

Armani shrugged. "Well, they don't have a virgin on their team."

"We're all virgins," said Tiffany sternly.

"You know what I mean."

"Whatever." Tiffany pulled a bag from her backpack. "Okay, now here are the key rings you'll give out when you're done, so they won't forget us. Don't they look cute?"

Leda took one in her hand. It was a large circle containing a photo of all three girls, arms around each other, grinning seductively. Over their heads was the line 2ND ANNUAL B.J. COMPETITION.

Tiffany handed her a stack of note cards. "And here are the ballots. Make sure you get them to mark it in front of you or they'll change their mind. That's what happened last year. I got totally screwed. Remember?"

"Totally," agreed Armani.

"Okay, that's about it. Next week's meeting is gonna be about how to present yourself. You want to be comfortable but elegant at the same time. We want to be a class act, know what I mean?"

Leda nodded. She couldn't believe these girls were in her bedroom, sleeping on her floor, talking to her. Her usual best friend, Beth, was going to be sooo jealous.

Armani dug into a bag of chips. "I heard Roseanne and Rachel are going all the way."

Tiffany reapplied her strawberry-flavored lip gloss. "Well, we're not going to worry about that. They're sluts. We're not." She held up her glass of apple juice. "I suggest a toast. May the best blow job win."

It was about five when Jack neared his place. The windows of the apartments lining the boardwalk shone like bronze. The sun had lowered to the edge of the horizon like a fiery ladle dipping into the sea. He stepped off the boardwalk and headed toward the water. The sand had emptied of people; their footprints were now covered with the small scratch of tiny avian claws. Seagulls and willets dashed madly back and forth with the waves.

He used to love to come here with Morgan. They'd grab a bottle of wine and sit huddled together in the sea breeze. He'd naïvely thought they would do this forever, until their arthritis made it difficult to bend down and they would have to collapse in a giggling bundle onto the sand. But within two years of their wedding day he'd started having to beg Morgan to come, and then he'd watch her sit an arm's length away, staring grimly out to sea.

A human jet droned by him and dove into the waves. Two seconds later, out popped a figure, which began jumping up and down and waving to him.

"It's freezing!" Molly cried.

She flapped her arms around herself like a great white goose and hopped back and forth in a futile attempt to avoid the water. Her skimpy bikini revealed the dead-white skin of a five-day-old flounder. Jack eyed her with fascination. Surely she was breaking some sort of L.A. environmental ordinance.

She finally dashed out and threw herself into jumping jacks, the tops of her thighs jiggling up and down with each outward thrust of her sturdy legs.

He nodded with approval. "Getting into shape?"

"What?"

"You toning yourself?"

She stopped and looked down at herself. "I don't know what you mean."

Jack swallowed uncomfortably. Molly looked up and grinned. "Race ya."

She turned on her heel and dashed houseward across the sand. He had to hand it to her, whatever she lacked in svelteness she certainly made up for with energy.

She was chopping garlic when he returned, scooping it by the palmful into the pan. The scent simmered in the air.

"You are about to experience nirvana," she promised, pushing in tomatoes and red peppers and swirling with a spoon, her nose wrinkling over the pot.

"I have plans," he said.

"Oh, pooh."

He stared at her. He'd never noticed it before, but she had a beautiful philtrum. That snug dip below the nose. Hers lifted her upper lip to a perky and kissable height. A man could ignore too much in favor of a small detail, he warned himself. But to no avail: "Well, maybe I could put it off . . ."

"Excellent. You pour the wine." She nodded at the three

bottles set out on the counter. She whistled as she stirred. He felt guilty.

"Look, I'm sorry about yesterday. What I said about your book."

"Nope, you were right."

"I was a bit harsh."

"You said what you thought. It was honest. I appreciated it. And it made me start thinking." She shook her head. "I mean, whew, you really have to believe in this stuff, don't you? I mean, you can't just fake it."

"No," he said. "You have to believe every word."

She shook her head in amazement. "I had no idea. It made me rethink my commitment."

He nodded. "Well, don't feel bad. A lot of people quit when they realize it's so difficult."

"Oh, God, no." She laughed. "I'm not quitting. I'm going into therapy. I figure I've been holding back. You know, emotionally. With my shrink's help, I'm going to break the bonds that encircle my heart. Touch my vulnerable core for the very first time. Put me in touch with my inner romance writer. And if none of that works, he says there are some excellent pills I can pop."

She placed a huge bowl of pasta in front of him. "Dig in."

Jack paled. "You're gonna pop a pill and become a writer?"

"Uh-huh."

"Can I have some more wine?"

By eleven, they were slithered low in their seats. Molly clamped down on her tongue as she opened the third bottle. It glugged garnet red into his glass.

"Cheers," she said.

Jack raised his glass. He took in the glisten of sweat above her lip and drank deeply.

She swirled the wine in her glass. " 'The caress of silk against her skin.' "

He looked up.

"You wrote that," she said.

"I did?"

"Yeah. Until I read you I didn't know how evocative words could be." She glanced at him sidelong. " 'The wet sweetness of her mouth.' 'The velvet of her breasts.' 'The suck of warm lips on her chilled nipple.' "

"Well, it's just a writer's trick. To use all the senses to . . ." He stopped to watch her lick her lips. "To . . . uh . . ." He forgot what his mind was talking about.

"To turn readers on?" She ran her eyes up and down his body. " 'The stroke, soft as down, against her inner thigh.' 'Her excited breath hot against his cheek.' "

He swallowed.

She leaned closer and drew her finger down his arm. " 'The jagged scratch of her nail against his back.' "

He closed his eyes and breathed in her scent.

" 'The pain, sharp and delicious, as he filled her.' 'The slick sweat on his gyrating buttocks . . .' "

His eyes popped open. Her lips were inches from his and coming closer. Jack felt his muscles ripple toward her as if pulled into a vortex. His mouth hungered for hers, his skin was desperate for her touch. But his brain braced itself with both feet against his lust. He groaned as he found himself hopping up. "Well, time to clean up, I guess."

She fell forward, incredulous. "Now?"

"We'll feel better about it in the morning." He grabbed dishes from the table and dumped them into the sink. He busied himself at the counter, his willpower fighting like a hapless gladiator against the ferocity and dirty tricks of his desires.

Molly sighed and got up. She leaned down and opened the dishwasher. She began loading. Jack found himself watching her, his body loose and revved at the same time. She glanced up and met his eyes.

Jack *tsk-tsk*ed.

She smiled. "Yes?"

He reached around her and grabbed every last piece out of the dishwasher. He laid them out on the counter, took their measure, then replaced them in the dishwasher, pots and pans arranged in precise rows.

She stared at him.

"The jets flow upward," he said, "so if you put a dish here you're cutting off thirty-five percent of the available stream."

He retreated to the other side of the dishwasher and pulled open the cutlery section and began rearranging the silverware by length.

"If you encase a fork on both sides with knives you reduce the cross flow."

He finally reached up and took down a dishwasher tablet. He broke off a quarter of it before tucking it into the soap section.

"I find that three quarters is more than enough. If you use more, the machine wastes too much water trying to rinse."

He closed the door with a click, snapped the control into place, and, breathing heavily, brushed his hands with satisfaction.

"You're a freak," she said.

That night, Jack lay on his bed his hands outstretched and listened to Mr. Winston's old hi-fi next door crackle out Wagner's Ring

Cycle. Mr. Winston was eighty years old. He spent most of his days drinking bourbon and tossing fistfuls of peanuts into his mouth between sips. He used to own the whole house but had chopped it over the years into three apartments, which he sold off one by one to single women marking their first rung on the property ladder, leaving himself just enough space to live in the attic with a microwave and tiny refrigerator. The women were for the most part quiet neighbors except for the occasional overzealous playing of Alanis Morissette.

Mr. Winston liked to talk to Jack about the times when men were men and the women kinda liked it. Jack enjoyed these rambling chats because he had never talked much to his own father. He couldn't figure out whether this was because his father had nothing to say or because his sister and mother never shut up. It always amazed him, the clannishness of women. How you could always count on them to coalesce. Even if they'd never met before, they seemed to slot comfortably together, like witches around a cauldron, perfectly in tune, nodding and eye-rolling at the world as one. And they always seemed so sure of what to do, as if their mothers had been whispering into their ears from birth. He scratched absentmindedly at the stubble that was starting to poke from his chin and thought how his father had never whispered anything into his ear, not even about the birds and the bees. His mother had been the one to accost him in the hallway when he was fourteen, barking: "Your penis in a girl's vagina will get her pregnant. Got that?" And she had flounced out the door, leaving Jack trembling against the wall in acute embarrassment.

So he had had to glean information on how to be a man wherever he found it. To be a man, he surmised, you fucked as much as you could. Unless you didn't, in which case you kept quiet about it. You were chatty and open with women, unless you fell in love with them, in which case you absolutely closed down. You opened doors, unless the woman looked at you as if you were crazy, in which case you pushed on through. You went Dutch, unless the woman disappeared to the bathroom at check time, in which case you pulled out your wallet. You didn't press for sex, unless she slathered herself with whipped cream, in which case you took an appreciative lick. You always asked about protection, unless she pulled out her own pack of condoms, in which case you prayed that they weren't jumbo size. In fact, it was all fairly straightforward. Unless it was not.

Jack closed his eyes and listened to the music. Some nights Mr. Winston spent too long on the boardwalk (or on Jack's front steps) with his bottle, couldn't make it up his stairs, and fell back, so Jack could hear him calling with his head lodged by the door, his feet sticking up. Then Jack would walk around to the side door and rescue Mr. Winston and then half carry, half push him up, and help out in more ways than he would be comfortable talking about. Then he'd lay Mr. Winston on the bed, a bucket next to him, a glass of water on his dusty night table, two aspirins within reach. The last thing he always did was lift the needle off the Wagner record, where it went around and around in aggravated silence.

Kate set down the phone and eyed the far corner of her bedroom, her relationship corner—the corner that, according to her new bible, *Feng Shui or Die*, regulated her love life. She had bought the book in desperation. The testosterone patches had been a disaster. They had done nothing but leave her cranky, with a burning urge to clip the hedge. She peered at the corner and gasped. It was as blank as a ream of copy paper. It even held, horrors, an overflowing laundry basket. Which explained everything. Of course, her marriage was sexless. She had dirty laundry in her relationship corner, for God's sake. How could she have been so blind?

She sped through the pages, looking for antidotes: mirrors; green, luscious, thriving plants; an erotic statue or two. And use lots of red, the book enthused, to add passion to your life. Kate looked up, her mouth open, as the bulb above her head exploded with light. The whole bedroom was in the relationship corner of the house. She glanced around at the tasteful cream-and-white interior: it was as sexually enticing as a mushroom. She would have to completely repaint and decorate it. She fingered through the Yellow Pages, looking for her man.

Molly whistled in the shower and reveled in the driving rain of water on her back. There was nothing like a hard, hot shower to get the morning started off right. She laughed out loud when she thought of Jack and his dishwasher. What a goon. What an infuriating, hilarious goon. She was going to have to break it to Kate that he was worse off than she'd thought. But still, there was something about him. Molly found herself wanting to reach out and hold him. And not just to maneuver him toward her own satisfaction but to caress his face, to lay her head on his chest and listen to his heartbeat. She wanted to find out what was on his mind and to soothe his furrowed brow. She realized with a start that here, for the first time, was a man for whom she'd be willing to take things slow. To curb her appetite. Maybe even take a chance. A chance. She took a sharp breath. She'd never thought she'd meet someone like that. Molly stopped and felt the warmth of hope spread through her body.

There was a banging on the bathroom door. "Molly!"

She reached over and opened the door a crack.

Jack stood wearily on the other side. "There's a man in black leather to see you. Says you ordered a restraining harness and a box of duct tape."

"Could you ask him to leave it in the hall?"

She closed the door and stepped out of the shower briskly. No use mooning about, she scolded herself; she had work to do, and she had to hurry. She had an informational S&M session for her novel in fifteen minutes.

Maryann sat close to Richard on Jack's settee. She smiled sweetly, her hands crossed on her knees, the finger with the large diamond wiggling back and forth to catch the light.

"Then we're going to go off on one horse," Richard was explaining. "After the ceremony. You know, Maryann in front of me like we're riding off into the sunset. Then we'll meet you at the reception. And party!"

Maryann rolled her eyes. "Richard."

Jack raised his glass of champagne to her. "Well, congratulations."

Maryann blushed. "Thanks. But you're supposed to say it to Richard."

"I have a toast," said Richard. "Thanks for making an honest man out of me."

She batted at him. "Oh, you."

He laughed and drank down half the glass. "It's your turn next, Jack. Maryann has lots of friends."

"Oh, lots," she said, gazing around the room.

"Maryann is a real matchmaker."

"Three weddings so far. And an engagement next week."

"And then she got her hooks into me."

"Well, someone had to put her foot down."

Richard winked at Jack.

"Jack, you in here?"

Molly strode into the room in black thigh-high stiletto boots and a rubber minidress. "Oops, I'm sorry. Didn't know you had company." She turned to go, but Richard hopped up from the settee and called out. "Hello."

Molly stopped and smiled. "Hello."

Richard turned to face Jack beseechingly.

Jack held out his hand to present her. "This is Molly." The resident whip mistress, he wanted to add, but refrained.

"Helloooo, Molly." Richard inhaled her. Maryann froze, her champagne glass still halfway to her mouth.

Molly turned to go. "Well, I was just making sure you were okay . . ."

Jack raised an eyebrow. "Why? Did you bring your riding crop?"

"Actually, I wanted to know if I could have the last of the Häagen-Dazs."

Richard jumped in. "Can I get you a drink?"

Molly glanced at Jack, then smiled. "Sure. That would be great."

Richard moved swiftly to the champagne and poured her a tall glass.

"Thank you."

She sat back and took a long sip. The tops of her breasts gamely tried to peek up from behind the bodice of her rubber dress. Richard gazed down at her in rapture.

"What an unusual dress," he said.

"Research."

"Oh, are you a writer, too?"

"Well, today I was a dominatrix." She clenched and un-clenched her fists. "I tell you, it is hard work."

Richard stared at her hands.

"Luckily they have all these gadgets that help with the more challenging projects. I don't know what people did in the olden days."

Richard swallowed. "I can't believe I've never met you before." He glanced at Jack. "Where's he been keeping you?"

Molly yawned. "Upstairs. Tied to a Regency desk."

Richard was hoarse. "Really?"

Maryann set down her drink. "Oh, honey, look at the time. We better get back. We still have the invitations to write."

Richard waved her away. "Oh, relax about the invitations. We'll get to them tomorrow."

"They need to go out tomorrow, which means we have to write them tonight."

"One day is not going to kill us."

"Yes, it will. You need a minimum of three weeks."

"Let's break the rules."

"Let's not."

He chucked her under the chin. "My ball and chain."

She stood up. "Come on." She gave Jack a limp hug. "Goodbye, Jack, we'll see you at the engagement party. We're registered at Macy's, just to let you know. I hate to mention it but I find it helps people to know where they can turn to." She dropped her voice. "I have women I'd like to introduce you to." She glanced at Molly and whispered. "Suitable mates."

Richard shook Molly's hand. "Come along, too, if you like. Sure to be a big gig. Maryann's parents throw great parties. One more won't make a difference, will it?"

Maryann smiled tightly. "It's a sit-down dinner."

"Pull up a chair, is what I say."

"Come along, Richard."

When the door closed on Richard and Maryann, Molly shook her head. "Oh, boy," she said.

"What?"

"I wouldn't buy the wedding present just yet."

"He's devoted to her."

She smiled. "What do you say to a nightcap?"

Jack swung his eyes up and down her trussed-up body and stepped back. "It's been a long night . . ."

"Oh, come on." She grabbed Jack's hand and pulled him back into the living room. She poured him another drink, then one for herself. "I feel we've gotten off to a bad start."

Jack chose the far side of the room and sat down. "How do you mean?"

"I feel I have trampled all over your sensitivity by putting you in a compromised position."

Jack was silent. He'd never heard it so well put.

"So I just wanted to say that I didn't mean to offend you in any way."

"Don't worry about it."

Molly handed him his drink. She then sat down next to him on the couch, close.

"I mean, it's so nice of you to let me stay here."

He stared straight ahead. "That's okay."

"And I won't intrude very long on your hospitality."

"Good."

She glanced at him.

"I mean, stay as long as you like," he said.

They fell into silence. Molly stood up suddenly and began to pace the room. Jack watched the way her rubber dress pressed against her strong thighs. He wondered what it would be like to be caught between those thighs . . .

"The thing is"—she came and stood before him—"I find you very, very attractive. Could I pour you another drink?"

Jack looked down, his glass was empty. He could not recall drinking.

"No, thanks." He set down his glass and crossed his arms.

She sat down next to him again. "You see, I find there are two types of men: those I call dalliances and those I call keepers. And I've always thought I liked the dalliances, but you . . . you . . ." She gazed at his lips.

Jack stared at hers.

She placed a hand on his knee. "Would you like to go out sometime?"

"No."

"Oh." She took back her hand.

"I mean, you're very nice and everything . . ."

She stood up. "I understand."

"It's just that . . ." Jack scrambled up.

"No need to explain."

Jack felt bad. She looked so dignified standing there, her arms at her sides. He feared for a brief moment that she was going to bow forward and click her heels. But she just smiled softly at him.

"I mean, we can be friends," he said.

"Of course." She stepped forward and kissed him on the lips, sucking them into her mouth and nibbling on their insides before letting go. She stuck out her hand. "It's a deal."

Jack hobbled to the door.

"Jack."

He looked back. She winked. "Can't blame a girl for trying."

Chapter Nine

"THE THING WITH YOU, Jack, is you're too nice," said Richard as he deflected Jack's blade in the ring of their fencing club off Santa Monica Boulevard. They both wore whites and circled each other, holding foils tipped with buttons.

"I know, I know," said Jack, adjusting the angle of his back foot before advancing again.

Their instructor called from the sidelines. "Wrist, move the wrist. Not the elbow."

Richard skipped lightly to the left. "Imagine coming on to you like that. What did she think you were?"

Jack shook his head in disbelief. "I have no idea. Do I give off these vibes? These just-screw-with-me vibes?"

Richard *tsk-tsk*ed. "Don't want her kind around."

"Watch it with that crossover!" barked the instructor.

Jack circled Richard. "I mean, these men who don't respect themselves. Those are the ones she preys on."

Richard counterparried. "You got that right."

Jack answered with a riposte. "She should have a sign on her: ONLY ONE THING ON HER MIND."

"I hear ya."

Jack changed engagement. "But sometimes, sometimes . . . I look at her and I think: Why not?"

"No. no. Absolutely not."

"Why not?"

Richard tried a feint. "Because she's not the one."

Jack saw it coming, and twirled. "But what if she was?"

"You're kidding me, right?"

"Yeah. No. I don't know. I mean, she's kind of growing on me."

"She's wearing you down, is what she's doing. Either way it's not a good idea."

"Why?"

"Simple: If you give in now, she'll never respect you." Richard lunged and pressed his sword firmly against Jack's Adam's apple. "Touché, bud."

It was like a bolt of lightning, a shock of recognition, a secret handshake. Jack could feel it even before they spoke.

"Heather?"

She stood in front of the Starbucks in a simple light blue sleeveless dress, her long blond hair pulled back in a black velvet bow. He had trotted across the street to meet her, holding out his hand, practically tripping over himself to claim her.

"Yes," she said, and they stood there, smiling at each other, drinking each other in, standing in everyone's way. Because how often does this happen? A meeting through a friend turning into something so . . . so . . . promising.

"You want a cappuccino?" he finally asked.

"Decaf latte, please."

Inside, they sat in the corner, looking out onto Main Street and talking in a rush, her tinkle of laughter playing like sunlight over their conversation. They talked about what a kind and generous person Maryann had been for setting them up. And how they had to rely on good friends to introduce them to quality people. The usual stuff. Too busy to find love in the workplace. Too shy to make the social scene. Too selective to sit on a bar stool waiting for the best offer. So there they both were, available, open-hearted, ready for anything.

"Of all the Starbucks to walk into . . ." he ventured.

She suddenly frowned. Jack felt a clutch of fear. What had he said? Did she not like *Casablanca*? How could he have been so stupid? Was it racist, was it sexist? He watched her eyes narrow, taking him in, measuring his worth. He held his breath.

"I know this is premature," she finally said, "but I just want you to know that I don't want to get involved, you know, sexually."

Jack let his breath out. "You're kidding."

She shook her head. She looked down at her hands as if ashamed. Jack couldn't believe his luck. What were the odds of him running into someone so . . . unusual?

"But you look so . . . normal."

She shrugged.

"You religious, or something?"

"Yes. But that isn't it."

"Then what?"

"I'm waiting for . . ."

"True love." He spoke for her.

She looked up, amazed. "Yes. How did you know?"

How did he know? Here was the woman he had been waiting for. Here was his angel. His salvation. He laid his hand over her soft and creamy one, careful not to press down in any suggestive way.

"I feel the same way."

She gazed up into his eyes, fearful that he was mocking her. "You do?"

"Absolutely."

Relief flooded over her face. Her back straightened. She set her decaf latte back on its saucer with a decisive clink and gazed into his eyes.

"Would you like to get together again?" she asked. "For lunch?"

Jack rode home, his head enveloped in a cloud of warm, fuzzy mist. He couldn't have told you which way he came back, whether it was up Pacific, right on Thirty-first, or perhaps straight over on Abbot Kinney and down North Venice Boulevard, but he could have told you how the sun gilded the trees, how the air had just the right degree of crispness. His self-satisfaction carried him along the streets like a magic carpet. He rode breathing deeply, shaking his head at his good fortune. Because he had found her: the Last Virgin in Los Angeles. He played back their conversation over and over.

"I'm saving my sexuality for my husband," she had said. "My chastity is my most cherished gift."

"That's a beautiful attitude," he replied.

"You may hold my hand."

And Jack had sat happily in Starbucks holding the creamy hand of this exquisite creature. Rosebud lips, heavenly blue eyes, long sleek legs leading to no-man's-land. Jack's groin had stirred in recognition. He had waited, and he had been rewarded. He would show them after all. He wanted to jump and punch the air with glee. But he suddenly frowned. It was going to be hell telling Molly. Very awkward. She had been so upfront with her feelings.

So heartbreakingly open about her desire. He had to hand it to her, that took true grit. Real force of character. But he had made his choice. He had found the one. Hopefully it wouldn't be too difficult for Molly to be around them, two lovebirds, brimming with that soft, woozy feeling called new love. It would hurt her terribly, he thought sadly. It would be a real blow.

But, he thought briskly, it couldn't be helped. For that beautiful chaste apparition was his future wife, his mate, the mother of his gorgeous children. He envisioned the house they would have in Palisades, the jungle gym in the backyard, the three towheaded children racing over the emerald lawn. He smiled as he saw the making of those children, the warm sensuous nights, her flowing nightgown, her long hair cascading down his chest.

He also saw, as he neared his house, Molly, upstairs, leaning out of her bedroom window. As he parked his motorbike he noticed that her face was moving in and out of the window. He could vaguely see a man's face behind her, a little above and to the left. Molly waved as Jack swung his leg over his bike.

"Lucinda left a message."

"Thanks."

He watched her. She had a small smile, the corner of her mouth lifted as if she was listening to a joke, anticipating the punch line.

She closed her eyes.

"Molly?"

Her eyes popped open. "Yeah?"

"Did she mention the conference?"

She closed her eyes. "No-oh, oh, oh, oh."

She growled, baring her small teeth, and then groaned and relaxed against the window ledge. Behind her the man's face came forward and nestled itself next to hers. He was meaty and sweaty. He was, Jack noticed, the Federal Express man.

"Oh, hello!" he called down to Jack.

Jack waved wordlessly.

Molly was up early the next morning in the garden. Jack watched her from his window. She wore a loose fuchsia sundress that came down to her shins. As she bent to examine a flower he could see her bony spine appear like a small delicate dinosaur's. Her arms were pink from the sun; her lips were parted in concentration. She was deadheading the rosebush, snipping old, faded blossoms, littering the lawn with their severed heads. Her dark hair shone almost blue in the morning light. She was barefoot, her feet caked with wet grass. He imagined himself there on the grass with her. The early morning dew soaking his back, her dress twisted, her heavy thigh exposed. The sun catching the rise of her small breasts, his lips drawing their outline. The warmth of her body pressing down, her eyes inviting him in.

As if knowing his thoughts, Molly suddenly turned and looked up. He stood still in the shadow and could tell from her squint that she could not see him. He then watched her smile as if, though she hadn't exactly seen, she knew. She returned to her guillotining.

"You want to know what I think?" said Primrose, who lay back on his bed, filing her nails. He had given up on Elfew. His vocabulary had been inadequate.

"Not really." He walked past her and slumped back in front of his computer.

"I think she has a lot of nerve coming in here, riling you up and not succumbing to your desires."

Guy looked over from where he was performing knee bends. "I say give her a quick poke and be done with it."

"Absolutely not."

"Come on, guv, no one will know."

"I will."

"Oh, 'oo cares," said Primrose. "Get 'er out yer system."

"There's nothing in my system. She appalls me."

"Yeah, you got 'appall' written all over your front. That's wot you got."

Jack looked over. "Why are you speaking Cockney? You're aristocrats."

Primrose raised her hands. "Don't blame us. Your characterization is undefined."

Jack took a deep breath, raised his fingers, and plunged in again:

Primrose murmured against Guy's insistent lips. "Don't, do, don't . . ."

Jack leaned forward and banged his fingers against the keys. "Oh, for crying out loud!"

Primrose jumped. "What?"

"Don't you just get sick of it? Complain, complain. Face it. He's an asshole. Just leave him."

Primrose placed a hand to her heaving breasts. "But I love him."

"He treats you like dirt."

"Yes, but deep down he loves me."

"Does he?"

Guy looked up from where he was now reading the sports page over Primrose's shoulder and shrugged. "Sure."

"Guy!" Primrose whined.

"I wish you'd put me in a contemporary where they're just giving it away. I'm getting tired of this." Guy went back to reading.

Jack gawked at Guy. "My God, that's it."

Guy glanced up. "What's it?"

"Why should you pillage?"

"Huh?"

"Why should you rape and plunder? I've been so blind. Get off her!"

Guy stumbled back. Primrose raised an eyebrow. Jack raked his hair with his hands.

"Why didn't I think of this before? The supersupersuper romance. That's what I'm going to write. A romance so sweet and tender and innocent it will change the world."

He paced the room. "Okay, now. Different names. Let's see. Beau. That's it. And . . . Chastity. Hmm. I like that. Good. Good." He sat back down at the computer. "Now, I want you to hold hands."

"Hold hands?"

"Wait, wait, wait, I'm just going to go back and delete. Okay, starting fresh. You've just met and you're talking and you're getting to know each other—"

"Oh, I get it," Primrose jumped in, "and she realizes his father was the one who raped her mother and they can never see each other again."

"No, no," said Jack, "they get to know each other and Beau asks Chastity for—"

"For all her father's money," Guy cried, "or he will seduce her love child, which she bore when she was thirteen."

"No." Jack shook his head. "For her hand in marriage."

"Which she rejects," said Primrose, "and he has to abduct her!"

"To his hilltop dungeon," added Guy.

"No, no, no," insisted Jack. "Which she accepts and they—"

"Are about to get married but she finds out he's really his brother's evil steptwin!"

"*No!* They live happily ever after. The end." Jack regarded them, out of breath.

Guy and Primrose were silent.

"Don't you see? My hero is going to be a nice guy. It will be revolutionary. Love, marriage, sex, and everlasting devotion with a . . . *nice guy.*"

Guy and Primrose exchanged glances.

Jack smiled at Primrose. "He's going to love you forever. From the start. What do you think?"

Primrose stifled a yawn.

Most of the chairs were taken in the games room by the time Rita arrived. The manic crossword trio was ensconced next to the Pepsi machine, holding their folded newspapers up to fading eyes.

"It's Friday," Rita called merrily as she breezed by, "you don't stand a chance."

The ambassador was holding court by the pool table. He gave Rita a long bold glance as she walked by, then returned his attention to Stella, who was pretending to read his palm.

"I see big things for you. Big things."

"How big?"

Stella brought his hand up to her cheek. "I see the stock market jumping seventy percent. I see them finding a cure for aging. I see you by the seaside, a piña colada in your hands."

The ambassador retrieved his hand. "Pimms. It would be a Pimms."

He glanced again at Rita, who now sat across the way, sketching three women who were getting a lesson in pool table etiquette. One leaned forward over the table, her glasses slightly askew, and walloped the eight ball into the far pocket.

As she sketched, Rita listened to Stella chatter.

"Now, the house I lived in as a child was bigger. Large hallway, pegs on the side for our coats. And Mama had a big rocking chair right by the door . . ."

The ambassador said nothing, letting his eyes rest on Rita's face while she sketched.

"We had two cats at the time. Twichet and Bess. Ah, Bess. She got run over by the milk truck. Never had a cat that I liked better. Mama said . . ."

The ambassador drummed his fingers on the armrest. He stood up suddenly. A hush came over the room. Rita continued to draw, concentrating on the long line of the pool stick.

He stopped by her chair. "I'm having drinks in my room at five o'clock. Would you like to join me?"

Rita looked up, taking in his fine blue eyes, his bushy white eyebrows, his ears, which balanced his head like training wheels. Still, she wasn't going to jump like a marionette to his tune. He was going to have to work a little harder.

"My grandchild is visiting me. Perhaps another time."

He inclined his head.

She watched him shuffle out. Stella sat where she was, her mouth pursed, staring down at her lap. Rita glanced at her and began to sketch her hands.

"Leda wants an orgy for her birthday. Can you emcee?"

Jack yawned. His sister's calls were getting earlier. "Orgy? What happened to Pin the Tail on the Donkey?"

"It was a nondemocratic, hierarchical game form. Only one person could win."

"The poor, poor donkey."

"She also wants to talk to you about something. Can she come over?"

"Sure. Is anything wrong?"

"No, I think it's homework. English composition or something. Though I don't know why she wants to see you. It's not like you're that kind of writer."

"What kind is that?"

"A good one."

"Good-bye, Kate."

Jack swung into Barnes & Noble and waved at the cashier, who nudged his fellow cashier. Jack sailed up to the third floor on the escalator, glancing around at all the men and women who wandered the aisles, touching the fronts of books as if they were the faces of prophets. In the back Jack found his books waiting like loyal friends. He chose one and leaned against a bookcase as nonchalantly as he could. For as any self-respecting writer will tell you, it wasn't enough to write. Self-promotion was a must. You had to make people buy. "I'm a publisher, not a publicist," Lucinda had brusquely told him, leaving Jack to flog the product like a rug merchant. So he did the usual book giveaways, the infiltrating of unsuspecting chat rooms, the whoring around at conventions. But there was nothing like a little strong-arming to really push the sales.

He looked around expectantly. Soon a woman meandered toward him, furtively glancing at where he stood and eyeing the selection next to him. She stood for a moment leafing through a book on funeral home franchises before taking a courageous breath and turning purposefully toward the romances. She turned her back to him as she read through the titles.

"May I suggest a Celeste d'Arcy?" he said.

The woman's back tensed but she continued to read as if she had not heard him.

"You *are* interested in romance?"

She looked over at the security guard, who loitered nearby. "What's it to you?" she said.

"We are kindred spirits. We must exalt in our yearning for a better, more passionate world. We can't let them beat us down. We must stick together. Remember—" he leaned close—"*we* are the silent majority."

She nodded.

"So tell me," he prompted.

She looked around, then whispered: "I don't know. I just like . . . emotion, you know."

He pulled out one of his books. "May I suggest a Celeste d'Arcy?" he repeated.

She made a face. "I heard it was a man."

"So?"

"I don't like the idea of a man prying into my inner thoughts like that. You know, looking into my desires."

"The better to fulfill them."

"Isn't he gay?"

"No. A common misapprehension. Gay guys write for gay guys. Straight men write for straight women. They do everything a woman does, only backward and in low heels."

"Hmmm," she said, and looked at the back cover. "Murder, abduction, and betrayal." She scratched her cheek. "Sounds good."

"It is. I assure you."

A large hand clamped Jack's shoulder. He turned to find the security guard looming above him. "You're going to have to move, sir. No harassing the customers."

"I'm just providing a service."

"So am I," he said, and escorted Jack out.

The thought occurred to Jack, as he stumbled out onto the sidewalk, that he should probably get a job. If this writer's block lasted, he calculated that he had about six months before it was time to downgrade to a two-bedroom in Studio City. The problem was that after a certain age, writers were basically unemployable. They were entirely too individual to be team players. Too opinionated, too charmed by the sound of their own mental mastication. They knew a little about everything and not enough about anything. Of course, he had done so much research on his last book, he could probably walk into an auction house and get a job as a Regency appraiser. And a few years ago he had managed a passable medical romance: no doubt he could fudge a day or two as a nurse. It was too bad there weren't a lot of openings for high-seas pirates, because he really knew the ins and outs of that field. Jack sighed. If his sales didn't pick up, he was in serious trouble. Besides, if he couldn't deliver with a female pseudonym, writing under his own name would be completely impossible. But as he sauntered down the sidewalk to where his motorcycle waited for him like a loyal steed, he found himself smiling. Thank God, he thought, his personal life was right on target. Heather was turning out to be everything he asked for. And more.

Heather stood before Jack in a one-piece bathing suit. She had a large black marker in her hand and was delineating private zones.

"So, for now, no touching above here," she said, drawing the marker three inches above the knee. "Eventually we can graduate to here." She made a dotted line three inches farther up. "But that's only after fifty good points."

"Good points." Jack sat on her couch in her living room, taking notes.

"Yes. You are allotted points after every date. Five for gentlemanly things like opening the car door. Paying for dinner. Active listening."

" 'Active listening.' "

"See, you're getting the hang of it already!"

Jack drew a question mark next to "active listening." He'd look it up later.

"Now, I'm afraid I'm pretty strict about chest-area touching." She drew a line across the middle of her throat. "So from here down is strictly off limits. Now, say if you're unbelievably good, and frankly no one's reached that, you may put your hands around my clavicle area."

"Gotcha."

"So. Do you want to sunbathe nude?"

Jack blinked. "You won't feel too . . . naked?"

"Well, now that we've established the rules I feel safe with you." Heathen shimmied out of her bathing suit and struck a pose. "God, you should see your face." She laughed. "You look paler than my cuticles."

She skipped outside to her balcony and lay down in the sun, her breasts standing suspiciously at attention. She closed her eyes and basked. Jack stood at the door and surveyed her, his eyes caressing her no-go areas. They twinkled and beckoned like a sports car in a shop window.

When Leda knocked on the door, Jack dashed down the stairs to open it. He was delighted his niece had come to him for help. He had spent the whole night working on a teaching plan, incorporating the secrets of good dialogue, plotting, characterization.

He'd even scribbled a few notes about his working habits—what kind of font he used, his margins, the philosophy behind his bio. It was going to be a fascinating afternoon.

He hugged her tight on the doorstep and helped her lug in her school bag. She twirled about in his hallway.

"I have so much to tell you about," she said.

"Good, good, come on through."

In the kitchen, Jack waved Leda to a chair and poured two tall glasses of cold milk. He set them down next to a basket filled with chocolate chip cookies. There was nothing like a child to give you permission to indulge in simple pleasures. "So," he said, wiping the milk mustache from his mouth. "What's on your mind?"

Leda collapsed into the chair. "Oral sex."

Jack choked on his cookie.

Leda pulled out an involved diagram, which had sections labeled "A," "B," "C," and "D."

"Now," she said, taking a pencil and pointing to each section. "In your experience, do you like the pressure put here, here, or here?"

Jack stared at her, open mouthed.

"Or do you like those big wave jobs where she's constantly vibrating with her mouth?"

Jack was speechless. Who was this woman-child majoring in men's anatomical studies? He examined the teenager in front of him, with her baby fat, her low-cut jeans laced across her crotch, a fake (he hoped) tattoo of a tongue plastered on the back of her wrist. What had happened to the child in princess party dresses who could tell you the difference between a Chasmosaurus and a Stegosaurus, who could name the moons of Jupiter and describe the composition of Saturn's rings, who knew that emperor penguins hatched their young upon their feet?

He'd heard the rumors about how fast kids were taking things these days, but he'd always dismissed them as urban legends made up to shock and confuse, to drive a further wedge between the generations. He liked to consider himself a staunch ally of the young, preferring to believe (against contrary evidence) that he was not so far from the roost. So he didn't want to judge Leda. He didn't want to make a fuss. Above all, he didn't want her to turn away. He had to keep the dialogue open.

He steeled himself. "Well, I'm sure your boyfriend would be delighted with any attention you care to give to him."

"Boyfriend?" Leda laughed. "I don't have a boyfriend. I'm only fourteen, for gosh sakes. It's for a competition. Best blow job. The winning team gets a trip to Disney."

Lord have mercy, he thought. Well, it had to stop. It was time to push this train, wherever it was headed, right off the track. But he had to do it with tact, with understanding, with cool. He took a deep breath.

"What would your mother say?"

"Oh, please. I wouldn't go to her for advice. I doubt she's any good."

He peered at her, then tried a different tack. "Now, sex is a big decision . . ."

"Sex? It's not sex."

"What is it?"

"It's . . ." She thought a moment. "Recreation."

Jack grimaced. "You are aware of the potential health risks . . ."

"I'll use a condom. I'm not an idiot."

"No one will ever marry you," he blurted.

Leda burst out laughing. "Oh, Uncle Jack, you are so funny."

She took a big gulp of milk and helped herself to another cookie. Jack racked his brain. There was only one thing left to do.

"How do you think that makes him feel?"

"Who?"

"Your victim."

"Victim?" Leda snorted.

Jack leaned forward. "Oh, sure he might say yes, but he's just bowing to pressure."

"I thought they liked it."

"Ah." Jack waved his hand. "That's so typical. The poor guy, he's bought into it. He thinks that's what he wants. He's been told that's what he wants. Every day he's bombarded by images, insinuating themselves into his psyche, force-feeding him his sexual desires. Perhaps he'd rather hold hands. Did you ever think of that? Perhaps he'd like to get to know you better instead of being coolly dispatched in the back of someone's car. Do you think he likes this expert handling of his zipper, this unveiling of his privates, this manipulation of his manroot?"

"Manroot?"

"And what about his heart? Do you even care? A young man's heart is still his largest organ."

"I—"

"Will you even speak to him in the hallway the next day?"

"Well . . ."

"Will you even recognize his face?"

"Of course I will."

Jack raised an eyebrow.

"But Armani said . . ."

"The ringleader, I presume?"

"Yeah. She said . . ."

"That you could practice your skills on these innocent men, notching grooves in your belt buckle?"

"Well, they're not saying no."

Jack shook his head. "Maybe they feel they have no choice. Maybe they feel you won't like them unless they submit."

"Oh, come on."

"Do you think we're so different from you? If you prick us, do we not bleed? If you wrong us, do we not cry? If you toy with us, do we not feel shame?"

"Gosh, Uncle Jack, I didn't mean to upset you."

He shrugged and sighed deeply.

Leda patted him on the arm. "I won't do it. Okay?" She kissed him on the forehead. "Please, don't cry."

Jack forced a brave smile and held out his hand. "I'm glad we had this chat."

Jack sat in Lucinda's office, having paid to fly to New York himself and deposit the manuscript into her lap personally, then insisting she read it right there in front of him, no, thanks, he'd wait. For two hours while she read Jack had sat gazing around her office, noting how prominently she displayed his books in comparison with her other authors'. Lucinda laughed. She turned the page. She laughed again. Jack smiled, encouraged, though uncomfortably aware that he hadn't written a comedy.

Lucinda snorted. "This Chastity, she's so . . . so . . ."

Jack nodded. "Thanks."

"And this Beau . . ."

"You like?"

"He's . . . he's . . ." she gasped.

"Too virtuous?"

"For starters—"

"I'll tone him down a bit." Jack jotted a note.

Finally, Lucinda leaned back and tossed the manuscript on the table. "May I ask what drugs you have been ingesting?"

"Excuse me?"

"This isn't a romance. This is a textbook on how to bore your readers to death."

"I don't know what you mean."

"Look at Beau. You have him thinking sweet innocent thoughts about her . . . he should be trying to ravish her in his every thought."

"But I thought . . . You know, times are changing and I thought maybe the readers were ready for a guy who wasn't enslaved by his dark passion all the time. Someone who was a regular guy. You know, a . . . nice guy."

Lucinda hooted. "Your readers will pass out in their cornflakes."

"But I wanted to keep up with the times. Men are nicer these days. Sensitive. Patient. Restrained."

"Have you read the newspaper lately?"

"Yeah, but that's the press. Your average guy is . . . a nice guy."

"I think you've lost the plot."

Jack stared at the pages. "I just thought I'd do something different. Shake up the industry. Set a new bar height."

"And run yourself into bankruptcy?"

Jack put his head in his hands. Lucinda grabbed the manuscript impatiently.

"Look, any nice stuff has got to be underneath where the heroine can't see it. So you have him reducing her to an emotional pulp in one scene and then have him have a quiet moment with his dog, scratching his ears. A connection that we can spy on and realize that past the ragged knuckles and grim mouth he's all heart. But, for God's sake, don't forget the ragged knuckles and grim mouth."

Jack looked up. "But I thought I'd branch out, try a book about someone who falls in love at first sight, and she, too, and they're both really nice, sensitive, and the only thing keeping them from each other is . . . society. You know, like *Romeo and Juliet*."

"*Romeo and Juliet* is about statutory rape, parental abuse, suicide, and murder. Now *that's* a romance."

She brushed off her lapels as if trying to brush him out of her hair. But he sat looking so forlorn she took pity on him.

"Look, if you want to continue to be a romance writer, Jack, you've got to understand a simple concept."

"Which is?"

"Women don't like nice men."

Her eyes indicated the door.

Jack hesitated. "Can I just ask . . . how did you find Chastity?"

"Truthfully?"

He nodded.

"I've got molding cottage cheese in the back of my refrigerator that's more enticing."

Jack slumped. Lucinda pulled out her notebook. "We'll knock this down to brief insanity. I'll give you another month to make good. Go." She pointed at the door. "Write."

Jack stood up wearily. Lucinda raised a finger. "Oh, I almost forgot. Thanks for sending me your friend's book. What was her name? Molly Desire? Fabulous."

"You liked it?"

"It has a certain joie de vivre."

"It's straight porn."

"Well, I think we need to keep up with the times."

"No moral element whatsoever."

"Well, the heroine gets her guy in the end. Guys, I should say."

She raised her eyebrow. "Frankly, I had no idea the male member was so agile."

"It's not."

Lucinda smiled. "If you say so."

Jack was insistent. "I mean it. Anatomically speaking, it can't do that."

Lucinda reached for the phone. "Well, it's all about wish fulfillment, isn't it? I think Molly has quite a career ahead of her."

It was late afternoon when Jack returned from his trip. He checked the status of his chandelier before striding into the living room for a stiff drink. There he found Molly reclining in the chaise longue. She looked up from the chessboard, where she was playing against herself.

"You're back," she said brightly.

Jack glared at her. "You're still here."

"I know. I'm sorry. The apartment I wanted fell through. I've got a lead on another one."

He poured himself a drink.

"I could use a fresh-up." She held out her glass.

He hesitated, then poured her one and collapsed into his chair. She settled back comfortably. "So how was it?"

"You showed Lucinda your book."

"Yes."

"Using my name."

"Yes."

"Without asking."

"I did ask. You said no."

She picked up the black queen from the chessboard and caressed the piece with her hand. "You play?"

"Of course, I play."

"Good." She began to set up the chess pieces. He picked up a book and pretended to be absorbed. When she was finished, she rubbed her hands and hunched over, hand to her head, like the Thinker. Then with a grand flourish she pushed forward a white pawn. She sat back, self-satisfied, and waited.

He continued to eyeball his book. Molly continued to stare at him. He finally dropped the book and dragged himself out of his chair.

He stood over her, staring down at the board, then finally pushed his black pawn up to meet hers.

She pushed forward another pawn.

He brought out his bishop. She countered with her knight.

He flopped into a chair and put his own knight into play. She chuckled and took his queen pawn. He took her king pawn. She brought out a knight to threaten his queen. He moved the queen. She popped the knight into the middle, thus threatening both castles.

Jack swore.

Molly laughed.

He saved one castle. She scooped up the second.

He viciously swept off the murderous knight with the queen.

She piously castled.

Jack retreated for a think.

"See the board, the whole board," she cooed.

He pictured her exquisite nose flattened by his lightning fist.

"Aha." She bore down on his second castle with her bishop and wiped it off the table. She whooped triumphantly. Jack glared at her long, breakable neck.

He sullenly took her bishop with his queen.

She slid over her castle from behind the pawns.

"Check," she said.

He grimaced; he'd forgotten about that castle.

"Mate," she added, and doubled over in glee.

He swept the pieces to the floor. Her eyes widened. He grabbed her shoulders and pulled her up from her chair, drawing her in, bearing down on her surprised lips with his hard mouth. He backed her against the wall. He could feel her soft curls as his hand closed around the back of her neck. She smelled of warm scotch. He could feel her responding, pushing into him, her mouth supple and inviting. His body was tensed, filled with swirling, driving urges. It was all coming back to him—his need, his dire need. He was all business now. He was crisp and exacting. Her skirt was soon hiked up, her panties shimmied down, her legs parted—

There was a loud banging on the window.

"Jack! Are you there?"

Jack groaned and loosened his grip.

"Who's that?" Molly whispered.

Jack cranked his neck around and found himself staring into the wizened face that peered through the window, taking in, no doubt, the exact roundness of his naked buttocks.

"My mother," he said.

Chapter Ten

"MOM, WHAT ARE you doing here?"

Rita sat at the kitchen table, a cup of tea before her. Her cheeks were pink with excitement. She looked as if she had just broken out of jail.

"I've come to live with you and this charming lady. You didn't tell me you had a girlfriend."

"I don't." Jack leaned against the counter, his arms crossed. "Well, not her, anyway."

Rita winked at Molly. Molly winked back. Rita shook her head at Jack. "You are such a blind boy."

Jack ignored her. "What happened?"

"They threw me out."

"Why?"

Rita shrugged. "Seems I got overly familiar."

"With whom?"

"Well, not with the manager, and I think he's a bit miffed." She turned to Molly. "You know how that is."

Molly rolled her eyes in sympathy.

Rita opened her arms wide. "So here I am. I hope I'm not intruding."

Jack put his glass down. "You've got to go back."

"Why?"

"Well, I'm in the middle of a book . . ."

She turned to Molly. "He's very serious. I've always admired his discipline."

Molly nodded in agreement.

"But he's a bit too much, don't you think?"

Molly smiled, hedging her bets.

Jack contemplated the two women, sitting at his table, drinking his tea, smiling at each other as if he were some amusing toddler.

"What is this? A hotel?" he said, too loudly.

His mother raised an eyebrow.

"I mean . . ." he started, then gave up. "I'll get the sheets."

Later that night, when the house was quiet, Jack, his hair sticking up, ran to the kitchen, where he thumbed through the yellow pages. The air was hot and murky. His skin prickled, his hair stuck to the back of his neck. What a close call. He had nearly ruined everything. Nearly terminated five years of self-denial. And for what? This vixen, this sly she-devil, this harlot in his house, who was sucking the very lifeblood from him, the very marrow of his bones. Who compromised him in the most base way.

He could feel his urges rumbling like distant thunder. She was under his roof, sleeping, bare-breasted no doubt, a long leg tangled in the sheets, her lips parted in slumber. His loins blossomed with desire.

It wasn't personal, he told himself. He was, after all, a man. Red-blooded. Virile. Was he not? Any woman would inflame his passions. Ignite his desires. Though Heather, for some reason, despite her outward perfection, was leaving him cold. Molly, though. You had to protect yourself from such a brazen lack of . . . propriety. Such a wanton display of availability. Such round puckery lips. Such thighs. Those thighs he wanted to caress with every inch of his body. Those thighs he wanted to hold him in a vise and never let go . . .

Born-again virgins, born-again virgins, he murmured, running his finger along the B's in the telephone book. He slammed the book shut. Nothing. He looked around wildly. There had to be someone he could call. He racked his brains and then—yes, he'd thought of just the man. He grabbed the phone and dialed.

"Simon."

"Jack, I terminated our therapy. I told you—"

"I need help." Jack raked his fingers through his hair. "I'm succumbing. Temptation is at the door. In fact, it's already in. It's upstairs, sleeping naked, lips parted—."

"Jack, relax."

"I'm going insane."

"Go with the flow. Take a deep breath and walk up those stairs."

"Never!"

"I think your time has come."

"No, it hasn't. I'm in a relationship! A committed relationship. And if I pass a few more zones, I'm in like Flynn. With a virgin. Do you hear that? A bonafide V-I-R-G-I-N. Miss Restraint herself. And when we commit we're gonna consume each other on a pyre of grand desire and burn the house down. So I can't let go now. Jesus, don't you see? I'm this close."

"Oh, Jack."

"You've got to find me someone to talk to."

"No."

"I'll tell the world you plagiarized half of *The Dark Side of Born-Again Virginity* from a government-sponsored abstinence manual."

There was a pause at the other end.

"Well, perhaps you could use a contact," Simon said.

"Give it to me."

"It's a bit hush-hush, you know." Simon paused as he found the number. "They meet at Sherman Oaks Mall. An informal thing."

"When?"

"Friday nights. Keeps them out of trouble."

Leda was standing at the mirror in the school bathroom when Tiffany and Armani walked in, all clicking heels and brass voices. Leda knew better than to say hello. She was being shunned. No hellos, no nods, just vacant stares when she passed through their sightline. They had not taken it well when she resigned from the trio. "Veil-wearing surrender monkey" was just one of the choice epitaphs. To others, however, Tiffany and Armani had been less than truthful. Leda was too trashy for their class act, they had declared. A real slut. And so Leda had been accosted twice this week in the hall by football players pressing their groins against her. She was miserable. She watched from under her hair as Tiffany banged the condom machine to produce a foil-wrapped disk, which she tossed at Leda. "Stick that where the sun don't shine." The others in the bathroom erupted in laughter. Leda let the condom glance off her, stepping on it as she rushed out the door. She should have gone through with it, she thought. Uncle Jack had ruined her life.

At the sound of the doorbell, Kate hopped down the stairs. She opened the door to find the man from Miller & Sons Painting checking his clipboard. He was young and tall, she noticed with a jolt, with lips as smooth as a baby's bottom. He touched his cap. "Afternoon, ma'am." Kate's knees softened.

"Hi, there," she giggled, stumbling back to let him in. He filled her hallway, all muscle and sweat. Kate closed her eyes and took a deep whiff.

"This way." She waved him forward and followed him up the stairs, her eyes glued to his backside.

Upstairs, he laid his stained hand on the cream wall.

"So you want it red."

"Yes, this Chinese red." She pointed to the cans of paint in the corner.

"The whole room?"

"Yes, it needs livening up."

"Is that right?" he said, glancing over at the white bed.

Kate ogled him, her whole body lit up like a pinball machine, and wondered whether he could hear all the pinging and dinging going on. Her eyes caressed his long lean arms, his beautifully molded seat, the impressive bulge at the front of his frayed jeans. If she reached for him, what would he do? Was he married? Did it matter? More important, would he still have time to paint the room?

"You in a hurry?" he asked.

"No, no, take your time."

"I didn't mean painting."

She raised her eyes to meet his. They peered down at her, dark coffee beans of pure want. She unbuttoned her shirt. He sidled up to her and pressed her against the wall. She closed her eyes as his lips found hers and his paint-stained fingers grabbed her ass.

"I'll get started," he said, and headed for the door. "I gotta get some sheets to cover the room."

Kate blinked from her reverie and sighed with disappointment.

While he was out at his truck, Kate rifled through her lingerie drawer. She changed quickly and squirted herself with scent. She worried about his disappointment when he plunged his hands under her Wonderbra. But then she heard him enter the house again. Her blood stilled. Her joints loosened. Her nipples tingled with anticipation.

He came into the room, carrying white sheets and wearing painter's overalls. Kate wondered how she was going to divest him of those overalls. In the small room, she stood beside him, reeling from his proximity and her desires. And it wasn't as if she were planning on doing the whole thing. She just wanted to touch him, to kiss him, to follow this raging feeling, so delicious and wild. And rare.

"Okay," he said. "I'll get on with it."

She nodded, but didn't move. He waited. She waited.

"What?" he said.

Her body was on fire. She raised her hand then dropped it. In the movies, the steps were easier—a glance, an understanding, a sweeping away of clothes and doubts. She continued to stare at him, words appearing and disappearing in her head.

Recognition dawned in his eyes.

"Lady," he said. "I'm here to paint."

Kate blushed to her ankles.

"Can I get you some coffee?"

"Yeah, black. Lots of sugar."

Downstairs, Kate flicked on the coffee maker and flicked off her erogenous zones one by one. She reached into the freezer for a comforting gallon of fudge ripple.

Jack found them sitting on the benches outside Victoria's Secret, watching the parade of teenage girls wandering in and out. There were five guys. Four, he was soon to learn, were Ralph, a forty-five-year-old cop; Eric, a thirty-year-old taxi driver; Tanner, an eighteen-year-old college student; and Gerald, a fifty-year-old laid-off McDonald's supervisor, who drove up all the way from Irvine.

Neil, the man Jack had talked to on the phone in an emotional gush the night before, approached him with his hand out. Neil wore khakis and a light blue button-down shirt over his large girth. His pillowy blandness was relieved only by a small blond goatee.

"Jack? Thanks for joining us. Come on over and meet our crowd."

He put a heavy paw across the back of Jack's neck and turned him to face the guys. "Men," he said "we have found another brother. Jack has been a committed Born Againer for five years."

The other men peered at Jack with a mixture of wariness and disbelief.

"Let us bid him welcome."

One by one they saluted him, hand to forehead like soldiers, and murmured, "I salute you, keeper of the spirit, brave of the heart, beater of the flesh."

Jack grinned self-consciously at Neil.

Neil patted him on the back. "We salute a guy who is man enough to self-regulate the passions of the body. Isn't that right, men?"

The men grunted. Neil waved Jack to a seat along the rails. "Why don't you sit down? See how it goes. And if you feel like joining in, feel free. We're here to listen to each other, provide support. It's a good group. Isn't it, men?"

The men grunted again. Neil grabbed a clipboard and sat back.

"So, Ralph, how did your week go?"

Ralph shoved a mess of popcorn into his mouth, chewed a few seconds, then swallowed. "Yeah. Okay."

"Anything to report?"

Ralph thought a moment.

"Nope," he said.

Neil nodded. "Anything you want to talk about?"

Ralph thought another minute. "Nope."

Neil checked him off. "Okay. Tanner?"

Tanner was staring at the poster in the Victoria's Secret window.

"Tanner?"

Tanner turned to him, mouth still open.

"Anything to report tonight?"

"No."

"No problems?"

"No."

"No temptations?"

"Not really."

"All right."

Tanner's eyes returned to the overflowing red lacy bra.

Neil glanced at his clipboard. "Eric. How's your fiancée?"

Eric sat with his arms crossed in front of him, rocking back and forth. "She's okay."

"Big day coming soon."

"Next spring."

Neil winked. "Think you can hold out?"

Eric stopped rocking. A look of sheer panic crossed his face. "I hope she's not frigid!"

Neil leaned back, hand to chin. "Would you like to talk about your concerns?"

"What if . . ." Eric stopped and stared straight ahead as if looking at an apocalyptic future.

Neil leaned forward. "Eric?"

Eric's eyes locked onto him. "What if she doesn't know what to do?"

Neil waved him away. "Oh, I'm sure your love will help smooth things over. It will be a beautiful moment. Isn't that right, men?"

The men glanced at Eric, lowered their eyes to his fly, then looked away. Neil smiled at Jack.

"So, Jack. Why don't you tell us about your commitment?"

Jack looked uncomfortable. "I don't know . . ."

"Don't be shy. We're all ears."

Jack cleared his throat then delved into the long, gory details about his past dates and his troubles with Molly. The men glanced at each other.

Neil cut him off. "So what exactly is the problem?"

"Well, I think it goes back to my ex-wife . . ."

There was an intake of breath. Neil laid a hand on Jack's shoulder. "We don't like to use that word here."

"Oh?"

Gerald jumped up with his fists clenched. " 'Bitch' is what we use!"

"Now, Gerald—"

"Shoulda hog-tied her to a tree and made her pay for what she did!"

"Gerald—"

"Slit her throat and let it ooze!"

"That's enough!"

Gerald bashed the Victoria's Secret window. "Bang her, bang her, bang her!"

Neil propelled himself off the bench and tackled Gerald. He held him to the ground while Gerald breathed heavily, like a fallen bull. Jack stared down at them, appalled. The other men looked on without a word. Neil finally stood up again and clapped. "Okay, okay, let's leave it there." He turned to Jack and smiled. "Some of us have exes who have . . . disappointed us."

He held out his arms. "Huddle time."

The men stood up and shuffled forward. They leaned into a circle with their arms around one another. Neil held out an arm to Jack.

"Join us."

Jack stepped back. "No, that's okay . . ."

Gerald grabbed him by the neck and pulled him in. "Dude, you're in the circle now!"

"Who are we?" Neil shouted.

The men yelled at the ceiling. "Born-again virgins!"

"What will we stay?"

"Born-again virgins!"

"What are we waiting for?"

"Love! True love! Rah! Rah! Rah!"

The men clapped and whistled. Neil raised his arms. "Go forth, my men. Stay hard, but stay firm."

The men gave a last clap and trudged away. Gerald gave Jack a bear hug. "See ya next Friday, big guy," he said and walked off.

Jack stared after him. Neil strode up. "You've come to the right group, Jack. We know the pressure out there. We know how hard it is to keep control." He patted Jack on the shoulder. "Luckily, you've got us now."

"I can't come again."

Neil furrowed his brow. "Why not?"

"Well, to be a born-again virgin is a very special proposition. It requires a certain . . . disillusionment."

"Yeah? So?"

"It's just that . . . the other guys?" Jack shook his head. "They're way out of my league."

When Jack got home, he found his mother rummaging around the kitchen, making tea.

"Molly has some good news," she said.

Jack's eyes narrowed. She'd gotten the call, he figured. The call every aspiring writer prayed for. The moment when an editor plucked your masterpiece from the pile and called to let you know it was going to be published. Frankly, Jack could tell her, it was all downhill after that. But when you got the call it was Christmas, your birthday, and New Year's Eve all rolled into one. He frowned. It must have been Lucinda. She probably offered Molly everything she'd never offered Jack: a six-figure advance, 50 percent royalties, a five-second-long credit on the movie screen. He ground his teeth.

"I'll kill her."

"She's pregnant."

"What?"

"Shhh. She's napping."

Jack strode out of the kitchen into the living room, where Molly lay on the couch enveloped in a pink billowing comforter, her eyes closed, her cheeks plump, a satisfied smile on her lips. Rita appeared at the doorway next to him.

"Isn't that sweet? She must be exhausted, poor thing."

"Yup, I imagine she is," he said.

"You'll need to take care of her."

"Me?"

"Well, obviously she'll need to stay."

"Until when?"

"Until the baby comes, of course. You don't want her gestating in a motel do you?"

"No, of course not."

"I didn't think so." Rita wiped her hands and headed for the door.

"But . . . but . . ."

She glanced back.

"But I'm not the father," he said.

"I know," said his mother with great disappointment.

Chapter Eleven

T HE NEXT NIGHT, Jack watched Molly from the corner of his eye. She reclined on the other couch, leafing through baby-and-mother magazines. She suddenly looked so peaceful, he thought. She would have looked like a vision of the Madonna were it not for the handcuffs still hooked to her belt.

"Good day at the office?" he asked.

She flipped through the pages. "I've discovered spanking isn't my thing."

"No?"

"A little light bondage, maybe a tickler or two."

"But spanking?"

"Nah."

"I see."

"What about you?"

"No, spanking has never done it."

She looked over. "What does?"

Jack paused. His fantasy life was rich and eventful, the latest successful images involving three-ring circuses, a nubile trapeze artist, and no end of jiggling tassels. Real life, though, required something much simpler.

"A pulse," he divulged.

Molly laughed. Jack watched her gaze at a picture of a woman nuzzling her baby. She sighed happily. "Did you know that, if she's a girl, the baby's ova are formed by now?" She leaned back, comfortable. "I just find that amazing. To think my DNA is ticking away, slotting itself in, growing hair and fingers and toes."

"Half your DNA."

"What?"

"It's only got half your DNA. The rest is the father's. And your DNA could be slack. Did you ever think of that? Maybe it's the other DNA who's doing all the work. Maybe your DNA is just lying on the couch, eating potato chips, clicking through reruns of *Friends*."

Molly looked over. "I take it you don't approve."

Jack shrugged. "A child should have a mother and a father."

"I think so, too. But it didn't work out that way."

"Because you didn't decide it was important enough."

Molly leaned up on her arm. "Kids grow up without a father all the time."

"But he'll never know his father's side of the family."

"Well, she'll know my side of the family. It'll be enough."

"What are you, an amoeba? Single-celled, just divide in two?"

"Not that it's any of your business, but I did check, all right? The father doesn't want to be involved."

"Now you find out."

She turned her eyes to him. "Would you prefer that I have an abortion?"

He paused. "No."

"Well, then, here we are."

"Yup, here we are." Jack flicked his newspaper back in front of his face.

Molly gazed down at her belly. "I wonder if I'll get really big.

My mom used to get bigger than a house when she was pregnant."

Jack felt contrite. "I'm sorry about your parents."

"Why?"

"Well, you know."

"No."

"About their minds? Their lost minds."

Molly stared at him blankly.

"In Florida?"

"My mom lives in Minnesota. My dad and his wife live in San Diego."

"Oh." He peered at her closely. "And your mom, she remembers everything?"

"Everything she wants to."

"Kate said they had Alzheimer's."

Molly laughed. "Kate is a good sister. But ruthless." She smiled sadly. "No, the real truth is a lot more mundane. My parents divorced when I was ten. They then decided they didn't like being parents anymore, and my sister and I got tossed back and forth like hot potatoes. So we try and help each other out."

"I'm sorry."

Molly shrugged. "What can you do?"

They sat in silence. He glanced over. She wore a khaki tank top and gray fatigue pants. The toenails of her crossed feet were painted lavender. He had never noticed her feet before. They were exquisite. Well shaped and smooth. Each toe a bite-size nugget. He was lost in her feet when he heard her sniff. He looked up to find, to his horror, her eyes watering. She wiped her nose with her arm. He dug into his jeans pocket and pulled out a clean tissue.

"Here."

"Thanks," she mumbled and blew heartily.

Jack cleared his throat. "It must be hard for you. On your own. No one to help you."

She blew again and overwhelmed the tissue. "Oops," she mumbled. He jumped up and raced to the other side of the room and came back with more tissues. He pressed them into her gooey hands. She honked.

"The problem is," he said, "there are no social constraints anymore. Everyone does exactly what they please. No thought for others. It used to be you had a community where people looked after each other, a community that regulated every-one."

"Mmmm," Molly managed.

"Everyone knew their place, knew what to do."

Jack stopped and watched fascinated as Molly dug into her nostrils with the tissue. "Don't you think that's what's wrong with today?" he prompted. "That there's no community to regulate us anymore?"

Molly gave a last blow and wiped her nose. "Did you know that until the twentieth century there were no apartments for women? Three women living together constituted a brothel? It looks to me like things are looking up."

Jack paused. "Then why are you crying?"

"I've got hay fever."

"Oh."

"Usually it's not so bad this time of year, but I've been honking up a storm. Thanks for the tissue." She handed it back to him and finally smiled. It transformed her, like afternoon light on a sunflower. So unexpected and endearing, it made his heart skip a beat. He stared at her, mesmerized.

"What?" She said.

"Nothing." He stood up quickly and shrugged on his coat. Molly looked up surprised.

"Where you going?"

"I've got a date."

"Oh, right." She began flipping through her magazine again. "Have a nice time."

Jack paused outside his house and spied on Molly through the window for a moment before setting off reluctantly into the night. Dating Heather was turning out to be less pleasurable than he'd expected. He had no idea what work it would entail—all the things you had to learn about another person. What was important to her. What was to be avoided. Figs, for example. Heather had a horror of figs. So any mention of the fruit, literal or figurative, was taboo. A fig, Jack soon found out, could trigger high screeches or worse, deafening silence. And silence between them was a mine field. He trod it carefully, looking both ways, lifting and setting down his feet with great care. But Heather kept reminding him that all good relationships required hard work and diligence. And she was a good trainer.

"Fetch," she said.

"Excuse me?"

"Fetch me at seven-thirty."

"Couldn't you just meet me there?"

"A gentleman always collects his date."

He sighed as he got on his motorcycle and strapped an extra helmet to the back. Why couldn't there be virgins west of the 405?

As he drove, he kept his eyes firmly on the road, trying to ignore the billboards that loomed all around him, sixty-foot-high mirages of glossy lips, deep cleavage, and asses waving in the air.

Everywhere he looked, he found naked female bodies draped before him. He felt like Odysseus, strapped to the mast, as he rolled past these Madison Avenue sirens all screaming at him, "Jack, Jack come to meeeeeeee." Ignoring his cock, which twitched as if wired, he gripped his motorcycle bars resolutely and thought about his Penelope.

But when he arrived, she made him wait.

"I'm not ready," she said and then closed the door again in his face.

He leaned against the whitewashed simulated-adobe wall and cooled his heels for a full twenty minutes until she appeared, looking as crisp and fresh as a plastic-wrapped cucumber.

She proffered her cheek for a kiss. As he leaned forward his nose was filled with the innocent aroma of lily of the valley. Her ear was so squeaky clean he had half a mind to take a big bite. He made do with a lingering smooch in the soft spot right below her jaw.

"Easy," she said.

"Ready?" He turned and made for the elevator. Halfway down the hall, he became aware that she wasn't striding along next to him. He turned.

She still stood at her apartment door, her eyebrow arched.

"What?" he said.

"I'm waiting."

His mind clicked like a video game, his mind's eye searching the screen. What was he missing, what was lurking, what was ready to pounce out at any second and annihilate him? He'd come to pick her up, he'd kissed her chastely, he'd brought a wallet full of dollars to pay her dinner with.

She crossed her arms.

"How. Do. I. Look?" It came out in crystal-cut syllables.

"Oooh." He knocked himself in the forehead. "Ya look great. Really great."

The elevator opened with a ding. He turned and dashed for the door. "Come on."

He jammed the door back with his leg and twisted himself around to look down the hall. She was still standing there, staring at him, like a poodle that wouldn't budge.

At his perplexed look, she turned and walked back into the apartment. Jack watched the elevator door close around his foot.

When he returned to the apartment, she was sitting, knees pressed close together, her hands wrapped around her purse.

"We need to talk," she said.

He hesitated. If they left now, they might miss the pre-dinner traffic. But he listened to his inner perfect date and sat down next to her.

"Now, I know that you're inexperienced with this," she began.

He nodded.

"So I'm willing to bend the rules a little. For your earlier infraction, I will not impose my usual correction of no zone policy."

Jack pressed his palms together in gratitude.

"But I need to explain some things to you. Obviously."

Jack glanced at his watch. There went the reservation.

She took out a notebook and began ticking things off. He sat nodding, his head thinking about the meal he would have ordered: Salmon carpaccio to start. Duck with apricots. A bottle of excellent Bordeaux. Maybe a small cognac to finish . . .

"So, in conclusion," she finally said, "I'm in charge of leading the relationship to its natural conclusion, and you're in charge of making me feel good."

"Okay." He stood up.

"Sit down."

He sat down.

She took his hands lovingly in hers. "It all comes down to this: You are to cherish my feelings, and I am to defer to your judgment."

Jack was silent. He rarely deferred to his own judgment.

She leaned forward and flicked an invisible piece of lint from his collar. "In this contract, I expect you to express your gratitude."

"For what?"

"For *what*?" Her tone was icy.

"I mean, for"—he blinked—"what?"

She stood up and put her hand to her hip. "For my being a woman who is willing to put up with you."

"Oh."

"Shall we?" she said. Jack followed her out the door, thinking that if he gave the maître d' a fifty he might give him back the table.

Molly sat in her bath and sang to her tummy, swirling suds around it as if washing the child inside. The nausea still plagued her, and she was so, so tired. Her breasts had been the first sign. The first sign that life was growing inside her. The awe of it. This ability of her body to create another human being. Within her grew the world. And what was she going to call this child of hers? Did she care whether it was a girl or boy? She only cared that it would have every opportunity for happiness. She was awash with love.

She closed her eyes and luxuriated in the warmth. She'd finally been caught. To think after such a long career, this was the first time she'd ever been pregnant. She'd always been so careful, but obviously the guy's Trojans had been defective. Of course, it wasn't the most optimum of moments, but there was no question about what she would do. You didn't look a gift horse like this in the mouth. After all, so many of her friends were single mothers and they had started out married.

Molly wrapped herself in a warm terry towel and padded downstairs for another bowl of Häagen Dazs. Jack had been kind to let her stay, but she really had to find her own place. Though there was something in her that didn't want to leave. She felt at home here. She remembered her happy childhood home. A long time ago, before her father left, walking out on Thanksgiving with the mashed potatoes and turkey leg still sticking to the wall.

Sure, she would have liked a father for the kid. But life had shown her that it wasn't strictly necessary. Nice, yes. How she'd envied her friends whose fathers would come home at night, breezing in and hugging the hell out of the kids before loosening their tie and telling them to get lost. When she slept over at a friend's, she used to wander around the house at night and quietly open the parents' bedroom door to watch them sleep. She got caught once. Because they weren't sleeping. And she was never invited back again.

Well, she wasn't going to let the past derail her. She wasn't going to spend the rest of her life moaning. She had her child to think about. And she wasn't going to give that baby the idea that anything was lacking. Of course, plenty of people were ready to do that. So she, Molly, would have to protect her.

Molly flicked on the kitchen light and padded to the refrigerator. She extracted the ice cream and sat back, eating it straight from the carton. She grinned guiltily. She knew Jack hated it when she did that. She would miss him. And the little things he did for her. The way he always left the hall light on when she'd been out. The way he remembered to buy her favorite tea. The way he sometimes watched her as if she were something very good to eat. Still, he had made his lack of interest very clear. And she'd never forced herself on anyone. She would accept his rejection with grace. You didn't have to tell her twice.

After dropping off Heather, Jack drove back on the Santa Monica Freeway, his lips red with the passionate kisses she had laid upon him like wreaths on a fallen soldier. At dinner he had tried to concentrate on her charms. His forehead had puckered with the effort. He gazed at her expensive silk blouse, her waterfall of pale hair, her bland, perfectly made-up face. Yet his heart sat in its case unmoved, twiddling its thumbs. Jack thumped it impatiently. Dinner, as usual, had run smoothly. Heather had been gracious, switching from topic to topic, summarizing and wrapping up their comments into neat consumer reports. She ate like a sparrow, her finger pointed delicately to the ceiling as she pushed her fork this way and that, expertly avoiding all contact with food.

Afterward, as he stifled a yawn and fumbled with his wallet, she sat with a fixed smile on her face.

"My wrap," she said, handing him her baby-pink pashmina. He hung it carefully about her smooth shoulders, leaning forward to drink in her scent.

"Careful," she warned, and he stepped back gratefully. Ah, finally, here was a woman who was firm in her convictions. Who would rein his swirling passions, who would be architect to the safe, nurturing world he wished to grow a family in.

At her door, however, he found himself asking to come in. "Well, just this once," she said. He cased the place as he entered.

"Tea?" she asked.

"Beer," he demanded.

144

She raised an eyebrow, but smiled. "I'll have one, too." She dipped forward when she handed him the bottle, showing off her cleavage, which she kept restrained behind a flowery cream bra.

"I'll put on some music," she said.

He watched her thin derrière twitch over to her tall, phallic CD rack. Finger to her lips, she made her choice and pushed the Load button on her CD player. It opened, well oiled and smooth. Jack stood up and like a tracker stealthily crept up behind her, blocking any escape. He placed a finger on her lips. Her eyes widened but she said nothing. He laid his hands on her shoulders, right by her throat.

"You be a good boy, now," she giggled, and swatted him away.

It was surprisingly easy. In one smooth movement, he pushed her over the floral armchair, ripped down her panties, and started making himself at home.

"Oh, Jack," she moaned. "Oh, Jack!"

He was in complete control and she loved it. She begged for more and he gave it to her. Deeper and deeper, on and on, until she was crying in ecstasy. With a final thrust he was done with her, and she shuddered. "Oh, Jack," she kept saying over and over, her face buried in the pillow. "Oh, Jack . . ."

"Oh, Jack, Jack, wake up!"

He woke up groggily. He had fallen asleep on Heather's couch while she put on the CD. He had dropped his bottle and the beer was pouring out. Jack shook his head to clear away his dream. Heather's fuzzy image came into better focus. She kneeled on the ground, dabbing impatiently at her rug with paper towels, her pink pashmina still firmly wrapped around her shoulders.

"I think it's time for you to go now." Her voice was clipped.

Jack closed his eyes again, desperate for sleep, but she shook his shoulder.

"Wake up!"

He tried to snuggle into the cushions. "I'm just sooo sleepy. Can't I stay? I promise not to do anything."

She ripped the cushions from under his head. "You can't sleep here. It's expressly forbidden in my mission statement."

Jack heard them before he saw them. As he let himself into his house, the low chanting seeped like noxious fumes beneath the shut doors of his living room. A drumbeat, continuous and slow, like a heartbeat. Through the keyhole he could see the naked bodies flash by. He rattled the locked doors, but no one answered, so he retraced his steps and peeked in through the outside window. The curtains were drawn, but he could see through a crack at the side. Seven women, drinking wine, sat naked on the floor around his elegant Victorian fireplace. One perched in the corner like a Buddha smacking the drum with her palm. Molly stood in the middle, stripped to her waist, swaying to the music, the light flickering on her belly.

Jack watched Molly turn languidly around, her arms undulating, her eyes closed. Her skin shone a pale gold in the firelight. Her hands skimmed the air in a silent monologue. Jack stood mesmerized, his eyes glued to her breasts, which had blossomed with pregnancy. He licked his lips in wonder. Her eyes suddenly popped open and stared right at him. Jack fell back into his rosebush and swore.

He returned to the house and found the kitchen strewn with dirty baking tins and a few remaining cupcakes decorated with fat pink babies. He bit into one and chewed. It was dark chocolate, moist and delicious. He wolfed down two, then rifled through the pile of gifts on the table. It was a varied collection; stretch-mark cream, sesame crackers, mother-

and–baby pampering kit, a big jar of calcium pills tied up with a bow.

When the living room door finally opened, Jack peered from the kitchen into the hallway. The women, now dressed, were filing out the front door, giving Molly's belly a farewell pat as they stepped into the night.

Molly walked into the kitchen wearing a T-shirt and shorts, her skin still burnished with sweat. Jack sat nursing a beer, cupcake crumbs around his mouth.

"What was all that about?"

"A conception party. Make sure everything's all right."

She picked up the tube of stretch-mark cream, hiked up her shirt, and began to smooth the cream into her belly, smiling down as if smoothing it into the baby's skin itself.

"And is everything all right?" he said.

"Hope so."

He gazed at her belly. She glanced down at him. "Do you want to touch it?"

He leaned back. "No, that's okay."

"Suit yourself." She gave it a last pat. "You can't feel anything yet, anyway. It's too small. But it's in there, twirling about."

He continued to watch. With a smile, she took his hand in hers and pressed it against her skin. Her belly was soft and warm. They stayed like that a long moment, not a word passing between them. In the quiet he could hear his heart pound. He wanted nothing more than to lay his cheek against the heat of her belly and stay there all night. He lifted his eyes to Molly and found her smiling down at him, peering through the windows of his lonely soul. He withdrew his hand and grabbed his beer.

"Couldn't rustle up the daddy for the party?"

"Daddy's job is over, isn't it? It's up to me to carry on."

She dug into her pocket and handed him a check.

"What's this?" he said.

"Rent."

"You don't need to pay me."

"Of course I do."

He tried to hand it back. She stopped him with her hand.

"Can you afford it?" he said.

"Don't worry about me. I'm making a fortune over the Internet. They can't get enough of my Zelena the Supreme Spanker. Though I think I'm going to wind up the series. Do something a little more traditional."

Jack pocketed the check.

She watched him. "You look very handsome tonight."

"And you look very . . . feminine."

She gathered her things and headed for the door. "Vive la différence, I say."

"I thought you guys wanted to make everything the same. Equality across the board."

"Not in everything. There are limits to biology."

He inclined his head. "I'm surprised to hear you so level-headed."

She stopped at the door. "Yup. I look at it this way. Pretty soon, male sperm will not be needed for the reproduction of the human species. If we demand equality now, you will be the beneficiary in a couple of generations. Because, face it, in a couple of generations you'll be obsolete."

"I will never be obsolete."

"Why not?"

"Because I could use my superior strength to enslave you, keep you captive, breed you like a mare, and control your offspring, selling them off for my own personal power and wealth."

She grinned. "Well, that's one tactic." She turned off the lights and left Jack alone in the kitchen, drinking in the dark, savoring the yeasty taste of his warm beer.

Chapter Twelve

ON THE WELCOMING plaque was written 21ST ANNUAL ROMANCE WRITERS' CONVENTION. In small print was added "Participate at Your Own Risk." Jack strode in and stopped to breathe in the rarefied atmosphere. Ah, pure romance, he thought. It was such a treat to be with his people again. People who understood the importance of emotion. Who reveled in the balm of a four-hankie ending. He approached the welcome table, which was being run by three very capable-looking ladies who with their sensible, short gray hair and ample girth looked like potbelly stoves.

"Name?"

"Celeste d'Arcy."

They all looked up. "Oh, Celeste d'Arcy," said the first one. "Oh, I know you. You're quite something."

"Quite something, indeed," agreed the second.

"Whew, boy," said the third.

They all looked at him, their eyes taking in every inch of him, their mouths hanging open and receptive. He grinned self-consciously.

"Well, you don't have to kill someone to write murder mysteries."

They laughed and one of them handed him his "Published Author" name tag, which right away elevated him above the aspiring authors from whom the conference drew most of its revenue. He walked through the lobby, carrying his goodie bag and schedule. He was glad he'd come. He had fallen into a rut; he'd lost his bearings. He needed to chop his writer's block and get back to work. He was here to make new contacts, forge new alliances, and let this atmosphere in which romance ruled un-abashedly fill up his well.

The hospitality suite was humming, packed with authors, readers, editors, and enough chocolate muffins to murder any-one's willpower. Along the wall, authors had laid out their promos. He glanced around at the cover art and was appalled. Draculas with come-hither eyes, vixens with red-hot lips, a bride dressed in black leather. The event had all the markings of an erotica convention. All that was missing were the whips and chains. He stopped in his tracks at the sight of a key chain in the shape of furry handcuffs.

He found his allotted table in the corner and busily started setting up, laying out buttons, stickers, and bookmarks. His job that week was to make as good and warm an impression as possible on the readers who wandered by, dragging their heavy book bags behind them like obstinate dogs. As an enticement, he pulled out a large bag of Reese's Peanut Butter Cups and sprinkled them like confetti over his table. He then sat down and waited, glancing around enviously at the other tables headed by women, which buzzed with activity. They sat there so comfortably in their leisure suits with big bright buttons declaring their romantic inclinations. Not for the first time he was reminded how he was not one of them, and never would be. Oh, they might smile, occasionally review his books, even let him onto their panels. But he could always sense the wry superiority, the head-shaking amusement, the silent exclusion.

In the corner, a couple of the male cover models were trying to promote themselves for the title of Mr. Romance. They had their own booth, which they had covered in eight-by-ten glossies of themselves. These were the men who made a living gracing the covers of the books, leaning over longhaired beauties, their shirts strategically ripped to reveal gym-enhanced pecs. There was one for every fantasy: bald and black, buffed Latino, a painfully thin young man with teased and highlighted long blond hair the top of which looked not unlike a rat's nest. Jack waved to Ken, the model he had used for his book signing, who was there offering the Native American option. His big arms protruded from his ripped sleeveless T-shirt; his long black hair shone like an oil spill. He had the stiff-necked look of a giraffe as he flipped his tresses repeatedly behind his back.

Jack would have liked to hang out with his male colleagues, but that was the trouble with being one of a handful of men in his field. There weren't enough of them to form a posse. He did hook up occasionally with one guy, a former fighter pilot who lived in the hills above San Bernardino and who, under the name of Tessa Bradley, wrote sci-fi bodice rippers populated with fishlike women scouring the underseas for their perfect mates. But he hadn't been able to come this year, so Jack was on his own.

He opened the conference schedule and thumbed through the choices of panels: "Sex Sells," "How to Sex Up Your Plot," "Sex and Dialogue," "Wet Dreams of Your Characters." Then he saw it, just what he was looking for: "The Nuts and Bolts of Romance Writing." That's what they all needed, he thought piously, a good old-fashioned reminder of the elements.

Abandoning his table, Jack grabbed his notebook and jogged

down the wide hotel corridors, searching for the Jefferson Conference Room. But there were several conference rooms, on different floors, in different buildings. The hotel was like a maze, intent on keeping its residents cluelessly huddled in the lobby bar.

When Jack finally found the room and swung open the door, he came to an abrupt stop. For there she was, standing at the podium in a bright red suit opened to reveal a black bustier. She wore a black feather boa flung around her neck and carried a pointer in her hand. She looked as if she'd just stepped out of a schoolboy's fantasy. Her name tag said "Molly Desire, Published Author."

She smiled with glee and raised her hand toward him. "Jack!"

Jack collapsed into a chair at the back of the room. He couldn't believe Molly was on a panel already. A story or two online, and the romance establishment was treating her as one of its members. It was ludicrous, recognizing online publishers of erotica who peddled their filthy wares to Saudi Arabia, exporting their obsessions with spanking and bondage. Jane Austen would twirl in her grave. He was surprised there was no international uproar.

He raised his hand. "I thought this was about the nuts and bolts of writing."

"It is. Your nuts and your bolt."

The class tittered. Molly swung her arm out to introduce him to the crowd. "Now, here's a man who could tell you a thing or two about turning our unspeakable urges into cold hard cash. Say hello to Celeste D'Arcy!"

The women clapped enthusiastically. Jack raised his hand in acknowledgment. Molly returned to her lecture. "The biggest problem, of course, is what to do with all the body parts. What do you call everything? With erotica you've got to check your romance sensibilities at the door. I call a cock a cock, and I'm very explicit about where it goes and what it does. It's a tool, right? A tool for pleasure."

"Don't forget the whips and chains," Jack called out.

Molly peered out at him. "It's not about chains and whips. It's about the psychology of power. It's not about positions, but about permission. I call it coloring outside the line. And, believe me, publishers are looking for writers to cross a few lines. But you have to remember to include the details. Be specific. How many fingers? Painful versus playful spanking?"

The women in the classroom nodded and scribbled notes.

Molly sauntered down the aisle toward Jack and stopped in front of him. "Our job is to heighten the sexy feeling. Which is why you have to be very descriptive." She placed his hand on the breast of her lace shirt. "Feel that lace. It's rough but evocative. Compare it to this," she said, sliding his hand down the thigh of her silk stockings. "Soft and inviting as a whisper." She leaned forward, her lips inches from his, her eyes veiled by her hat. "Do you see my eyes? Have I become mysterious to you?" She circled his neck with her feathery boa. "Go on, stroke my kitty," she whispered in his ear.

Jack found Lucinda in the lobby bar guzzling old-fashioneds and staring at the football players barreling back and forth on the TV. She looked tired. She didn't acknowledge Jack. She just watched the carnage on screen, open mouthed.

Jack slid into the seat next to her. "I need to talk to you."

Lucinda took a big sip of bourbon. "If I hear one more pitch, I'm going to scream. I got one just now in the elevator about a dog who's a wereman and desperate to find his true love before he's neutered. Lord, lend me strength."

"I thought you liked these conventions."

"Too much of a good thing is not necessarily a good thing. How many books did you sell?"

"Let me get you another drink."

She rolled her eyes but didn't protest.

Jack handed her the complimentary bowl of broken potato chips. "So, uh, did you get a chance to read my latest?"

"Yup."

"And?"

"I hate this part of my job."

"Well, it was really just the first draft."

"In that case, you won't mind tossing it."

It was Jack's turn to take a long drink.

Lucinda popped an olive into her mouth and glanced over at him. "Paranormal is in. Have you any green aliens pining away for their orange counterparts?"

"No."

She gazed back at the football. "Pity."

"What am I going to do?"

"Sometimes people need a break. They get burned out."

"Well, maybe I could change era."

"I suggest a change of pseudonym."

"It's that bad?"

"Well, the figures have not been good."

He slumped on the bar.

Lucinda waved her glass at the waiter for another. "Don't be glum. It happens to everyone. Hell, even Nora Roberts can't do Nora Roberts anymore."

"What if my next hero is green?"

Lucinda cocked her head. "What color green?"

"Chartreuse. He turns to emerald when he's really turned on."

She nodded. "Antennae?"

"I suppose."

"Would they be fuzzy or smooth?"

Jack looked at her.

She looked back. "Jack, you can never underestimate the importance of the texture of a man's antennae."

That night, Jack dressed carefully. Black on black, topped off with a large werewolf mask. He placed it over his head and scrutinized himself in the mirror. The effect was mesmerizing: rough tufts of hair, bloodied teeth, gleaming eyes. He'd never written a werewolf romance, although werewolves were one of the most popular alpha males. He was grateful Lucinda had never pushed him in that genre direction. Dog fetishists, he called those fans.

He was still bristling from Molly's lecture. Okay, she wanted erotic? She wanted tantalizing and explicit? He would play her game. He threw his cape over his shoulders and opened the door. Molly was in the building somewhere; he was going to sniff her out and devour her.

Downstairs the conference attendees gathered in costume outside Ballroom A for the annual Vampire Ball. It was a motley crew, with witches in fishnet stockings, several Elviras, and plenty of grinning vamsels in distress. There was every range of vampire, mostly the bland tuxedo-and-whiteface variety, though one was sashaying around straight-backed in a black corset, looking like a cross between Nosferatu and Scarlett O'Hara.

Jack looked around but didn't see Molly anywhere. He waded into the sea of self-promotion. A pirate grabbed a vixen from behind and she fell into his arms with a swoon. "Hold it," someone barked, and a flash went off. As Jack stalked around the party's edges, women surged around him, batting their eyelids.

They loved his look. They reached for his gloves, tried to kiss his mask. He finally had to dash through the crowd, clutching his costume to him.

Then he caught sight of her, leaning against the wall next to the ballroom doors, looking demure and wildly seductive in a long white Regency-style wedding dress, with a tiara in her hair. He stared at the way her breasts swelled snugly in her tight bodice. His mind swirled around her body like a mist. Lucinda was wrong. His book wasn't over the top after all. For there Molly was, his pregnant princess bride.

This was his chance. Jack approached her from behind and breathed her in. The darkness of his mask heightened his awareness. He could smell her, that intoxicating musky smell. Like the forest bed after a spring rain. He could hear the rustle of her dress as she moved. Her slow, steady breath. He could almost hear the baby inside her swirling around. She was ripe, open. Her lips plump, like freshly picked raspberries. He reached out and drew his finger down the back of her neck. She turned around and peered up at his mask.

"Hello?" she said.

He leaned close. "I ache for you."

Molly laughed.

He tried again. "I want to take you."

"Who are you?"

"Anyone you want me to be. Anonymous, faceless. A stranger."

She reached for his mask. He held her hand away. With the other he let his finger stray along the bodice of her dress.

"Tell me," she said.

He pushed against her. Her eyes widened as she felt his intent. She lowered her eyes. He knew that look; he'd seen it all too many times before, and he knew exactly where it would lead her. He would tantalize her until she begged for more. His nostrils flared as he bent down and bit her on the shoulder.

She slugged him in the stomach.

"Ow!" he cried.

She grabbed his testicles and gave them a good twist. "Look, pal, I don't know who you are, but you can take that shit and shove it up your ass."

She released him and disappeared. Jack doubled up and leaned against the wall, gasping for breath.

He stumbled into the men's bathroom, where he found Ken standing at the mirror, dressed with Elizabethan flourish with a Mr. Romance contestant number on his back. He was applying blemish cream.

"Of all the nights," Ken said.

Jack ripped off his mask and dropped it on the side of the sink. He washed the sweat from his brow.

"Hey, it's you!" Ken said.

Jack stared dully at his reflection. "It's me."

"Got any more books coming out?"

"You'd have to ask my publisher."

Ken flicked back his hair and regarded his image in the mirror. "Well, wish me luck." He ambled over to the urinals. Jack stared at Ken's back in the mirror. This was one of many men who had slept with Molly. This one, he remembered, had left with Molly after Jack's book signing and had made her moan and groan and thrash about until the chandelier nearly fell down. He narrowed his eyes and popped his mask back on. He strolled over next to Ken at the urinals and unzipped as casually as he could.

"Think you'll win?" Jack said.

"I'm hoping for Mr. Congeniality."

Under the cover of his mask, Jack glanced down and over. He grinned and zipped back up.

"Don't worry," he said, "you got it in the bag,"

By the time he got back, everyone was filing into the ballroom for dinner. Inside, witches and dominatrixes were tripping over one another to grab the best tables near the stage. Jack went from table to table looking for Molly, but couldn't see her anywhere. "You're going to have to sit down, sir; the show's about to start," a harried waiter said, so Jack finally slid into a seat between a vampire and a succubus. They turned and smiled, their fluorescent fangs white and dripping with blood. He took off his mask and lay it on the table beside him, then settled his napkin on his lap and dug morosely into his chicken breast.

"Ladies and gentlemen, it's time for the Mr. Romance Competition!"

Jack looked up. Twelve men stood under the glaring lights in billowing white pirate shirts and tight black pants. The women hollered like truck drivers and clapped wildly. Jack watched appalled as, one by one, the men strode down the catwalk, some waving swords, some ripping off their shirts (those who did and shouldn't have got a sympathy clap). The last one to parade down the catwalk was Ken. His hips pumped back and forth like pistons and his lips were curled in mock disdain. The women around the edge of the catwalk bellowed with desire. The MC crooned into the microphone. "Let's give it up for Ken Bullfeather. He likes surfing, singing, and his two Dalmatians, Jack and Jill!"

Ken stopped at the end and, fixing the crowd with a pout, untied his shirt.

"Woo woo woo," went the crowd. Ken turned and slid the shirt up his bronzed, buff back. He stopped halfway and glanced back.

"Oh, baby, oh, baby." The woman next to Jack had her hand to her heart and looked in serious pain.

Ken slid the shirt over his head and, whirling it around a time or two, tossed it to the crowd.

"Oh, God, give it to me now!" A Victorian damsel in distress leaned forward and yelled.

Ken pranced back along the catwalk, glancing left and right, lips curled, eyes hooded, chest flexing with each stride. He stepped back in line and winked.

"And there you have it, ladies and gentlemen, our twelve contestants for the title of Mr. Romance!"

The women stood and whooped.

"And now please take your seats as the models and authors reenact some of your favorite scenes."

Ken stepped from the line and walked to the middle of the stage. He plastered on a brooding face and flexed his muscles. The crowd yowled. Spotlights flicked on to reveal Molly, also on the stage, draped over a chair in a tight black low-necked sweater, a mid-calf skirt slit up the side, and a beret perched cockily on her swept-back hair. Jack dropped his roll.

A reader stepped up and began to read: " 'How many days does a girl have to wait for a guy to make his intentions known? How many nights does she have to sleep alone and fantasize about the moment he comes to his senses . . .' "

"Oh, I love this one. It just sizzles," the succubus leaned over and whispered into Jack's ear.

Ken prowled up to Molly, his arms swinging back and forth, his gait long and low. He swung her back and leaned over her, raking her body with his nails. She grinned up at him with pleasure.

" 'And then, one day when you least expect it, sanity arrives in the form of a big . . .' "

Ken jutted forward his chin and kissed the hell out of Molly. The crowd howled its approval. Jack jumped up. Heat built in his brain; the pressure was unbearable. He rushed forth and hopped onto the stage. There was a gasp from the audience. The woman reading the passage stopped in surprise. Jack strode toward Ken and Molly. Ken looked up and immediately stepped back. Molly stood up unsteadily and squinted toward the oncoming black shape, silhouetted by the lights.

Jack paused, struck dumb.

Molly blinked. "Jack . . ."

Her eyes shone like moonstones. Her lips were parted in that half smile that drove him wild. He wanted to grip her, to kiss that grin off her face, he wanted to . . . He grabbed the microphone from the reader and turned to the crowd. There was a hush. He cleared his throat.

"What happened to romance?"

There was complete silence. You could have heard a fluttering hankie drop. He took a deep breath.

"What happened to the emotional coming together of two people? A man and a woman, I don't care, a man and a man, a man and a genetically modified woman, a man and a centaur."

The audience looked at one another curiously.

"Love is not about body parts. Or positions. Or size. Love is about you and me. It's about finding your soul mate. The yang to your yin. Your sun and moon and star. But it is here." He pointed to his heart. "Not here." He grabbed his crotch.

There was a delighted gasp.

Jack observed his audience. They stared back, open-mouthed. He glanced over at Molly.

"It just seems to me that we used to have a tradition here. Men and women behaving like civilized people. Learning to relate with dignity and affection. Not all this jumping into bed on page one. Penis size detailed before we even know the guy's intentions. Characters screwing in the streets, faceless, nameless."

"I give them names," Molly interjected.

"But forget to use them."

"Is that a personal attack?"

"Look, all I'm saying is, let's get back to romance. Let's get back to delayed gratification. To honor, and beauty." He looked out at the audience and smiled sadly. "After all, what are we? Animals?"

"*Yes!*" the ladies roared.

The sound was apocalyptic. It blasted back like a fireball and singed his heart. Jack handed back the microphone, bowed to Molly, and made his way down the catwalk. There was silence as he stepped off. The crowd parted around him as he headed out the doors.

Chapter Thirteen

J ACK RECLINED ON his couch, a pile of empty beer cans around him, trying to figure out what to do with the rest of his life. The fallout from the convention had not been good.

"I'm considering not offering you another contract," Lucinda had said. "I just don't think your heart's in it anymore."

"Maybe if you let me use my real name, I'd have more invested."

"I just don't think you're ready."

"To be a man?"

Lucinda sighed. "I really don't see what the big deal is."

"I'm hiding behind this false identity. I feel like a fraud."

"Ginger Savage doesn't care."

"Who?"

"He's new. I signed him at the conference. He writes his novels in text messages and draws little pictures in the margins. You should read him. He's so now, so cutting edge."

"So illiterate?"

"Don't be testy. You've no idea the pressure I'm under. I have to attract a younger crowd."

"But does he make you moan the way I do? Make you quiver, make you beg for more?"

"Now, Jack."

"I'm serious. What am I supposed to do with all this love, this knowledge, this passion?"

"Why don't you try real estate?"

Disheartened, Jack had stopped the charade of disappearing upstairs every morning and instead lay in front of the TV, munching potato chips and flicking through cable channels. Now he clicked on MTV to find Christina Aguilera prancing around in leather chaps and little else. He scratched his groin and sighed. Leather and skin, he had to admit, a wholly good thing.

Molly appeared at the door. "Well, if it isn't the best-selling romance novelist hard at work."

Jack's eyes didn't leave the screen. He was still red-faced about the scene he'd created at the conference and had been avoiding Molly. "I thought you were going to the animal sexual rights conference today."

Molly stretched. "I was too distraught. I killed him."

"Who?"

"Jes Hardy. My hero."

Jack looked up. "You can't do that."

Molly shrugged. "Well, it just happened. One minute, they're laughing, eyes shining, hearts bursting, groins tingling, and then suddenly a single shot is fired and he falls down dead. Poor Cassandra." She thought a moment. "Poor me."

She glanced through the *TV Guide*.

Jack continued to stare at her. "That's awful."

"Yeah, it was too bad."

"No, I mean, that's bad writing. You've got to put him back."

"No can do."

"Look, you're just going to have to work harder, beef up his character. Make him strong, sincere . . ."

"And sexy. Did that. Not enough."

"Then you've got to add to him."

"Oh, no, he didn't need anything more. He already had everything a man needed."

"And what was that?"

"Well, he had the most gorgeous steel-blue eyes, for one. They were like the sea on a stormy night." Molly smiled dreamily. "And he had a chest that just made my mouth water. And buns . . . babeee." Molly sighed. "But that was nothing compared to his inner beauty. He had an inner core you couldn't break. He believed in something, you know. Something bigger than himself. He was heroic. A shining star."

Jack gazed at her curiously. Past the jungle of clichés, he could see a sliver of civilized truth. Molly shook her head sadly. "But then he died. A smile on his firm lips. All his appendages lying there, useless. Oh, poor Cassandra. Poor me."

"A real stud, huh?"

She waved him away. "Oh, he was more than just a stud. He stood up for what he believed in. I think in the end every woman wants a man who stands for something."

Jack crossed his arms. "Okay, I'll bite. What did he stand for?"

She thought a moment. "He stood up for the less able."

"What, like on a bus?"

"He stood up for people being who they are. Freedom, I guess. He stood up for freedom."

"And that's a turn-on?"

"And how."

"But you killed him."

She shrugged.

Jack leaned forward. "You murdered him. You put your hands around his neck and snuffed out the life of a decent man."

"Let's not get over—"

"There he was trying to do his best, trying to please you, trying to make you happy—and what do you do? You destroy him. You annihilate your hero."

"It's okay, I'll create another one."

Jack stood up. "You don't deserve another one!"

Molly blinked. "Jack."

He threw her a dismissive glance and headed for the door.

She called after him. "You want to know why I killed him?"

Jack rested his hand on the door handle but didn't turn.

"It's because he didn't love Cassandra. All right? I worked and reworked his inner monologues until I was blue in the face, and he just stood there, arms folded, unconvinced. A million words down and he never warmed to her."

"That happens."

"Well, I don't know what he was waiting for. Something better, probably. Always looking for something better. Prettier. Nicer. Bigger breasts." She collapsed back into the couch. She looked up. "So I shot him." She shook her head solemnly. "So I shot him," she said again. She then grinned. Then chuckled. Then laughed out loud. Guffaws burst from her like hiccups. She abandoned herself to laughter, laying her head down on the coffee table, her shoulders jiggling with mirth. Jack watched her, stone-faced.

"Whew," she said, finally coming up for air, wiping her eyes with the back of her hand. "Look at me. I've run the gamut of emotions and I haven't even brushed my teeth yet."

Later, when Jack was still clicking through channels and Molly had long ago gone upstairs to work, there was a pounding on the front door. Jack looked through the peephole to find Richard cowering on his front stoop.

166

"You've got to help me!" Richard cried when Jack let him in. He slammed the door behind him. "Zara's found out about me marrying Maryann. She's trying to kill me."

"Can you hear that?" Richard put his ear to the door. A faint buzzing leaked through the mail slot. "She's got a chain saw." He pulled Jack into the living room and barricaded the door behind them. Jack sat back on the couch, his hands behind his head. Richard yanked the curtains closed. "I think I eluded her. I had to run down the alley. It was unbelievable. There I was sitting at the Sidewalk Café with Maryann, minding my own business, and Zara walks up and cuts our table in two. I had to run for my life. It was chaos. It was primal. It was—"

"What happened to Maryann?"

Richard paused. "I don't know." He poured himself a drink. "Oh, God, why does this always happen to me?"

Jack raised an eyebrow.

Richard paced the room. "You know what Zara said to me? Just as she's sawing my daiquiri in half? She said, 'You don't like women.' Can you believe that? She's talking about me here. Of course, I like women. I like everything about them. I like the way they look. I like the way they keep conversations going. Asking me questions about myself I've never thought about. I like the way they fuss, buying me cashmere sweaters for my birthday. I like them too much. That's the problem: I can't choose. But I have to. I want as good a marriage as my parents have. And I've chosen Maryann."

"Lucky girl."

"You can say that again. But she's perfect: lovely, devoted, great with kids. And she's smart, too, so she can work. Because, you know, life is much more expensive now. We want to have a big house. And travel. And I'm gonna make sure she exercises so she keeps those great legs."

The chain saw was getting louder. Richard flicked back the edge of the curtains. "You ever seen a woman with a chain saw?"

Jack shook his head. "Can't say I have."

"It's spectacular." Richard peered out the window again. "Stirring. It's hotter than hot." He hesitated. "Well, thanks for the drink." He slapped Jack on the shoulder and dashed out the door. "Zara," Jack heard him cry as he ran down the path. "Wait for me!"

Leda sat alone in the school cafeteria. No one would talk to her. Beth, her usual best friend, was not taking her back, and Tiffany and her crowd were definitely not an option. There was no chance of sauntering up to the beautiful people and setting down her lunch next to their homemade fat-free salads. Besides, most of them had sneaked out to McDonald's anyway. She didn't really want to sit with the goths, had no interest in the potheads, and wouldn't touch a nerd with a ten-foot pole. So she sat alone on the end of a long table and sucked unhappily at her chocolate shake.

"Hi."

She looked up to see a girl whose name she didn't know. She'd seen her once or twice passing her in the halls, noting only that she was usually alone, dressed in overalls, and walking quickly with her head down.

"Can I sit here?" The girl held her tray to her side like a football.

Leda shrugged. "Sure."

They sat for the next five minutes, staring downward, eating in silence, until the girl picked up her chocolate shake. "Look. Same."

Leda nodded and smiled wanly. "Yeah."

The girl leaned forward. "I've noticed you before. I like your hair."

"Thanks."

"It's a pretty color."

"I wish it was blonder."

"No. I like it just the way it is."

Leda smiled. She picked up her tray. The girl pointed quickly to the band sticker Leda had stuck to her books. "They rock!"

"Yeah, he's really cute."

"What's your name?"

Leda hesitated, then set down her tray. "Leda."

"Mine's Susan."

Leda nodded.

The girl made a face. "I hate it."

They laughed. And Leda relaxed a bit and thought, Hey, maybe she can be my new best friend. She leaned forward to confide the way best friends do. "You know what makes me happy?"

Susan was all ears. "What?"

"Fresh bread."

"Me too! Cinnamon rolls."

"And I love the smell of clean laundry."

"Totally. My mom uses this stuff with lemon in it? Makes it smell like lemonade."

"Know what I really like? Seeing the Crest Whitestrips actually make my teeth whiter."

"Me, I like shoes that fit me without making my feet look like they're a yard long."

They leaned toward each other and giggled. But then Leda's eyes grew wide as she saw three boys approach behind Susan. Football players. Their necks were the size of boulders. They bore down on the table and stopped abruptly, looming over the two girls' heads. Leda flinched at the oncoming assault but they addressed Susan instead. One knocked her milk shake onto the floor.

"Lezzie, lezzie," they chanted, then moved on, leaving the two girls trembling in their wake.

Susan didn't budge. Leda stared at her, horrified. Leda quickly looked around. Everyone was staring at them, pointing, laughing. Leda's stomach sank to the bottom of her boots. She pushed back her chair. "I gotta go."

Susan squinted at her milk shake and didn't move.

Leda perched on the edge of her chair, her hands around her tray. "I'm sorry."

Susan looked up. "Yeah, I mean, no. I mean, it's okay. Whatever."

Leda stood up, feeling guilty. But her life was intolerable already. This was the last thing she needed. She rushed away.

On the top floor of Jack's house, in his third bedroom, Rita lay in bed, looking through her photo albums. She wasn't prone to nostalgia, but she'd been feeling old and tired lately so she thought she'd have a nice relaxing cup of tea and reminisce about her past. Such a short past, it seemed. Especially the last ten, fifteen years, when she hadn't bothered to take many pictures. There were dozens of pictures of the children until they were about ten or eleven, and then the photos just petered out. A few special occasions, graduations, a couple of summer trips, two weddings. But nothing like right after they were born, when a crooked smile had been occasion enough to pull out the camera.

She gazed at a picture of her late husband, taken on the dock of their summer rental in Big Bear. He was laughing, contemplating plunging in. His hair was crew cut, as had been popular at the time, making him look more masculine than she remembered. She regarded his stocky physique wistfully. She'd never known whether her husband strayed. She was too exhausted, first by the children and then by her late career as an early reading specialist, to think too much about that. Every once in a while she would ask herself what she would do if he had had affairs and she'd found out. But infidelity never reared its head, even though her heart had always slowed when she unfolded stray bits of paper from his coat pocket. The question, and their physical relationship, passed into history. He died a loved man, a quiet man who did his duty. He had been closer to Kate than to Jack. Behind closed doors, he would criticize Rita for holding on to Jack too long, for not letting him go. And look at Jack now, Rita thought ruefully. Maybe he was right. But what mother doesn't love her son with unspeakable passion?

Chapter Fourteen

THEY WERE MADE of steel and had no faces. They loomed before Jack, sixty feet high, thin silvery arms turning slowly but relentlessly. He raised his arm and urged his lathered horse forward. As he rode by, he slashed with his sword at the air above him, but the arms were miles up, and they continued to turn. He pulled his horse up at the top of the hill. Sweat poured down his back. The sun tore at his eyes. His nostrils flared with indignation. He tightened the reins with one hand and stretched out the arm holding the sword. He took a deep breath, filling his lungs up with hope. There was grace in trying to avoid the inevitable, he thought, as he dug into his horse's sides, bellowing as he leaned forward. The thunder of the hoofs filled his ears, but as he neared his prey thunder gave way to the sound of silence. And all he could hear as he turned his steed around for another go was his jagged breath and the soft *swoosh swoosh* the arms made as they skimmed through the air.

Jack jolted up in bed. He blinked in the blackness. The *swoosh* had sharpened into a hissing. Then a howling, which broke sharply. He stumbled out of bed and ran to his window. He placed his face flat against the glass and could just make out a shadow below struggling with a bulging black bag. The fuckers were trying to steal Tom. He shouldn't have let his guard down.

"Drop him!" he yelled. He whirled around and ran down the stairs. He barreled through the kitchen and pushed through the door. But he missed his step and lost his balance. He just caught sight of a big black jacket and a cowboy hat before the screen door swung back, caught him on the forehead, and he dropped like a sack of potatoes.

When Jack woke up he found himself in bed, a woman asleep in the chair beside him, her head fallen back, a rip-roaring snore shaking her nose. He eyed her a long time, taking in her spiky hair, her apricot kimono, her smooth, creamy skin, and wondered who the hell she was.

He glanced around the room, his eyes alighting on the dresser and desk, the computer and all the books. A slow panic began rising: he couldn't place any of it. He scanned the room again. He didn't recognize a thing. He examined the woman, who by now was leaning precariously to the side. One more snore and she might topple. Had she kidnapped him? In a panic, he rubbed his feet together. But they were intact. Was he tied to the bed? He swung up his hand to check and smashed himself in the side of the jaw. He winced. He threw back the covers and swung his legs out, then groaned at the ache in his head. The woman snorted awake. She jumped up and pushed against him as he tried to get up.

"Whoa, take it easy."

"Where am I?"

"Your head still hurt?"

"Where am I?"

"At home. In your cozy bed. Here"—she pushed him gently back—"just rest."

He shook off her hand. She didn't look like a nurse. Why was she so insistent that he stay in bed? What did she plan to do? He pushed himself up and grabbed the bedpost for support. His legs were jelly.

"Jack, stop. I'm going to call the doctor."

"What's wrong with me?"

"You fell. You hurt your head."

"God, I can't remember anything."

"It'll come back. Just sit down."

He collapsed back and let her lift his legs onto the bed. He watched her teeth clamp down firmly on her tongue as she leaned over and tucked him back in. Her worn robe fell open and revealed ivory skin caressed by a slip of a camisole. He gazed in rapture but she whisked the feast away, settling herself on the edge of his bed and patting his hand.

"It's okay, Shhhh. It's okay," she said.

She smelled of lavender. Was it lavender? Something fresh. A touch of sweetness. He allowed himself to relax. She was soothing, whoever she was. He examined her funny lips. Infinitely kissable, he thought. And her eyes, though tired, were beautiful, gold and brown, like a caramel swirl. He lost himself a moment in those eyes.

"Are you all right?" she said.

Then it dawned on him. Of course: This must be his wife. That's what wives did, right? Patted you on the hand when things went wrong. And what they wore. Ratty robes. He suddenly laughed. Everything was okay, then. Here was his wife. She was kind. And caring. And—he swept his eyes across her succulent body—hot.

"What's so funny?" she asked.

He shook his head. He couldn't admit he didn't recognize her. Wives, they got touchy about that sort of thing.

174

"Just you, me . . . everything."

"Yeah. Pretty funny."

He peered at her in the dim light. He noticed she sat with her hand absentmindedly rubbing her tummy. He stared at it. She smiled.

"The morning sickness is gone, I think."

Oh, God! His *pregnant* wife. He fell back.

She touched his forehead with the back of her hand. "You okay?"

He gazed at her and wondered whether he loved her.

"What happened?" he said.

"Someone tried to steal your cat."

"Oh?" he said noncommittally.

She leaned forward. "Jack, do you know who you are?"

"Jack?" he said.

She smiled. "All right. How old are you?"

He thought a moment. "Do you have a mirror?"

"You don't remember anything?"

He couldn't break it to her. It would be too cruel, to know that her husband, the father of her child, had lost his marbles. He would have to protect her from the truth. He would get to know her again in time. And love her. Luckily, he could begin afresh with the baby.

"I was just kidding," he said.

She smiled, relieved. "Okay . . . Well, probably the best thing you can do now is rest."

He reached out and stroked her shoulder. "Okay, dear," he said.

She looked down at his hand. "You sure you're feeling all right?"

"Fine, fine." He glanced at her tummy. "How are you feeling?"

"Oh, good, thanks." She straightened up and patted her belly. "Yup, I definitely think I'm over the worst. Until the birth, of course."

"Do we know what it's going to be?"

She smiled. "A baby."

"I mean, sex."

"Oh, I don't plan to find out."

"Don't have a problem with that."

She smiled. "Well, that's good."

He nodded. He patted the side of his bed. "You must be tired. Why don't you take a load off?" He raised his eyebrows suggestively.

She laughed. "I'm glad you haven't forgotten your sense of humor. Now, I've got to go out. Why don't you take it easy? Your mom's here. She's making you scrambled eggs."

"I love scrambled eggs," he said agreeably, then paused. Did he?

Later, his mother brought up a tray. He watched the woman walk in. She was trim, with flame hair and very bright blue eyes.

"You gave us a fright," she said, arranging the breakfast tray across his lap. "Imagine, getting all worked up over that randy old fart."

"Who?"

"Your cat."

"Oh."

"Molly said you were a bit hazy."

Molly. So that was his wife's name. Molly. He liked that. Molly. And she was having his baby. He grinned. He was looking forward to trying again.

His mother plumped up his pillows and settled him back. "I

think you should stay in bed today. I don't think you should write."

Write. Write what? He glanced at the nightstand and saw a stack of books with women swooning on them. His wife's reading, no doubt.

When she closed the door, Jack closed his eyes. He felt so sleepy. He thought of Molly and shook his head in amazement. A baby. She was having his baby. How perfect. He tapped at his chest with manly pride, then pumped his pelvis in celebration. He sighed as he leaned back. There was nothing sexier than a woman's rounded belly, filled with his child. Jack fell asleep with a smile on his lips.

When Jack woke, he found Molly sitting on the bed, staring down at him. She had placed her hand on his as if keeping it warm. At his glance, she blushed and retrieved her hand, burying it deep in her pocket. They sat in silence, examining each other's faces. Jack felt as if he had had a very good dream and awakened to find it all true. He could hear the rain outside, tapping at the windows like an instrument.

"How long have I been asleep?"

"About an hour."

"Rain. That could be a good name for the baby."

She laughed. "Maybe."

"God, a baby. Such a big thing."

"I know, Jack," she said wearily. "I know it's a big thing."

He was confused. Had they been discussing it like that? Was it an issue between them?

"I just meant—"

"I know. But I'm dealing with it, and it's no concern of yours." She stood up to go.

He reached up swiftly and pulled her onto the bed. She fell over on him and gazed down with surprise.

"Let's talk about this later," he said, his voice husky. His arms circled her. He nuzzled her neck. "Do you know how delicious you are?" he said.

He quieted her astonished laugh with his mouth. He delved into her skin with abandon. It tasted of salt and sand. He noticed as he rushed to divest her of her clothes that she was wearing a bikini. He pulled the top down and licked at the sprinkling of sand around her nipple. She alternated between batting him lightly away and moaning deeply. It was a tantalizing combination and he pressed into her, urgent.

With a groan she pushed him away and sat up, slipping her arms back into the top of her bathing suit. He sat up, confused.

"What?"

"We can't do this," she said.

"Is it the baby?"

"No, it's you."

"Should I shave?"

"You know who I am, right?"

"The mother of my child?"

"Oh, dear," she said.

He reached out and traced a line down her arm. She closed her eyes. He traced a line around her breasts. His fingers continued down her stomach, farther down, and began swirling around her inner thighs. Molly fell back, panting. He untied her bikini bottom. She watched in a trance as it fell away. He pushed forward, covering her body with his. She sighed with assent as his mouth found hers. It was a perfect molding of skin now. Jack's hands were everywhere. Molly murmured with pleasure. But her eyes popped open when he maneuvered himself into position.

With a groan, she pushed him away. He fell back out of bed, striking his head on the nightstand.

"Jack!" Molly jumped out of bed and rushed to him. "Are you all right?"

He opened his eyes and looked up at her. "What are you doing?"

"I need to tell you—"

"What are you doing in my bedroom?" he said. "Naked," he added, glaring at her body.

Molly leaned forward. "Do you know who I am?"

"The unwed mother who's stealing all my work?"

Molly threw her arms around him. "Welcome back, Jack," she said and kissed him on the lips. Jack dove into her lips, pushing her back onto the bed and sliding all over her, drinking in her scent. But then he stopped, leaning over her, panting, like a wolf hovering over its feed. He loosed his viselike grip and climbed off the bed. Molly sighed with disappointment. He finally tore his eyes from her body and pointed at the door. Molly gathered the bottom of her bathing suit and, with as much dignity as possible, sidled out.

Chapter Fifteen

MOLLY STOOD IN the middle of her room and waved her arms about like a conductor. "Okay, leg up and over. That's right. Now, you, twist left, now right . . ."

The threesome on the bed—two men in leather chaps and dog collars, and a severe young woman in an executive suit—had been scooting about with alarming precision, but they'd been at it awhile and were starting to stumble.

"Will you watch it with that thing? You nearly poked my eye out."

"Sorry."

They collapsed in a heap, exhausted. Molly shook her head. It was always a complicated process writing these sex scenes. Six hands and feet: where to put them all? Molly let her arms fall to her sides and sighed. She was exhausted herself. She'd been working round the clock to meet the insatiable demand, and she'd grown frazzled. She was turning into a factory. She gazed at her lead character, Esme, a nubile dominatrix with a heart of gold.

"What's going on with you?"

"I just don't get it."

"Get what?"

"Why I'm here. What's my motive?"

"Love, of course."

Esme looked over to where one of the characters, a young man named Devon, sat languidly in the corner, drinking champagne. "You mean I'm in love with him?"

"Why, yes."

"Oh."

"Didn't I make that clear?" Molly looked around. They all shook their heads. She sat back down. "Damn."

She stared into space for a long while. The characters looked at each other nervously.

"Okay." She addressed Esme. "So, you love him. But he barely knows you exist. And the little he knows of you, he doesn't seem to like. He thinks you're too much, too this, too that. What would you say to him?"

Esme crossed her arms. "I'd say, Get a life."

"What if you know deep down he's a good man, he just doesn't know you very well. What if you'd fallen in love?"

"Can I make a suggestion?" Devon said.

"Please."

"Strap him to the bed and make him bark."

"Devon, we're trying to think here," Esme huffed. She returned her attention to Molly. "Why don't I just lay it on the line? Say, 'Hey, I love you.'"

"But what do you think he'd say?" Molly looked at Devon.

"Before or after he dashed out the door?"

The other man nodded in agreement.

Esme shrugged. "You never know. Maybe he'll crush me to his heart and kiss me deeply and won't have to say a thing at all."

Silence descended as they all thought about that one.

"What's wrong?" asked Devon, peering over at Molly.

"Nothing." Molly shook her head brusquely. "Okay, every-body, enough of a break. Where's the whip?"

By Jack Carter.

By Jack Carter.

🖎 ☺☾ⓜ&; ♦☾□◆ⓜ□✍

Jack hunched over his computer and doodled. He typed his byline again and again and again, trying different fonts, different sizes, even different colors. He was typing it in Bookman Old Style, italic, when the doorbell rang. Jack rolled his eyes with annoyance. Interruptions, constant interruptions, he fumed. He went back to doodling. The doorbell rang again.

"Oh, for God's sake, will someone get that?" he heard his mother call.

In front of his house, Jack found an older man in a wheelchair, jabbing the doorbell with a long stick. At the sight of Jack he dropped the stick and made a slight bow in his chair.

"Good morning. Is Rita in?"

"Rita?" Jack glanced up the path behind the man. There was no car, no van. The man was dusty and windblown and looked as if he'd ridden for miles. "Why, yes. I'll go get her." But he hesitated. Should he offer to help the visitor in with his wheel-chair? The small dignified man had "Don't Touch" written all over him.

"I'll wait," said the man crisply.

Jack nodded. He left the door open while he walked to the foot of the stairs and yelled up. "Mom!"

No answer.

He cleared his throat and tried again. "Mom! You've got a visitor!"

"No!" she yelled down.

Jack grinned sheepishly at the man, then hopped up the stairs.

He found his mother in her room, playing solitaire by the window. She was dressed, made up, and slapping down the cards as if her life depended on it.

"Someone's here for you."

She didn't look up. "Tell him to go away."

"But . . . he's in a wheelchair."

"So?"

"But he looks like he's come miles. I think by wheelchair."

"And he can go back again."

Rita slapped down the ace of spades. "Ah, there you are, you little sucker."

Her hands flew as she got rid of half the cards in her hand. She leaned back in relief. "That's better."

"What do I tell him?"

"Nothing. Just shut the door."

"I can't—"

"Oh, all right. I'll do it."

She laid down her cards and stood up. She glanced at the mirror and licked back a strand of hair before passing Jack and making her way downstairs.

Jack stood on the top landing, listening. He heard murmuring. Then a haughty laugh from his mother. Then the slam of the door. He ran to the window and watched as the old man motored himself down the path, his leg stuck in front of him plowing through air. He stopped at the stop sign, looked both ways, and sailed on through the intersection with the imperturbability of a four-star general. Jack stretched his neck to watch until the man had rolled out of view. His mother made her way back upstairs and into her chair.

"The nerve of that man."

"What did he do?"

"It's what he didn't do. He didn't invite me to the Valentine's dance."

"How neglectful of him."

"You can say that again. Biggest event of the social calendar. And he thinks he can wait until the last minute to see if I'm free. Well, he's in the doghouse now."

"Did he apologize?"

"In his way."

"Which is?"

"He said he was sorry."

"Sounds good to me."

His mother flicked her hand at him. "Oh, Jack, do you really think I'm the kind of woman who settles for an apology?"

Jack sighed and sat down. It was going to be a long conversation.

"He seemed like a nice guy."

"You're just saying that because he's in a wheelchair."

He shrugged.

Rita's hands flashed as she flipped through her deck three cards at a time. "He's not particularly nice. And he's become less so since he's got an entire floor of drooling women drooling for him. This is a man who was married to the same woman for forty-five years, who married the second woman he'd ever slept with. He hadn't a clue that this is what old age had in store for him. And he's so busy living his fantasies he keeps forgetting to take his medication. The nurses give him lectures and he just laughs. He forgot his teeth at Mabel's and he had to send someone back to get them. He can stew a bit."

Jack raised his hands in defeat. "Fine."

"You know how he got in that wheelchair?"

"No."

"Mary Jane Wilcox took exception to him messing around with her best friend of fifty-three years and was banging on the door. He tried to climb over the balcony to the next apartment and slipped. Luckily the fire escape broke his fall and he only broke his leg."

She slapped down the final king. "Get me another cup of tea, would you, dear."

A few days later, Jack was sitting at his computer, waiting for Heather to arrive. It was the first time she'd agreed to come to his house. So far they had spent their dates at her place or on neutral territory. It was better for her safety, she said. Who knows, she smiled, you could be a bloodthirsty ravager. Jack always obliged by baring his teeth, and she would shriek with delight.

He could hear Molly typing next door. He tingled with Pavlovian response. He realized with a sinking heart that he was starting to lose all control. She had to leave as soon as possible. He wasn't going to hold on for very much longer. Soon his urges would take him hostage and frog-march him to her door. At the moment he was fighting an overwhelming desire to just slide into her room, sit on her bed, and watch her work. He wanted to watch her grip her tongue the way she did when she was concentrating. He wanted to massage the tension from her shoulders. He wanted to . . .

"Jack."

Jack jumped. Molly stood at his open door.

"Thanks for the organic iron cookies," she said.

"No problem. I was in the neighborhood."

"Well, I appreciate it. I feel a lot better."

He nodded. "Good."

She looked around. "It's so quiet."

"Yeah."

"Where's your mom?"

"On her way to a Mexican extravaganza in San Diego with her friends from Sweet Endings. With any luck, they'll miss their exit and end up in Baja for the real thing."

She laughed. He fiddled nervously with the computer keys.

"Sorry," she said. "I didn't mean to interrupt."

"Oh, no, that's okay. I'm just bidding on eBay. So far today, I've bought an ebony Masai warrior club, a 1970s Randall Bowie knife, and an eight-inch Egyptian dagger."

Molly shook her head, smiling, then turned to go.

Jack called after her. "Big plans today?"

"Yeah, I'm thinking of starting a mainstream single title."

"Good for you."

"It's an old-fashioned love story set in L.A."

"Really?"

"Yeah. I thought I'd see how it goes."

"Well, if you need any help . . . on what not to do."

She smiled. "Thanks."

They stared at each other. Molly turned to go again. Jack stood up. "Molly . . ."

"Yes?"

The doorbell rang.

Heather was standing on the doorstep with a clipboard snug in her crossed arms.

"I've come for your inspection," she said.

Jack shook off the annoyance that bubbled up from his insides like indigestion. Wasn't that what he admired about Heather?

Her determination to see their relationship as a psychological construction project? How had she put it so well? "We must investigate our motives and our responses until we've taped down all the sides of the box and it's impossible to get out."

He slapped on a welcoming smile. He even opened his arms to hug her, but she stepped back to take in the whole house. "It's a very intimate moment when a woman goes to a man's place for the first time," she said.

"Well, it's just a little place."

"I sincerely hope not," she said, glancing around at the broken pavement. To distract her, he bent to kiss her. She jerked her head away. "Who's that?"

She pointed up at Molly, who was standing on the upstairs balcony, shaking out a beach towel. He'd forgotten to get her out for the day. He glanced at Heather. He hadn't mentioned Molly to Heather. He knew the rules of engagement. No fraternizing with other females whatever. If Heather found out that Molly lived with him, he could kiss her expensively highlighted locks good-bye.

"That's—" he thought quickly—"the maid."

She brightened. "You have a maid? Gosh, you didn't tell me you have a maid. How . . . executive." She checked off a little box on her form and then ran her hand up his arm. "How . . . manly." She looked back at Molly. "Have you thought about putting her in uniform?"

Jack opened the door to his house and stepped back to let Heather through. She swept into the hall, her head held high, her eyes lighting on everything. Jack could hear Molly walking around upstairs. He would have to find an excuse to go upstairs and somehow prevent Molly from appearing. Could he lock her in her room? Was that within his landlord rights?

"Let's start with the living room." He led her in. Heather stood at the entrance.

"Who does your rooms?"

Jack looked at her blankly.

"Who is your decorator?"

"Oh. I don't have one."

"You did this?"

"Yes."

"Really, Jack." She laughed, patting his arm. "You amaze me."

"Thanks," he said cautiously. He watched her march into the room and stop in deep meditation at the window curtains.

"Maybe I'll leave you to have a good look," he joked.

"That's a good idea," she said as she turned over a dish to check its make.

He turned to dash upstairs, but Molly had been quicker. She was at the door. "Hi, there. You must be Heather." She strode into the room and stuck out her hand.

Heather offered a limp jellyfish.

Molly gave it a good pump. "Gosh, it's so nice to meet you. Jack's told me so much about you."

Jack flashed her a warning glance.

Molly shook her head in amazement. "I mean, a virgin, whew. That takes a lot of . . . well, frankly, I'm just curious. How can you be a virgin? That's, that's like impossible."

Heather arched her eyebrow, her eyes sweeping over Molly with disdain. "Well, maybe I never got to know anyone well enough."

Molly cocked her head. "But really, what's there to know? You say, 'Hello, you're hot,' wham bam. There's not much more to it than that. You can even drop the hello. 'You're hot'—that's just polite chitchat, to get them in the mood. In fact, what you're left with—"

"She gets the picture," Jack barked.

Molly smiled and clasped her hands. "Well, better get back to work." She patted Jack on the back. "I'll leave you to get to know each other." She winked.

Heather followed Molly's weighty bottom up the stairs with her eyes. "Jack," she said. But Jack had already disappeared into the kitchen. Heather followed him and stood at the door with her arms crossed.

"She came highly recommended," Jack said defensively.

Heather watched him loading the dishwasher from the sink full of dirty dishes.

"Doesn't she do that?"

Jack stopped mid-load. "She never gets it right."

"What's her name again?"

"Molly."

She put her head out the kitchen door. "Molly!"

Jack put his fingers to his lips. "Shhh. What are you doing?"

"Yeah?" Molly called down.

"I'd love a cup of coffee," Heather called up.

"Coffee? We keep it in the fridge," Molly responded. Heather turned to glare at Jack, but Molly suddenly appeared at the door behind her. "Hope I didn't use the last of it," she said. She opened the refrigerator door and rummaged about. "Here it is. And the coffee maker's here. You know what? I better make it. It's pretty temperamental. You want one, too, Jack?"

"Uh, sure."

"Three cups coming up."

Heather glanced at Jack. He smiled. She sat down and smoothed her long tresses with her hand. "Do you cook also?"

Molly opened the coffee container and took a deep whiff. "Yeah. Occasionally. Jack chokes it down, don't you, pal."

Heather's eyes swept the room. "I see you don't do windows."

Molly laughed. She finished scooping and flicked on the coffee maker. "All righty, that should do it. Well, I'll leave you guys alone." She walked out.

Heather stared after her. "Really, Jack, you've got to be harder on her. She'll walk all over you. I mean, what is she doing up there?"

"I have no idea."

Heather rose from her chair. "I'll just go check."

"No!"

"Jack, you've got to learn to deal with these people. The next thing you know, she's going to be using this place as her own."

Molly popped her head back in. "Know what? Screw work. I think I'll go to the beach. It's beautiful out."

Heather raised an eyebrow. "I hope you don't expect to be paid."

"That's the beauty of the line I'm in. I get paid half before I've even started."

Heather turned to Jack. "Say something," she hissed.

Molly looked at Jack. "What?"

"Have a nice time," he said.

"Thanks. Hey, Heather, if I don't see you later, it was nice to meet you." They heard the door slam.

Heather glared at Jack. He rummaged in his cupboard for dishwasher detergent, avoiding her eye. "She's incredibly good," he said. "I don't want to lose her."

Heather took a delicate sip of coffee. "Well, when I'm your wife I'll change some things. It takes great skill to deal with staff."

Jack swallowed. "Wife?"

She smiled back. "Well, it is where we are headed, isn't it?"

"I thought we were still getting to know each other."

"We are." She glanced around the customized kitchen. "And I feel I've gotten to know you enough to take the plunge."

She set down her coffee and stood next to him. "We still have so much to learn about each other, Jack, let's not wait."

Jack's shaking hands broke the dishwasher tablet in half. He swore under his breath.

"Are you resisting, Jack?"

"No, no."

"Because I've always felt that with relationships if you don't go to the next step, they begin to smell. Sort of like cheese."

Heather slid her hand up the back of his neck and tousled his hair. "I could be so useful to you. We could be a great team. I could be your muse."

Jack looked up at the ceiling. He could hear the thud as Primrose fell out of bed laughing.

"And your collaborator," she continued. "Even your manager. And when your time comes, I can manage your estate. Make sure your name and image are used in the most tasteful and lucrative way possible."

"Oh, I don't know if I'll have much of an estate."

"Well, you'll have to work hard, of course. But I would make sure you kept to a tight schedule."

"I have been kind of slack lately."

"I'll change that."

He slumped back in his chair. "It's just so hard . . . and no one seems to care what I write."

She leaned over and patted him on the shoulder. "Oh, Jack, you are a great writer. Everyone knows it. It's just a matter of time before you're discovered and treated with the respect you deserve."

Jack looked up, his eyes brimming with desperation. "You think so?"

"I know so." She took his face in her hands and peered into his eyes. "*You* are a great writer."

He shrugged and looked away. Then glanced at her again.

She gave his face a little shake. "Really."

It was an attractive proposition. Complete devotion. Encouragement. Adulation.

"Okay," he said.

She dropped her hands. "You will, of course, ask me correctly. With champagne and a ring." She rummaged in her bag and handed him a Tiffany card. "They have my preferences and ring size on file."

"I suppose that's necessary?"

"Oh, Jack. You know as well as I do that first weddings are precious. It's nice to get the details right."

Richard was set. He wore his new Boss jacket with a crisp white T-shirt and his favorite worn jeans. He was relying on his Timberland boots to give him that understated, rugged look. He picked up his pace and strolled into Starbucks as if he were squeezing it in between two very important meetings.

Maryann was already there, businesslike in a sleeveless oatmeal-colored shift. She looked up from the corner table and waved.

"Hello, honey."

"Hi ya, sweet stuff." He bent down and gave her a long lingering kiss, until she took him firmly by the shoulder and pushed him away. "Okay cowboy, why don't you get yourself a drink."

He chose a cranberry walnut muffin and a raspberry tea. No use getting all caffeinated and strung out about the whole thing. When he got back, she had removed a file from her purse and was thumbing through.

"I've calculated my assets to the nearest thousand. It's more considerable than when I first talked to you. I forgot about my shares of SexToysRUs. These are the papers my lawyer put together. Just initial at the bottom of each page and sign where I've got an arrow."

Richard took a large bite of muffin. "Do I really have to?"

"Richard, we've been through this."

"It's just that . . . well, God, it's so unromantic. Whatever happened to 'What's mine is yours, what's yours is mine'?"

"You don't have anything."

"So I wasn't as astute as you were. I wasn't savvy enough to buy SexToysRUs at four bucks a share."

"You bought cheek implants."

"You've got to stand out from the pack."

"You spend everything you earn."

"Life's expensive. I've got the gym, I gotta go out. A week here and there skiing is not going to break the bank."

"But it doesn't add up to anything. I scrimped and saved. And now I have an apartment in Marina del Rey, the time share in Cabo San Lucas, and an impressive stock portfolio."

Richard opened his arms. "Don't you see? We'll be perfect for each other. You save, and I make sure we have a good time."

"Richard . . ."

"It just seems to me that if we're going to be a union, we should be a union." Richard stopped and stared intently at his iced tea. "I mean . . ." he stopped. He shielded his eyes with his hand. He tried to speak again but, overcome, he bit his lip.

"Oh, honey." Maryann leaned forward. "Tell me what you're feeling. I'm listening."

Richard raked his hair with his hands. "Well, it's just hard, you know? This finding of a mate."

Maryann nodded vigorously. "I know. Believe me, I know."

"I mean, because once you settle on one you kind of get involved emotionally."

She smiled and patted his hand. "Aw."

"I mean, you spend a lot of time taking her out for a spin, imagining what kind of state she'll be in in a couple of years. Figure out the resale value if times get hard. And then you realize she might not even be for sale."

Maryann removed her hand.

Richard shook his head. "I've been getting tired. I gotta tell ya. It's been breaking me up. But you know"—he looked into her eyes—"I'm glad we're talking. I'm glad we're communicating. I feel closer to you."

Leda sat at the top of the bleachers, watching the football game. The cliques from her school were arrayed in the seats below her. Every group she had tried to sit next to had stared at her dully until she had mumbled some excuse and tried another spot, which was how she had ended up at the very top, alone.

Well, not quite alone. At the other end sat Susan, wrapped up in an oversized sweatshirt with a hood. They had glanced at each other and then quickly looked away, for fear that just their eyes meeting would elicit persecution. They sat tense as crouching tigers until finally Susan took the plunge and slid all the way over to Leda.

Leda stared straight ahead. "I like boys," she said.

"No problem."

There was silence.

"Well, not every one of them," Leda admitted.

Susan smiled.

Leda nodded down toward the popular crowd, each girl in which was dressed in kilts and tweed as if attending an English shooting party. "Jenny Harris still looks like a hooker in that skirt, doesn't she?"

"You can say that again."

"Jenny Harris still looks like a hooker in that skirt, doesn't she?"

They snorted with giggles, but stopped abruptly when eyes turned toward them. Luckily, Tarzana High scored a goal and they were quickly forgotten.

Chapter Sixteen

J ACK STARED GLUMLY around his café. The barmaid, he
noted, had cornrowed her yellow hair and looked like a tall
Nordic mistake. Across the street, T-shirts demanded, "Shut
Up, Bitch." A nymph on Rollerblades glided by, her hair flying
behind her like the last ray of sun. The man sitting next to Jack at
the window took a deep pull of his Marlboro and looked after
her. He nudged Jack. "If I don't find a mate soon, I'm gonna buy
me a dog and move back to the mountains."

Jack understood the feeling. There were days when he contemplated the South Pole. A cold, barren place where he could
write in peace, take cold showers, and commune with the
tuxedoed penguins. Penguins, after all, mated for life. They
managed to stay together through thick and thin ice, clinging
together in the open seas, mating with great delicacy on pre-
carious ice cliffs. The males even incubated the eggs under their
feet while their females snacked in the ocean. Talk about
commitment.

But he shouldn't be envious, he reminded himself. He had
found his mate. Beautiful, lovely Heather. And she had agreed to
take the next step. All was going as planned. To think, here he
was, on the brink of achieving his personal goal. He had played

his cards right and he was finally staring success in the face. He and Heather had restrained themselves and they had long last been rewarded with a perfect union.

So why did he feel like hell?

"Can I sit here?"

Jack looked up to find a statuesque blonde in a neon-green bikini wobbling on Rollerblades and balancing a tray precariously. Jack pushed his papers together. "Sure."

She collapsed into the chair and rearranged her breasts in her top. Jack blinked his gaze away.

"Whatcha doing?" she asked.

"Nothing."

"You're just sitting here talking to yourself?"

"Oh, that. I'm writing."

"Really?" Her eyes lit up. "You're a screenwriter?"

"No. Books."

"Books? Oh." Her large lips sucked at her Coke. "Anything I'd have read?"

"Probably not."

"You think I'm dumb, right?"

"No!"

"You think I'm blond, got knockers, I must be dumber than an ox."

"Really, I didn't—"

"Just so you know, I'm a smart gal. These"—she indicated her massive breasts—"are silicone. I bought them because they will further my career. They are an investment. You buy stocks, right?"

"Some."

"Well, these are my stocks. And as the rest of me goes down, they can only go up."

"Very astute."

"You probably figure I don't know what that means, right?"

"No, I assumed—"

"Because I know words, I'm college educated."

"So I gather."

Jack watched her as she nibbled at her hot dog. "So what *is* your career?"

"I'm a mathematician. I teach applied probability theory at UCLA."

"You're kidding."

"See what I mean? You've got preconceived notions."

He stared at her breasts. "And your investment?"

"I teach an eight o'clock class. Nobody falls asleep on my time."

"That's very . . ."

"Astute? I know."

She daintily patted her lips with her napkin before leaning closer. "Do you like girls?"

"What?"

"I'm a nice girl looking for a nice guy. Do you like girls?"

"Of course, I like girls."

"Yeah? How many dates have you been on in the last month?"

Jack thought a moment. "I don't really date."

"No?"

"No, I fantasize about ideal women. I dress them up in whatever I want, the more corsets the better. I put them through excruciating psychological trauma before having fifteen-second sex with them, and then I delete them."

She stood up without a word and rolled away. Jack looked after her. He hadn't meant to scare her. He was just being truthful. Just telling her how it was. Because maybe Molly was right. Maybe he was a freak. A control freak who wasn't the slightest bit in control. He stood up to go.

"Jack!"

He turned and there she was. His ex-wife. Sleek as a well-oiled seal, with a belly that protruded from her shirt like the nose of a B-52 bomber. She waddled like mad to catch up to him.

"Oh, my God, Jack. Oh, my God. Oh, my God."

She barreled into him and flung her arms around his neck. Her belly bore deeply into his. She finally stepped back and clapped her hands together in amazement.

"I can't believe it's you."

"Morgan?" He stared at her belly. She grabbed it with both hands as if about to pass it like a basketball.

"Can you believe it? It's due next week. A girl. We're calling her Carly. What do you think? Isn't it cute? Are you still in Venice?"

He nodded.

"I'm in Malibu. Love it. The sea breeze up there. Magical."

"You're . . . um, you got . . . um . . ." He stared at the ten-pound rock that weighed down her finger.

"Married again. I sure did. Fred's in the business. You know those little hoods that go over the back of video cameras so you can avoid the glare? He makes them. I read one of your books. Too hilarious."

". . . Thanks."

"Who'da thunk it, huh?" She whacked him on the shoulder.

"You still working for . . .?"

"Oh, God, no. Way too busy. What with the house and Fred, and now the baby. Crazy." She took him in head to toe. "So. How you doing?"

"Fine."

"Still single?"

"Well . . ."

"Great! I'll have to hook you up with one of my girlfriends. She's desperate. You'll love her." She glanced at her Rolex. "Better go. If I don't sit down soon, I'm going to have this baby splat on the sidewalk." She reached over and kissed him on the cheek. "It was really good to see you. Keep in touch. You look great."

Jack stared at her intently. "You said you didn't want kids."

"Oh, well, you know . . ." She waved her hand.

"You said it would ruin your career."

"People change." She shrugged and turned to go. Jack stepped in front of her. "You said you had too much to do. That you couldn't fit it in. And now look at you, waddling like a duck, bigger than a mall."

Morgan's eyes narrowed. "What can I say, Jack? Maybe I just didn't want to have a baby with you."

Heather was right, Jack thought as the armed guard ushered him into Tiffany's. It was time to close the deal. Become a member of society again, instead of a lone wolf at the edge of the pack. He had found his alpha bitch. And together they would have alpha puppies. Little people he would be willing to lay down his life for.

Heather had been so exacting lately. He had barely been allowed to gaze upon her, much less touch her. But he felt it was the only way she could express her love. She had been hurt, as he had. She wanted to get it right. He just wished she'd relax a little. But she knew best; she was the keeper of their honor. And what a pleasure it would finally be to divest themselves of it. Though, truth be told, he was strangely unaffected by her package. He was hoping that their engagement might jump-start them to zone five, or, as she put it, a hair's breath from her nipple. He had almost fainted when she first said it. She had such a way with words. Now, though, it seemed as impersonal as a pit stop on a road map.

Still, love would conquer all. Love would fuse their disparate selves into one single-souled being. And the fire to begin the meltdown would be the ring. He glanced around the store. All around him men and women gawped down into long cases, their faces lit by the jeweled glow. Jack blinked. The sparkle burned his eyes. Row upon row of flashing necklaces, bracelets, and rings, each accompanied by a price tag that made him wince. What ever happened to two months' salary? he thought. These cost a private pension.

The precious stones seemed to hum with vibrations. Diamonds. Millions of diamonds. White ones, blue, even yellow. They all winked at him as if in on a joke. He had always used jewels to help him with the plot points in his book. They always had the ability to divert a heroine's desires in the direction he intended. So, as he made his way around the room, he searched for something that would nudge Heather in the right direction. But he was having trouble. The sapphires left him cold. The emeralds looked sickly. And the rubies reminded him of spilled blood. After all these years of writing about jewels in his novels and interviewing jewelers about special cuts and antique settings, he suddenly realized that this was the first time he'd ever been in the market. Morgan hadn't wanted a ring. She'd asked for a new computer.

"Ooo, baby, baby." Jack looked over. In the corner, sitting on a velvet chair, a young woman crooned adoringly to the ring on her finger as her fiancé wrote his check.

Jack was lost a moment, thinking about their life, wondering how they'd met, how long they had been together. What had possessed them to take this final step? They were acting as if they barely knew each other. They'd probably met last week, Jack thought grimly, and had such a great time snorting coke and performing unspeakable acts upon each other's anatomy that they decided to spend the rest of their lives together. Until one of them found something better. That one would probably be her. She looked like she had a lot of mileage still in her. Maybe she had a string of diamond rings she had finagled out of her other boyfriends. Maybe at night, when the lights were low and she was alone, she took them out of her treasure box and put them on all her fingers and danced naked in the candlelight, a goddess of thwarted desire. Maybe, just maybe, Jack thought, he was getting a bad attitude.

"May I help you?"

He looked up to find a salesman bowing to him, his hands clasped together. He reeked of spice soap and cigarette smoke.

Jack shook his head. "I don't think you can."

"We have a very good return policy if the lady in question does not accept the gesture in the spirit in which it was intended."

A ray of hope beamed over Jack. He hadn't thought of that. What if Heather said no? What if he went down on bended knee and she shook her head? He grinned. Then frowned at himself in reproach. A hero did what a hero had to do.

"I'm looking for an engagement ring."

The man drew out a tray of dazzling specimens. "I think you will find that these rings say, 'Will you marry me?' in a most spectacular way."

Jack observed them wistfully. "But do any of them say, 'Will you love me?'"

The man picked up a three-carat pear-shaped diamond with a

multi-thousand-dollar price tag. "I think this one could be quite convincing."

In the corner of the last case, Jack caught sight of a small white gold ring exquisitely etched with what looked like a rose vine. Not really an engagement ring at all, more like a ring of lifelong love with no beginning, no ending. Simple, serene, and elegant. Molly would love that ring, he found himself thinking, and he stared at it a long time.

"You have excellent taste."

Jack tore his eyes away, then pointed to the other end of the case, where diamonds erupted from a wide gold band like a rash. "I'll take that one. Wrap it up."

He would spare no expense. For he was on the cusp of marriage again. And this time, it would work. He folded his receipt neatly before sliding it into his wallet. Life, like books, he had learned, required concise plotting when it came to planning a happily ever after. You needed to have firm control of your characters. With the weight of the ring in his pocket, he felt himself relax. Soon he would have his happy ending. Someone to be with forever and ever. They would be partners in love and family. They would bounce their babies on their knees. They would grow together like two saplings planted close on the forest bed and stretch to the heavens, their gnarled branches entwined. He swung out of Tiffany's a determined man.

"Next."

Tansil, the head varsity cheerleader from Tarzana High, walked into Leda's family room. Leda sat behind a teak desk, a pile of applications next to her. She couldn't believe that this girl, who walked down the school hall every day like Miss America before the bowing, scraping masses, was now applying to her for a job.

Well, that's the kind of thing that happened when you took control of your life. She and Susan had started up their own business, offering cash and excellent references. People were now falling all over themselves to be their best friend.

Leda put up her finger and answered her mobile. Tansil stood awkwardly at the door.

Leda clicked her tongue into the phone. "What do you mean, the quality wasn't good? That shot left nothing to the imagination. Fine. All right. All right. I'll see what I can do."

She hung up and waved Tansil to a seat before glancing at the paper in front of her. "So, I see here you're a ballet dancer."

"Yes, I was second in my ballet class."

"Excellent. We need lots of flexibility. Want a Coke or something?"

"No, I'm okay, thanks."

"Can I ask how you found out about us?"

"Cheryl Dean mentioned it in PhysEd."

Leda ticked off a box on the form. She sat back. "Well, let me tell you a bit about our company. We started two weeks ago. We're going to provide high-quality footage featuring high school women. We'll offer links to various pleasure product companies. Our employees are students like yourself, looking for a bit of extra cash. We don't plan to go public yet, but when we do, we will offer our employees the best possible IPO stock option. That said, we do require freedom from certain constraints. Clothingwise."

Leda leaned back in her chair and put her hands together. "So. Why don't you tell me a little about yourself and how you would contribute to our company?"

"Well, I like people . . ."

"You won't be meeting any."

"Oh. Well, um, I am enthusiastic. And I take direction well. And I'm really punctual . . ."

"Can you do the splits?"

"Yes."

"Touch your head with your feet? Backward."

"In my sleep."

"Hook your legs behind your ears and rock back and forth?"

Silence.

"Great. We'll try you out. I've got a shoot tomorrow at three. Be here promptly. We've got to be finished by six. My mom comes home at seven."

Kate lay in bed in her new Chinese red bedroom. It gave her a splitting headache. She closed her eyes against the glare, but it continued to burn into her retinas. She was either going to have to repaint or go mad. She'd thrown away the feng shui book. The changes to her relationship corner had done nothing for her libido, and had only inflamed Carl's further.

Carl came in whistling from the bathroom, wearing only a towel around his expansive waist. He'd taken a shower. Kate knew what that meant. When he slid into the bed beside her, she smiled wanly. When he made his moves, she made her best effort to get into it. She even tried fantasizing about the painter, but Carl's belly kept knocking her out of that. When he tweaked her nipples a small stirring arose. She tried to follow it, doing her best to concentrate and fan the flames like a squaw huddling over a half-burning ember. But then she realized she'd forgotten to call the accountant back about the tax forms, and Leda's class project, she needed to buy paint for it, and had she remembered to bring her blue shirt to the dry cleaner? By the time she had wrestled her attention back to the show, the show was over. Carl was peppering her with kisses and edging himself back over to his side of the bed.

Kate sighed and, turning her night table light back on, picked up her latest mystery.

He was swinging closer and closer. She was on the next branch and she was trapped. She bared her teeth at him. He pounded on his chest, grabbed the vine, and swung over. She backed against the tree trunk, hissing. He grabbed her and tore away her loincloth. The monkeys in the next tree let up a roar—

Jack blinked in the sudden light from his nightstand lamp. Molly was standing by the bed.

"There's something wrong. I'm bleeding," she said.

Her face was awash with terror and she was shivering. "Here," he said, jumping up and swallowing her shoulders with his arm and leading her down the stairs. "It's going to be okay."

The emergency room was chaos. Friday night. Two A.M. More misery billowed in with each opening of the door. A child with a gash above his eye. Two bruised men twitching with pain. An old woman clutching her stomach, a bucket at her feet. A drunk banged on the bulletproof glass that encased the receptionist. Everything was blue from the walls to the floor to the hard molded plastic chairs as if some professional had deemed the color to be the most soothing.

In a row of seats against the wall, Molly sat staring straight ahead, an unopened bottle of water in her hands. She had not moved for the thirty minutes they had been there. Jack leaned forward.

"Do you feel okay?"

"No."

"Anything I can do?"

"No."

He patted her awkwardly on the back. She flinched. He took his hand away.

He checked his watch. Jesus, what a thing to happen. He felt a pang of guilt as the next thought that occurred to him was that it was probably for the best. The easiest solution. After all, Molly was unmarried, essentially homeless. Motherhood material she wasn't. Maybe the reprieve would allow her to get on with her life. It had been an unwise decision in the first place. In the future, she'd have to be more careful. Did she have any idea how much it took to raise a kid? Yes, this was definitely for the best. A blessing in disguise. He leaned back and opened a magazine. He glanced at her face. She sat hunched over, misery etched in her eyes. He put down the magazine.

"Does it hurt?"

"Everything hurts," she said.

"Molly Macintyre?"

The nurse stood at the door, her white uniform stained, her ankles swollen like plums over her white shoes. She looked tired and ruthless. Molly shrank back.

"Molly Macintyre," she barked again.

Molly stood up and inched her way toward her.

The woman eyed Jack. "You coming?"

Jack froze. "Oh, I'm just . . ."

"It's just me," Molly said.

The woman nodded, adjusted her clipboard under her arm like a sergeant stick, and led Molly through the fortified doors.

Jack sat back down and hiked his foot over his other knee. It shouldn't take long now. Probably just a check, a quick pre-scription, and out back through the doors Molly would come. Saddened, certainly, but probably, if she was at all realistic, relieved. Yes, he thought, rubbing his eyes awake, it was definitely for the better. Life would go back to normal. Molly could carve out a niche in her genre. She could eventually get a nice place, meet a nice guy, and have lots of nice babies. Jack settled back, his arms folded, and watched, unseeing, the flickering images on TV.

Two hours later, Jack hunched low in his seat. It was now four o'clock in the morning and the flow of broken people was finally drawing to a trickle. The only ones waiting now were two drunks with plastic bags for shoes and a young mother trying to soothe her child's fevered cry. The little girl was very sick. He could see that at a glance. Jack tried to tear his eyes away, to give the woman some privacy, but his eyes kept sliding back toward her of their own accord. The mother rocked her daughter back and forth in a futile effort to comfort her, sitting at a pinched angle so as not to disturb her child more, attempting to draw the pain into her fingers with each smoothing of her brow, trying her very best to help. She caught Jack watching her.

Her eyes teared up. "I can't bear for her to be in pain."

Jack suddenly stood up. From behind the bulletproof glass, the receptionist eyed him as he strode to her.

"I changed my mind. I should go in."

"Too late."

"It'd be better if I was in there with her—"

"She'll be out soon."

"But—"

"Back off!" She pointed to the sign: VIOLENCE WILL NOT BE TOLERATED.

Jack retreated and began to pace. And while he paced, he watched the receptionist watching him. With one hand she dug

208

deep into an extra-large bag of peanut M&M's and popped one after the other into her mouth. When her eyes finally returned to her magazine, he moved slowly, stealthily toward the doors that led to the inner sanctuary of emergency medicine. He peered through the windows of the doors to see two more doors which had to be penetrated before he could find her. Somewhere beyond those doors was a damsel in distress. He eyed the receptionist. She was sucking at a Big Gulp, her eyes glued to the pages.

He walked right in.

"Hey!"

He pushed through the two sets of doors and barreled into the emergency corridor. He stopped confused. It was surprisingly quiet. A nurse sat in a chair with her eyes closed and an uneaten sandwich in her hand. He whirled around, looking for a clue to Molly's whereabouts, but there wasn't one. He dashed past the nurses' desk. He could hear the doors behind him slam back and the pounding of footsteps. He looked back to see two security guards gaining on him, their large bodies jiggling down the hall. He swung his head back and forth, peering into the tight cubicles filled with machines, registering as he loped by the blurred faces of families caught in tragedy. And then he heard her cry out.

He stopped as if shot. He looked desperately around. Again she cried out. He followed the voice to a plastic yellow curtain. Behind it Molly sat on a bed, unhooking herself from a monitor. She was fully dressed, her bag beside her. She held out her hand, her smile tremulous.

"Jack, is that you?"

Jack reached for her. "Molly," he murmured before being bounced against the wall by a massive belly. His knees crumpled where they were bashed with a stick. His chin smashed into a water dispenser. He slid down the wall, face forward.

"Hold him."

They leaned on his arms. He was turned over, his legs spread-eagled, the bloated bouncers pinning his arms. A doctor, young and sleep deprived, leaned over him with a scalpel. "We're sick of you guys making trouble."

Jack watched the blade descend toward his face and thought, What an unexpected way to go.

Molly fell to her knees and leaned over him, shielding him with her body. "It's okay. He's with me."

The doctor hesitated.

"Please, it's been so stressful for us." She smiled beseechingly at the doctor. "Please."

The doctor, taking in her delicate state, reluctantly got up. "I think you would benefit from some anger management before the baby comes," he called to Jack as Molly dragged him down the hall.

They tumbled out the hospital doors, which shut behind them with a snap. They leaned over, hands on knees, panting and laughing. Their eyes locked. Jack suddenly reached over and grabbed Molly and hugged her fiercely. The street lights flashed in his bruised eyes. He finally released her and checked her for signs of despair. "You okay?" he asked.

Molly wrapped her sweater around her belly with care. "Yes, I'm fine. It was a false alarm. Everything's fine."

Jack nodded. He watched her. She suddenly seemed so small, so vulnerable. He grew hot with anger. "You shouldn't have to do this on your own. Where's the father?"

"I don't know."

She was on the verge of tears. He breathed deeply. "I'm sorry," he said, patting her on the shoulder. They stood in awkward silence.

"You were great in there," she said.

His eyes swung over to her. "Really?"

"Really."

Jack's mouth bled where he cracked a smile.

The next morning, Jack felt more energized than he had for months. He picked Primrose back up, shook the dust from her long, tangled hair and flung her back into the arms of her true love. Guy hitched up his pants and caught her.

"My love," he said, gazing down into her azure eyes. "I cannot bear it another moment if you do not know how much I love you."

Primrose blinked with surprise. "But I thought you hated me."

"Ah, that was merely a heart besieged, trying its utmost to stand erect. But the battle is won and I lay down my arms before you."

"Oh, my lord." Primrose trembled.

"Oh, my lady," Guy said, his voice thick with emotion.

Guy found her lips and Primrose was swept away with a passion she had not known existed. Outside, the sky darkened and the sea rumbled. Inside, in the grand estate that would be her home, Primrose finally surrendered her virtue, sure in her knowledge that Guy and his wealth would be hers forever and ever.

Jack sat back and let out a sigh of contentment. As Guy's head descended to claim her heaving breasts, Primrose looked over at Jack, raising her eyebrows appreciatively. "Well, it's about time," she whispered.

His outpouring was copious, a thousand words without a blink. It was over by ten A.M. and he faced the day with zest. It was amazing what a few hours could do. From rudderless to purpose-ful. From directionless to single-mindedness. Because now, in Molly, he had a project. He would make her comfortable, keep her safe, make sure she birthed with great success. He had taken it upon himself to help her. And help her he would. A hero sacrificed. And Jack would sacrifice. He was a hero. Someone's hero. And what a relief that was. He brought tea up to Molly's room where she was still in bed.

She looked at him warily. "What's this?"

"Tea."

"Why?"

"You need to rest."

"I'm fine."

"It could be you have an incompetent cervix."

"Excuse me?"

"Yes, I've been doing some research. Women your age have a thirty percent chance of developing one. And with your history . . ."

"My history."

"Well, it's been worn down, I suspect."

She pointed to the door. "Out."

He threw back her covers. "That's a good idea. Time to go baby shopping."

"What's gotten into you?"

"You have a duty to your baby to be prepared. I've looked on the Internet." He slipped a long piece of paper from his pocket and unfolded it. "And the first thing we need is a portable changing cot/playpen/cocktail bar."

"But the baby's months away."

"No time like the present."

"Well, maybe later. I'm really busy—"

"Can't we just do what I want for once! I want to go baby shopping. Let's go baby shopping."

Molly raised her eyebrow. "And will you be bringing your whip, too?"

Jack sighed. "I just want . . ."

"All right, all right." She dropped the pen she had been chewing on and got out of bed. She wore a short tank top, which revealed her slightly protruding stomach.

"Looks like you ate too many pancakes," Jack commented. Molly thumped her belly with satisfaction.

They drove to Sid & Me, a baby store on Lincoln, Jack glancing over at Molly every now and then and smiling. Molly looked over.

"What?"

"Nothing."

But he was bubbling inside. They were just like an old married couple, he thought. She looked so beautiful, sitting there, her face scrubbed and glowing, her dark eyes shining. She'd tied her hair up in a bright green bandana. They parked next to a car outfitted with a baby car seat in back.

"Look!" Jack pointed eagerly at the car seat as if it were a wildly expensive gadget he'd set his sights on. Molly pulled him along. Inside, the shop was painted womb-pink and offered every notion of baby thing.

"What's this?" Molly picked up a box labeled Postpartum Support. They both stared at it in wonder.

"It's to help tone your tummy. Afterward," said the crisp Mary Poppins saleswoman behind them. She regarded Molly's belly a moment with an arched eyebrow, then switched into a beatific smile.

"Can I help you with anything this morning?"

Molly shrugged helplessly. Jack took out his list. "Okay, let's see. We need cribs, changing mats, nursing pads, bottles, sterilizers. But I want to know about the steam versus gas factor. All those ions, are they medically proven to be safe?"

While the saleslady showed him around, Jack watched Molly from the corner of his eye as she made her own way around the store. He couldn't help watching her. There she was, suddenly the center of his universe. His heart caught a moment. He gazed at her as she read the back of a box, and he suddenly wondered whether this was the moment he'd explain to his grandchildren. He stood a moment in stunned silence at what that thought meant.

"Hey, Jack, look at this," Molly held up a limp plastic flap. "An Inflate-a-Potty."

They laughed together and riffled through tiny sleep suits. Jack held up two. "What do you think? Blue? Pink?"

Laughter erupted in the next aisle. Molly and Jack peered over. Several women surrounded a large-bellied woman, squealing with laughter. Jack glared at the sparkling rings that shone from their left hands.

"First wives," he hissed.

They went in for the basics. They came out with a disposable swim diaper, a heart-shaped Wee View Mirror, a Stroll'r Holder, a prenatal listening kit . . .

"Oh, we forgot the car seat," Jack cried as they walked out to the car.

"That's what baby showers are for," Molly said.

"Oh, yeah. Will your mom fly over?"

Molly stopped, her shoulders hunched.

"You haven't told your mom."

She shook her head.

"Why not?"

"I think I was hoping I'd get married first." She laughed and climbed into the car. Jack shoved the key into the ignition.

"Maybe you should."

"I was only kidding."

"Well, maybe you shouldn't kid. Marriage doesn't always have to end up badly."

"Jack, I don't know if you've noticed, but I'm not dating anyone."

"I know. It doesn't have to be like that. Maybe it could be more of an arranged thing. You know, like what people do for a green card. Did you ever see that movie? And they ended up falling in love."

"Life is not a movie, Jack."

Jack slowed at the stoplight. "But people do it all the time."

"You mean, marry someone just for the piece of paper. And then fall in love with him?"

Jack gazed at her funny face, at her crooked front tooth, at her crazy hair so bent on escaping. "Why not?"

"But I don't know anyone like that," she said.

Jack swallowed. He opened his mouth, then closed it. He tore his eyes away from her face and stared straight ahead, his Adam's apple bobbing in distress.

"It's green," Molly finally said. Jack shoved his car into gear and drove off in silence.

That night, Molly and Jack maneuvered around the kitchen in a familiar dance. He fixed the salad; she dressed the pasta. She served them both and sat down. He made a lame joke about the zucchini. She smiled. She sneezed explosively. He passed a tissue. They ate quickly. Afterward, she washed the pasta pot, leaving

Jack to the dishwasher. He gazed at the back of her neck, which suddenly looked very small and tender. He reached out involuntarily, but the neck disappeared as she shrugged her sweater back on. His eyes followed her across the room.

She stopped at the door.

"Jack, I'm moving out."

Jack's eyes widened. "You are?"

"Yeah, I got my advance and . . ." Jack looked so distressed, she stopped. "I thought it would make things . . . easier for you."

He turned away. "It does."

She watched him fidget blindly with the dishwasher's salt container. "I mean . . . I drive you nuts."

"You do."

"You need your space back."

"You can say that again."

"So I'm leaving Thursday."

He looked up. "But that's Valentine's Day."

"Is it?" She shook her head and laughed. "What a marketing trap that is, huh?"

He blinked. "Yeah."

"Well, good night."

"Good night."

She turned to go.

"Molly."

She stopped.

Jack gazed at her. "You'll find someone to love someday and you'll be very happy."

She regarded him a quiet moment before speaking. "Maybe that's the difference between you and me, Jack. You think falling in love will make you whole. I think it could crack me wide open."

Chapter Seventeen

KATE STARED AT Carl's side of the bed. It was empty. He was gone on business again. He was staying away with increasing frequency. A small alarm bell was going off somewhere inside her head, but she waved it away. What she wanted right now was some peace and a good book. She picked up her mystery and began to read, then tossed the book down with a choice word. She'd already read this one. She did that all the time: pick up books from the library and not remember she'd read them until she got them home and was on page two. She fumed. What on earth could she read now? She glanced over at her well-stocked bookcase. Her eyes fell on Jack's books. He gave her one every year for Christmas, but she'd never read any of them. She always thanked him politely and tucked the new book into the back of her shelf. No one could understand why she'd never cracked one open. It was hard to explain her intense jealousy, her need to believe that Jack wasn't as bright as she was. After all, he was younger, the apple of their mother's eye. It wasn't fair. And the fact that he was now a highfalutin writer was just beyond her endurance. Of course, she loved him. Of course, she wanted the very best for him. But did he really have to be so successful? How to describe her feelings? Green-eyed, thrilled, envious, protective, horrified, proud . . . All the classic signs of A.S.S.: acute sibling syndrome.

Kate sighed and picked up Jack's *The Virgin and the Rake*. She was desperate, she reminded herself. She hopped back into bed, pulled her covers to her chin, and opened the book. Soon, her eyes grew wide.

> *On the riverbank at moonlight, she surrendered and bared herself before him* . . . Kate's lips parted. She turned the pages with urgency.
>
> *In his hurry, he ripped her dress. His rough hand closed over her porcelain skin* . . . Kate swallowed.
>
> *Never had she known such strength, such tenderness* . . .

It was three o'clock in the morning before Kate managed to put the book down again. She lay back in a near swoon, her loins on fire.

The next day Jack sat in his chair staring blindly at the computer. He'd been there an hour and nothing had registered. He finally jabbed Print, hoping the hard copy would entice his eye. He sat there drumming his fingers while the section printed and then hunkered over his manuscript, trying to concentrate on the puzzle of words. But he failed. He tossed the pages back on his desk.

Primrose, wedding ring on her finger and socks on her feet, lay back in Jack's bed. She nudged Guy, who lay snoring beside her. "Aw, isn't that sweet? He's in love."

Guy groaned and pulled the covers over his head. Primrose reached over and patted Jack's hand. "I was hoping you'd see the light."

Jack jumped up and paced the room. "I don't know what's wrong with me. I can't think. I can't sleep. I can't eat."

"Oh, yes," said Guy from under the blanket, "I noticed you had trouble with that massive frozen pizza you just polished off."

Primrose patted Jack's hand again. "Ignore him."

Jack shook his head. "I don't know what to do."

"I think you should tell her."

Jack stopped and stared out the window. "You think?"

"Tell her what?" Guy said.

Primrose sighed. "Guy, are you really so obtuse? Have you missed everything? Can't you see there's a woman in the house who is fertile, radiant, and unavailable. Naturally, he's mad for her."

Jack glowered at her.

Primrose shrugged. "Am I right?"

"So you think I should tell her."

"Yes," said Primrose.

"No," said Guy throwing off the covers.

Jack looked up. "Why not?"

"What are you going to do with the child in her belly? When you claim her you'll have to do something with it. You can't waste your energy raising someone else's genes."

"I didn't even think of that."

"Well, you should. You should have its exit strategy ready."

"What do you mean?"

"In the wild, lions who take over prides kill all the cubs."

Jack put up his hands. "Oh, no, I don't think . . . Well, I was just going to . . . um . . . maybe he or she can go to boarding school?"

Primrose nodded vigorously. "That's an excellent idea."

Guy thought a moment. "Or you could make it clean the stables while you sire your own heir."

Primrose waved him away. "Oh, don't bog Jack down with details. We should help him woo her."

Jack sat back in his chair. "Okay, shoot. What do you suggest?"

Guy rubbed his chin in thought. "I've always found that a good swift kick in the pants gets them going."

Primrose untangled herself from the covers. "Don't listen to him. He's a Neanderthal. Listen to me. Just kiss her and she'll be swept away. She won't know what she's doing. All she'll feel is the wild beating in her breast and your hands masterfully taking command of her body. Oh, the thrill," she said, glancing over at Guy with disappointment.

"What if she rejects me?"

"Why would she reject you?"

"I . . . I'm not . . . I haven't been . . ." Jack paused. "Well, it's true, I am kind of a catch, aren't I?"

"You are."

"I mean, I'm employed, sort of. Not bad looking. Got a good relationship with my mother."

Primrose clasped her hands together. "You're a dream."

"Still, she's kind of quirky; what if she says no?"

Guy collapsed back into bed. "You can't think about it. Women are a wall, just a brick wall. One says no, you move on to the next one. You don't get personal; you don't leave your heart behind. Cut, dried." He drew a finger across his throat.

"What you need, though, is appropriate attire." Primrose padded over to his closet and pulled out some shirts. She placed one against his chest.

"I think the blue. Yes, definitely. And please, no Tevas. Real shoes for real men. Can't go flopping up to her.

"Here, let me." Primrose gave his hair a little brush back and forth. "A certain insouciance. Voilà, perfect. I wouldn't change a thing."

"Yeah?" He looked at Guy.

"For a twenty-first-century white guy, not bad."

"Okay." Jack headed for the door. "I'm off."

"Good luck!" They waved to him from the bedroom window as he set off down the boardwalk.

He found Molly at her favorite haunt, the Figtree Café, reading through a manuscript. She wore a loose flowery dress and a line of bright orange bangles. She sat next to the railing at a table for two, stuffing large rolls from a bread basket into her mouth. What a picture, he thought. What a gorgeous, beautiful, sexy picture.

She smiled when she looked up to find him standing at her table. "Hi."

"Can I join you?"

"Sure." She moved her mess of books and papers to make way for him. "I just ordered. Want something?"

"Is that wine?" He fastened his eyes on her large glass.

"Australian chardonnay. You want one?"

"No, I was just thinking," he said, as he settled in, "don't they say alcohol's not good for the baby?"

She waved away the notion. "I only drink half. It relaxes me. As far as I'm concerned, stress is worse. You look like you've had a tough day."

Jack reached for her hand, then stopped. Maybe that was a bit premature, he thought; better to take it slow. He fumbled with the salt shaker instead and took a deep breath. "I woke up this morning and realized something."

"Yeah?"

The waiter set Molly's plate in front of her. She grabbed her knife and fork with a gleam in her eye.

Jack reached over and took her plate. "I don't know. Tuna, that's a lot of mercury." He placed it in front of himself. "I'll order the chicken burger and you can have that." He forked in a mouthful. "You can't be too careful. Everything you eat goes into their little bodies."

Molly stared at her fish.

"So," he said, reaching for the bread basket and helping himself to the last roll, "I know I probably haven't been the most welcoming person in the world, but now that you're leaving I realize"—he gazed at her in rapture—"I'm going to really miss you."

"Well, that's nice. I'll miss you, too." She took a sip of wine.

Jack stopped chewing and watched her intently. He pushed forward her water glass. "Maybe you should have a drink of this at the same time, water it down."

Molly shook her head, smiling.

Jack polished off the fish. "What I guess I mean to say is, I want you to know you can stay longer."

Molly nodded. "Thanks, but I think it's time to move on. Get my ducks in a row before the birth."

Jack used the last bite of roll to wipe the dish clean of its sauce. "But it's kinda sudden, your leaving and everything, and I thought, maybe . . ." He popped the bread in his mouth and chewed. He finally swallowed and patted his lips carefully with his napkin. He looked at her bashfully. "What are you doing the rest of the day? Maybe we could . . ."

Molly rubbed her neck. "I'm going home and having a hot soak. I'm beat."

"Is that a good idea? I've heard hot water's unsafe for the baby. Sort of boils them in a bag."

Molly reached over and speared a slice of chili from his plate and swallowed it. Jack looked up. "Hope you don't regret that."

She crossed her eyes at him.

He took a deep breath. "I just feel I haven't gotten to know you."

"Really?"

"Well, not . . . I mean, we know each other. Like friends."

"Uh-huh."

"But I was thinking maybe . . . I don't know how you would feel about this . . ." He stopped and looked deep into her eyes. "I'm gonna be honest here. I've never felt this way before. Molly?" He reached for her hand.

"Here we go. You want ketchup with that?"

The waiter set down Jack's chicken burger in front of Molly. She was about to dive in when Jack reached over and snatched the side sauce away. "You got to be careful about sauces. You only need three hundred extra calories while you're pregnant. Whew, I watched my sister blow up like a tree trunk. A fat tree trunk. Believe me, you'll thank me later."

He swiped one of her fries. "What I'm trying to say is, I was wondering if you wanted to sort of . . . get together?"

"Jack?" She was smiling sweetly.

He held his breath. "Yes?"

"I mean this in the nicest, most sincere way: Fuck off."

Later that day, Jack viciously stuffed his cornbread mixture into two Cornish game hens, then trussed them up hard with string. That crazy, ungrateful woman. He was only trying to help. Touchy, touchy. Okay so she was pregnant. But come on.

Was that any reason to be so nasty? He was just trying to be helpful. But that's what women were like. God forbid you should give them any advice. No, you had to just listen to them complain, complain, complain. Okay, so maybe Molly never did complain. And, okay so maybe she never had asked for the advice. Still, shoving her pickle into his mouth was a bit excessive.

Well, she would rue the day. She'd had her chance, and it was gone. The last single heterosexual man willing to commit, or at least consider the option, after careful thought and thorough investigation into their mutual compatibility, not to mention prenuptial vetting, was no longer available. Someone else got him. Sorry. In this market, you had to jump, have your financials ready, and sign on the dotted line.

He attacked the potatoes, skinning them with relish, then digging and goring out their eyes. He laid them out in a row and began chopping them mercilessly.

Good thing she was leaving. He had to get on with his life. It never would have worked out. She was too . . . and he was too . . . Anyway, it was all best left unexplored. It would have ended in disaster and she would have gotten her feelings hurt. And he would have lost more time. Really, this was the best way. A bird in the hand. Wasn't that the conventional wisdom? This could be his last chance. Or he could wind up like Mr. Winston next door.

Heather had waited long enough. He was going to make an honest woman of her. Okay, so maybe she was already honest, to the point of being a corpse, but the important thing was, he was going to do right. He took a deep breath. He was about to commit rightism. Yes, that's what he was going to do. Jack plopped three tomatoes into boiling water and watched them turn in agony.

★ ★ ★

Molly strolled down the boardwalk, shaking her head. Who did he think he was, the procreation police? So she had been a little harsh. But geez, she'd been starving. She was not a nice person when she was starving. Any of her friends could have told him that. They knew the procedure. Molly, starving: Make room, clear the floor, provide massive doses of fat-laced food. It didn't have to be gourmet. She was easy to please—fries, potato chips, white bread, didn't matter. Just stand back and don't get in the way.

Jack obviously had a lot to learn. It was probably best that they'd never gotten together. And what was he going on about, not knowing her? How many months had she been washing his stray curlies down the shower drain? That added up to some serious bonding, as far as she was concerned.

She smiled. It *was* kind of cute, though. It had been a long, long time since anyone had worried about her. Usually it made her feel so uncomfortable she shied away; she didn't want to owe anyone. But coming from Jack, she realized, she found it kind of sweet. Comforting. Lovely, in fact. She stopped in the middle of the boardwalk, causing a pedestrian pile-up behind her. Still—she shook herself and resumed walking—it wasn't meant to be. He had his fancy girlfriend, his life all planned out. It was time to get on with the rest of *her* life.

Chapter Eighteen

W<small>HEN HEATHER ARRIVED</small> on Valentine's evening she wore an elegant black pantsuit. "Roses," she said, accepting her bouquet. "Really, Jack. How quaint."

She strolled into the living room and dumped the bouquet on the couch. "I hope your mother appreciates the significance of this meeting."

Jack looked away. Rita was upstairs, beside herself with rage and painting her toenails fuchsia. She had been so certain the ambassador was going to call and come crawling back. But it was too late now. The dance was this evening. The old man hadn't blinked, and his mother was fightin' mad.

"She's looking forward to meeting you," he said.

"I bet she is. I'm taking you off her hands."

He glanced at her. Her eyes were blue and empty, her philtrum flat. He took a deep breath. Her heart, he reminded himself, was pure. Like rubber sap.

"Heather, do you love me?" he said.

"Of course." She swatted at him. "Silly."

"And you want to have kids, right?"

She glanced at him quickly. " . . . Sure."

"How many?"

"Oh, I don't know." She smiled sweetly. "How many can you afford?" She lay back on the chaise longue. "Could do with a glass of wine."

"Red or white?"

"Champagne."

"Naturally." Jack went into the kitchen. It would be fine when they were married. She would relax and be accommodating. They would warm up to each other. She would relax, finally secure in the knowledge that he would love her forever. He stopped dead in his tracks. Love her forever. For ever and ever. First thing in the morning, last thing at night. Over breakfast, lunch, and dinner. He grabbed a paper bag and blew into it desperately. He then shoved his fist through the bag. Love wasn't for pussies, he reminded himself. He leaned down to see how his birds were browning, gave a quick stir to the baby carrots, and popped open the champagne.

Meanwhile, Rita shuffled into the living room, wads of cotton between her toes. She stopped and glared silently at Heather, who jumped up and held out her hand. "Oh, Mrs. Carter. I'm so glad to meet you. Jack has told me so much about you."

Rita let her hand be pumped. "Who are you?"

"Why, I'm Heather. I'm sure Jack has told you all about me."

Rita padded over to the sideboard and poured herself a hefty drink. She tossed it back with a practiced jerk of her head, then sat back with her feet splayed out and pulled out a folded crossword puzzle. Heather perched on the edge of the couch with her back straight, her hands folded neatly on her lap. She took a fortifying look at the expensive marble fireplace in the corner and leaned forward.

"I just wanted you to know how fond I am of Jack," she said.

"Fond, shpond. What that boy needs is a good—"

"Here we go." Jack returned, holding high the tray of bubbly. He did a double take when he saw his mother.

"Mom, what are you doing here?"

"What does it look like I'm doing? I'm drying my toes."

"So you two have met." He nodded at Heather.

"We sure have," said Heather brightly.

Rita shrugged, not looking up from her puzzle. "What's a three-letter word for loser?"

Jack regarded his mother, who sat on his couch like a stiff-legged chicken. She would have to be removed. Romance withered under the envious eye of a parent, especially one going through her second adolescence. "I found a blank Monday crossword puzzle," he said.

"You did? Where?"

"I left it in your room."

"Well, why didn't you say so?" Rita hopped onto her heels, ready to shuffle out, but caught sight of the table set for two. "What's this?"

"It's Valentine's Day," said Heather.

"I know what day it is," snapped Rita.

Heather stood up and curled her arm around Jack. "And Jack has something he wants to ask me. Don't you, honey pie?"

Rita looked over at Jack sharply. "Yeah? Well, I'm sure you won't mind a poor old lonely woman joining you." She sat down at the table and shoved aside the perfectly laid cutlery to fit herself in. "Need another fork here."

"But . . ." Heather said.

"What?" Rita barked.

Heather looked at Jack. Jack stepped in. "It's supposed to be romantic."

"You think you young people are the only ones who know

about romance?" Rita pointed a knife at Jack. "The things I could teach you, if it wasn't against the law."

Jack crossed his arms. "We're having Cornish game hens. There's only two."

Rita swatted that away. "Oh, those things are huge. You never can eat a whole one. Just rip me off a little thigh. I don't need much." She patted the chair next to her. "Come on, dear, sit down. Let's get to know each other."

Heather eyed Jack, then sat down carefully next to his mother. The front door opened. They looked up to see Molly stride in, sweaty and flush-faced in track shorts and tank top. She stopped and took in the strange gathering. "Well, well, the gang's all here. Hello, Heather."

Heather frowned. "Is this your day?"

"You bet it is. I'm all set. Brought over everything this morning." She gave Jack a triumphant look. "Here you go." She handed him the keys.

Jack contemplated them. Molly peered at them, too, as if all the world's answers were etched in their nickel.

Jack finally pocketed them. "Good," he said.

Molly nodded. "Yup, I think it's for the best."

Heather leaned over to Rita. "Is she quitting?"

Jack stuck out his hand. "Well, have a nice life."

Molly blinked, then shook it. "Thanks for everything."

"Don't be a stranger."

"Take care."

"Safe trip."

"See ya around."

Having run out of good-byes, they stared at each other.

Molly released Jack's hand and turned to go.

"Wait." Rita jumped up, grabbed Molly's arm, and pulled her

over to the table. "Sit down, dear. We're just starting. You look famished."

"But . . ."

Rita sat her down firmly. "You don't eat enough. Sit. Consider it one for the road."

Molly reached over and popped an olive into her mouth. "Well, now that you mention it, I *am* starved."

"Of course you are. Jack's just about to serve, aren't you, dear?"

Jack paused, staring at the three women gathered around his table set for two. It wasn't as if he didn't have a choice. He could serve, or he could put out his eyes with the ice tongs. He returned to the kitchen and bucked himself up. So there had been a bit of a hiccup in his plans. Not insurmountable. He could turn dinner into a family affair. There was even a scene in one of his novels where the hero went down on bended knee before his surprised intended at a candlelit dinner attended by her mother. It was one of his better efforts. Lucinda had said she'd cried at the end. Maybe Molly, too, would be moved to tears. Maybe she would gaze at him with utter regret, firm in the knowledge that the last good guy was gone. Maybe she would lay her head down and pour out all her disappointment right there on his special Valentine's place mat. Yup, he smiled, that's what he would do, pop the loaded question. Right in front of them all.

When Jack returned with the Cornish game hens, Molly was tossing olives into her mouth by the handful and eyeing the butter dish like a lioness on a hunt. The two others leaned back, keeping their appendages securely out of her way. He deposited the platter on the table with a flourish. He then drew out a massive knife and, gazing at Molly, began to sharpen it with long sharp swishes. The women at the table watched with bated breath.

"So this is where everyone is."

Kate stood at the doorway. She looked hot and frazzled. Jack plunged the knife deep into the Cornish game hen's heart. "What are you doing here?"

"I can't be alone on Valentine's." She glanced at Heather. "Hello. You're . . .?"

"The virgin," Rita said.

"Oh, right." Kate dropped her coat on the couch and disappeared into the bathroom. It had been a dreadful week. Carl had called to say he was going to be delayed again and wouldn't make it home for Valentine's. She had let out a long moan and broken out into a sweat: Jack's book had left her so randy she had half a mind to hump the tree in the backyard. All those images of restrained heat, heaving breasts, throbbing loins. It made her want to yowl at night.

In the bathroom, Kate rummaged in her bag until she found the box she wanted. In it sat a small robin's-egg-sized vibrator with a remote. She'd bought it on the Internet. She was going to release all this sexual tension even if she had to do it herself. "Happy Valentine's Day," she said to herself and kissed her image in the mirror leaving a perfectly formed red-lipped smooch. She slipped the vibrator into her panties, flipped the remote to On, and gave it a zing. She squealed and dropped the remote behind the sink. "Damn." She dropped to all fours. Outside, she heard Carl's voice. She scrambled up and dashed out.

Carl stood in the dining room. He wore a creased shirt and looked exhausted.

"Carl," she said.

"Hello, Kate," he said. "I've been looking for you."

She raised her chin. "Have you?"

His eyes were brooding and dark. "Yes. I've ridden miles to be with you."

Jack, Heather, Rita, and Molly watched them open mouthed, moving their heads back and forth as if watching a tennis match. They all looked over to Kate for her return. She walked past Carl without a word, her head held high, and sat down. Carl stood awkwardly behind her. Jack jumped up. "I'll get you a chair." He dashed into the kitchen and stopped in his tracks.

"Hey, Uncle Jack, I didn't know you were having a party." Leda was lounging against the kitchen counter, digging into the chocolate mousse.

"Neither did I." Jack collapsed into a chair and laid his head on the table. "No date tonight?"

Leda shook her head. "Tansil was having a party, but I have a stack of 1099s to fill out. My mom here?"

"Yup."

"And Dad?"

"Just arrived."

"Are they talking?"

"Yup."

Leda smiled and took the last bite of chocolate mousse. Jack lifted his head weakly. "Want to join us?"

"No. I think I'll just hang out in here and work on my business module."

"Suit yourself." He flopped his head back on the table.

The doorbell rang. Jack sighed and went off to answer it. Richard stood on his doorstep, dressed in casual chic, shaved to perfection, and reeking of expensive whisky.

"Hey, hey, hey." He leaned forward in a blast of hot, soused breath. "Whatcha doing tonight?"

Jack looked behind Richard. "Where's Maryann?"

Richard sighed deeply. "It was getting too serious."

"You were getting married."

"See what I mean?" Richard grinned, leaning heavily on the door jamb. "What do you say, let's go get drunk."

"I can't." Jack pulled himself to his full height. "I, for one, am celebrating commitment. What this world needs more of. I'm celebrating the uniqueness of one woman. Her modesty, her sensitivity, her femininity. Her singularity."

"Jack?" Heather, Rita, Kate, and Molly called out.

Richard peered around Jack into the dining room and its over-populated table. He raised his eyebrows, impressed. "Looks like you could use some help." He stumbled past Jack and waved to Molly at the table. "Well, helloooo there."

Molly smiled, amused. "Hey, there, Dick. Sit down. Have a breast."

Jack stayed at the door, gazing at the path that led out his gate toward the sea. He imagined himself walking down the path into the cold black water and swimming with long, bold strokes to China.

"Jack?" Heather called out again.

Jack returned to the table to find Molly and Richard, giggling softly in the corner, pretending they were at a table all their own.

"Delicious," Richard said, leaning toward Molly. "Did you cook this?"

She shook her head, grinning.

His eyes raked her body. "You look lovely tonight."

"So do you."

Richard made a muscle. "I've been working out."

"Oh, I can tell."

Jack glared at them. He stood up, peered around at his over-burdened table, and raised his glass.

"I have a toast."

Rita stood up. "Can you wait a minute? I need to go to the little girl's room."

"Me too," said Molly.

"Might as well," said Richard. One by one, they took station breaks while Jack stood stiffly with his champagne in his raised hand. The last one to go in was Carl. As he washed his hands he noticed something shiny behind the sink. He reached around and picked it up, accidentally pressing one of the buttons. From the dining table he could hear Kate yelp. Carl cocked his ear. He gave the button another zap. Kate delivered. Carl laughed, palmed the controls, and sauntered out to find, everyone looking at Kate.

She shrugged apologetically. "I'm sorry, I don't know what's gotten into me."

Jack cleared his throat. "I have a toast," he said again. They all looked up.

"As you know, Heather and I have been seeing a lot of each other. And we've enjoyed each other's company. And she's nice and everything . . ."

Heather raised an eyebrow.

"So we've decided to . . . ah . . . to . . . ah . . ." He stared at Molly. "We . . . ah . . ."

Kate cried out.

They all looked at her. She smiled with embarrassment. "I'm sorry. I . . . oh. Oh. *Oh*." She gripped the edge of the table and closed her eyes. Across the table, Carl watched her, grinning, his finger on her power points.

Kate opened her eyes and fanned herself with her hands. "Oh, don't mind me. Go on, Jack. I just . . . ohhhhhhhhhhh, oh. *Oh*." She leaned forward, her body shaking. "Ooooooh . . . !" She banged the table. "*Hot damn, give it to me, baby!*" She howled at the ceiling, then fell back. At peace.

Jack looked at his sister. "You finished?"

Kate raised her eyes to Carl, drowning him in gratitude.

"As I was saying . . ." Jack fumbled in his pocket and pulled out a small blue box. Heather's eyes lit up. He bent down on one knee and presented her with the box.

"Heather, would you do me the honor of becoming my wife?"

Heather looked triumphantly around. There was complete silence. Molly stared down at her plate. Kate's mouth fell open. Carl peered down the table at Heather curiously. Richard shook his head and took a long drink. Rita put down her glass. "Oh, Jack, really, you didn't," she finally said.

Heather took the box into her hands and opened it. "Nice," she said. She slipped it on her finger and assessed it. "Very nice."

Jack nodded.

"But no," she said.

"No?"

She took the ring off, popped it back into the box, and handed it back to him.

"You're a nice guy, Jack. But I find you . . . a little too needy." She stood up.

Jack scrambled up. "But I thought you said . . ."

Heather gathered her purse and flicked back her hair. "It became apparent to me quite early on that this wasn't going to work, but my therapist told me to see it through. I needed an imprint, you see. I'd never gotten this far before. So, thanks for that. I now can visualize fully what it's like to be proposed to. If you need someone to help you visualize someone saying yes, I'll give you the number of my shrink. I'd offer to do it, but I don't think it would be sensible."

She walked to the door. Jack ran after her and caught her in the

235

hall. He grabbed her arm and leaned into her. "I tell you what. I'll let you into zone 5. After all, I understand that a woman has her needs. And if we were officially engaged, I don't see why we have to wait until the day of . . . I mean, it's just a precaution, you know . . ." He smiled at her seductively. She stared up at him, as if considering. She shook her head. "No."

Jack dropped her arm. "It's not fair. I did everything I was supposed to do."

"Maybe that's the problem, Jack."

Jack grabbed her and kissed her firmly and thoroughly.

When he was done, she smacked her lips. "Nice," she said. "But too late." She stepped out and closed the door in his face.

Jack stood immobile in the hallway.

A blast of music shuddered through the window.

Rita clasped her hands together with glee. "Well, it's about time." She jumped from her chair and ran to the window. Chairs scraped as the others all joined her.

Outside on the sidewalk the ambassador sat in his wheelchair, holding a large boom box over his head, his face set and determined. Glenn Miller's "Little Brown Jug" poured out into the night. Rita ran through the hall and flung open the front door.

Jack started after her. "Mom!"

Rita ran down the steps, her arms wide. She hopped into the ambassador's lap and peppered the man with kisses. The boom box fell to the ground with a crash.

Jack stood at the door and watched his mother make herself comfortable, resting her head on the ambassador's shoulder.

"Don't wait up for me, dear," she called to Jack as the ambassador threw his wheelchair into reverse and maneuvered them down the road. The rest, including Leda, gathered at the window and stared after them wistfully.

"I wonder what the horsepower is on that thing," Richard mused.

Jack walked back into the kitchen and stood with his palms on the counter. He thought of the look on the ambassador's face when his mother ran down the steps. It was love. Or, at the very least, grand infatuation. That look that said, "I want you however much of a pain in the ass you are."

Molly, he thought. He wanted to see Molly. He ran back into the living room. But it was empty. He rushed through the house. It was empty. They were all gone. Kate and Carl and Leda. Richard. And Molly.

He dashed up the stairs.

"Molly!"

He ran into her room. The Regency desk had been polished carefully and shone in the lamplight. The closet door was open. Hangers hung bare. He sat down in the middle of the bed and picked up her pillow. He buried his head in it. It smelled of nothing and he laughed at himself.

Chapter Nineteen

J UST THE WARMTH of him soothed her. His breath on her cheek made Rita forget the ache in her bones. She lost herself in the softness of his forearm, the small wiry hairs that bent like trampled wheat. She sighed, feeling the tension between her eyes melt away.

He smelled like mint. Just tart enough to spike the senses. His hands were stroking her breasts now. They surrendered to his touch. The swirl of desire moved slowly through her, from the head down, toward a place she had long thought dead. But it had only been dormant, as things turned out, and now it perked itself up from its long comatose sleep. Ah, yes, she thought, ah yes, I remember. He watched her face as his hand roamed over her body, sliding up and down her torso, pausing over her hips to tickle her. She laughed in surprise. He continued his journey downward to her thighs, which he glided over with a feathery touch. He pressed against her, pecking at her with little tender kisses.

"I'm not going to break, you know," she said.

He locked her in a soul kiss that ground her very bones. Their mouths skimmed over each other like fingers reading Braille. He held her arm down against the bed and a bolt of desire shot through her. She held his cock in her hand and stroked it like an old friend. Such a wondrous thing in a man. The rise, the press against skin, the rooting, and then a peaceful sigh as it found its place. She tried hard not to distance herself, not to float above the coupling the way she often did, commenting on the action. Oooh, look at those two, at their age. Still she smiled with acknowledgment at the slight absurdity of it, even as she bared her teeth at the rightness. He kept pressing her, rocking her. She closed her eyes and felt him sink deeper and deeper.

"Hey, how 'bout I be the Earl this time," Kate cried, standing in the middle of her bedroom in nothing but a frilly apron. Carl shrugged and pulled off his black boots. "Where's your feather duster?"

"I think it fell under the bed."

Carl leaned over and retrieved it. He struck a pose. "Okay, I'm busy cleaning and you sneak in through the window and surprise me."

Kate threw a cape over her shoulders. "Okay, you don't see me coming until the very last minute." She climbed up onto the windowsill.

"Don't chip the paint," he said.

"Jesus Christ, Carl, it's just paint."

"Okay, okay."

Kate balanced on the sill and beat her breasts. "Ready?"

Carl began sashaying around, dusting madly.

"Here I co-ome!" Kate landed with a thump. "Ow! Damn it." She rolled around on the floor, clutching her ankle. "Uh-oh, I think I sprained it."

Carl bent down. "Does this hurt?"

"*Ow!*"

Leda barreled into the room. "Mom, are you all right?"

She stopped and stared at her mother, who sprawled on the floor in black boots up to her thighs and not much else, and at her father, who was trying desperately to hide his manhood behind a starched white maid's apron. And Leda fainted dead away.

Molly unpacked the last of her clothes. There weren't many. Sarongs had become her uniform. Unlike jeans, they draped around her increasing girth with no complaint. She gazed at herself in the mirror. What a different person she was from the one who had first arrived on Jack's doorstep, unemployed and homeless. Look at her now, a pregnant professional writer. But then, her life always tended to be extreme. Which was why she yearned for a little quiet, a little constancy. She was going to concentrate on making her life absolutely ordinary. For the baby. She planned to work hard, buy a little house, send her kid to a good school.

The best part was that her baby wouldn't have to rely on her parents' relationship for happiness. Molly was going to be happy, and that would be enough for both of them. No highs or lows, no departures, no screaming, no being passed back and forth like a baseball card. They were going to lead a very quiet life, a happy life, with no surprises.

She peered around her new two-bedroom apartment. It was small but bright, with a lovely brick fireplace in the living room. And if she was still and there were no cars driving down Pacific, she could just hear the muffled thunder of the waves along the beach. Her apartment had been carved out of one of the big beach houses on the avenues just five streets down from Jack's. No, her choice of apartments had nothing to do with Jack, she would have said defensively if asked. It was a great neighborhood. Why would she move away?

Next week, she'd start fixing up the second bedroom for the baby. Right now it was filled with all the things she and Jack had bought that day they spent together. She smiled at the memory. God, she missed him already. She still woke up every morning disappointed not to hear his typing next door.

Jack glared at the phone, willing it to ring. It had been a tough couple of weeks. He'd tried to enjoy the peace and quiet but he kept ending up downstairs, sitting at the kitchen table, waiting for Molly's return. He shook his head at himself. He should be on top of the world. He had sent his latest manuscript to a new publisher and they were salivating to print it. Under his real name. He should be triumphant, celebrating, crowing, instead of sitting miserably by himself, holding an orange bangle Molly had dropped behind the door.

So he finally decided to visit his sister. Misery loved company, and he knew her love life was even more disastrous than his. But Kate received him fresh from bed, in her bathrobe, looking smug and—Jack did a double take—satiated.

She poured them coffee, then collapsed into her couch.

"That ambassador must be some man," she said.

"I hope he has a license for that thing."

She yawned furiously. "I thought it was very romantic."

"You've changed your tune."

"I've always wanted Mom to be happy."

Jack laughed harshly. Kate dangled her leg. A black garter peeked from under her robe. "I gotta tell you," she said, "you look about as happy as a shucked clam."

"Heard from Molly?" It came out of his mouth before he had a chance to stop it. He'd been planning on slipping it in on the way out, as if it had just then occurred to him, as if it carried the same weight as discussing the turn in the weather.

"Yes," she said.

Jack nodded and leaned toward her. He waited. She didn't elaborate. He poked again.

"Seen her new place?"

"Yes." She took a sip of tea and readjusted her robe. Again she dropped the ball. Again he picked it up.

"And?"

"It's cute. She drew a huge whale on the wall. The landlord's going to kill her."

He laughed. He sounded like a hyena. She looked at him curiously. He choked softly into his fist. "I better give her a call."

"Oh, I wouldn't."

"Why not?"

She shrugged. "Just wouldn't."

He stared at her.

She set down her coffee. "I like Molly. She's a nice woman. She's got a lot on her plate, and the last thing she needs is someone who can't make up his mind what the hell he wants."

"I know what I want."

"Okay, what do you want?"

Jack opened his mouth. He wanted Molly, that's what he wanted. He wanted her with him every moment of the day for the rest of his life. But how do you reach for the sun when your heart is smothered by dark clouds? He closed his mouth again.

"See? You have no idea. I mean, jeez, I practically threw her at you. What was I supposed to do? Chain her to the wall? You missed your chance. Instead you choose someone like Heather." She slapped her knee. "Whew, boy, you know how to pick 'em."

Jack pushed out his chair and grabbed his keys. If he had wanted sanctimonious advice and gloating, he would have talked to his mother.

His mother, the Sweet Endings receptionist archly told him, would no doubt be found in room 143. So Jack walked down the long mile of corridor and knocked on the door. The ambassador opened it.

"Come in," he said. "She's in the shower."

He led Jack into a sun-bright room and offered him a drink. Soon Jack was sitting on a gray-and-blue-checked couch, holding a well-made G&T and listening to the shower in the next room noisily wash the old man's lust off his mother's body. They sat a moment in silence until Jack finally nodded toward the window.

"Nice view," he said.

"Yes, it reminds me of Biarritz."

They both took deep pulls and gazed into their glasses.

"Are you really an ambassador?"

"I believe strongly in the American ideal of self-actualization."

"Which means . . .?"

"I'm a used-car salesman from Pasadena."

The shower turned off. They both focused on the door from which Jack half expected his mother to appear, hair wrapped in a towel, her naked and cocked leg coming first around the corner.

"Nice lady," the ambassador said.

"Yeah."

"Great tits."

Jack looked over. "What?"

The ambassador looked up. "What?"

"Did you say something?"

"No."

243

"Oh."

Jack returned to staring at the door like a retriever. He could hear his mother singing softly. She was taking her damned time, flitting about, no doubt, cannibalizing tunes from *West Side Story*. The ambassador settled back into the couch and swung one leg over the other.

"Know what I like about your mother?"

Jack eyed him nervously.

"She's a woman who doesn't play games."

Jack hesitated, then nodded.

"She takes a bull by the horn, if you know what I mean."

Jack stared at him with horror.

The old man grinned into his G&T and took another swallow. "Yup, diamonds and pearls are good, but what a woman really wants is some passion. Some good loving. You've got to put a little oomph into it."

The ambassador glanced at the closed door and leaned forward.

"I'm going to speak to you from the other side, son. I hope you don't mind if I do. But there is going to be a point in your life when all those organs that up to now you've managed to ignore, things like your intestines, your lungs, your prostate, will suddenly rise up and introduce themselves. That's just the same time when the most important organ of all shrivels up to nothing. And let me tell you, I'm not going to meet my maker regretting all the times I schtupped. It's the times I didn't that I'll be thinking of."

Jack set down his drink. "Why are you telling me this?"

"She told me about your mission."

"What mission?"

"Finding your true love."

"Oh, that." Jack laughed bitterly. "That was a long time ago."

"Glad to hear it. Sounded like you were going about it a

strange way. Because I don't know, call me a dirty old man, but I always felt that true love showed no restraint."

A flush grew over Jack. A warmth glowed through him, as if he had just downed a fifth of the best whisky made. He stood up unsteadily. "I better go."

"Sure. I'll tell your mother you stopped by." The ambassador led Jack to the door and patted him on the back. "Good luck, son."

Jack strode down the boardwalk, holding a bright red bouquet in front of him like a gushing heart. Rollerbladers, tourists, muscle men, they all pointed at him and laughed. He marched resolutely, looking neither left nor right, until he turned and walked up the alley and stopped in front of her door.

The ambassador was right. It was time to divulge his love with no restraint. It was time to lay it on the line. To declare himself. Even if she collapsed on the floor laughing. A hero took a chance.

He had pried her telephone number out of Kate, but refrained from calling. He wanted to show up at her door and make his case more personally. He wanted to be memorable about it. He wanted to tell their children about it. He wanted it to be the moment he remembered when he died. His heart thumped painfully when he knocked. But when Molly opened it, he knew he had been right to come. She was everything he'd ever wanted. Her smile lit up at the peonies, which he presented with an awkward flourish.

"I love you, Molly. I want to be with you. Let's love each other. Let's depend on each other. Let's create something beautiful in this world. So say yes, Molly, say yes, I will, yes."

She stood motionless, her eyes wide, her mouth frozen.

"Molly, say something."

"I . . ."

"Hey, hey, hey, look who's here." Richard appeared behind her. He glanced at the flowers and smoothly kept talking. "Where ya been? We thought you'd dropped off the face of the earth."

Jack stared at his friend in disbelief. Molly glanced away.

"Come on in, buddy. Good to see ya. Man, it's hot." Richard slapped him on the back and led him in. "Hon, how 'bout an iced latte?"

Jack watched mutely as Molly trotted over to the open kitchen.

"Come in, come in. Where ya been, big guy?" Richard hooked his large paw over Jack's neck and led him into the living room. Jack moved as if sedated. He felt white hot and chilled to the bone at the same time. His brain turned to sludge. His eyes never left Molly as she went about the ritual of making espresso from a massive machine on the counter.

He noticed two used coffee mugs, two half-empty juice glasses, two plates with the remains of croissants, and the scattered *L.A. Times*. Richard finished off one of the juice glasses.

"Did you get my messages? Hell, I must've left three. I couldn't for the life of me figure out where you'd run off to . . ."

While Richard talked, Jack suddenly became aware of Richard's bare feet. He peered down at them. What did they mean? Was he hot? Had he just come in from the beach with too much sand on his shoes, so he took them off? Or had he just woken up and swung his legs out of . . . Jack suddenly laughed. Jesus, what was he thinking? Had he completely lost his mind? Molly might be loose but she wasn't desperate, she wasn't crazy, she sure as hell wasn't fucking Richard Mann.

"We're getting married," Richard said.

Jack's brain caved in. He could feel the rumble as the hard bits of skull splashed down into the warm goo that was his cognitive center. His fist flashed out and caught Richard below the chin. Richard fell back and landed crookedly on the couch. He blinked up at Jack, surprised.

"Hey, buddy."

"Jack!" Molly rushed over.

Jack stood over him. "Married? Married? Why the hell are you getting married?"

Richard climbed back to his feet, nursing his jaw. "What can I say, Jack? I'm in love. It still can happen. I've found my ray of sunshine." He smiled at Molly, who looked at his bruise with concern. "It's okay, hon, why don't you get that coffee."

"Besides," Richard whispered to Jack as Molly walked back toward the kitchen, "she's playing hard to get. No nookie until the day, she says. Been around you too long. But what can I say, I'm a licked puppy." He gazed after her happily.

Jack turned on Molly. "But what about the sex?" he yelled. "What if you don't have good sex?"

Richard and Molly stared at him. Richard coughed into his fist. "That's a good point. I'm glad you brought that up. And it takes a true friend to be so honest. But, you see, we've talked about that, and we've concluded that when we get going it's gonna be all right." He grinned.

Jack felt ill. "But what about the baby?" he whispered.

"What about the baby?" Molly's eyes were cold.

"I mean . . ." He stopped.

"Know how I look at it?" Richard jumped in. "Plenty of women have kids already these days. They're like accessories. Used to be women brought a hope chest; now they bring diapers."

Jack's body slumped as the news settled. "Congratulations." He held out his hand to Richard.

Richard clasped it with both hands and gave it a good pump. He threw his arms around Jack and slapped him solidly on the back. "Thanks, buddy," he said. "Know where we're going to honeymoon? Oahu. Awesome. Sit down. I'll get the brochure."

He dashed into the next room. Jack watched Molly, who had retreated to the far corner of the room.

"So you want to get married?"

She shrugged. "Well, Richard's pretty keen."

He stared at her.

"Don't look at me like that," she said. "You're the one who suggested it. Get the piece of paper, you said. Make it legit. And Richard will be a good father. So why not?"

Jack's mouth was dry. "Do you love him?"

"Oh, please, Jack." She waved her hand at him angrily. "Let's not talk shop."

Chapter Twenty

LEDA AND HER new best friend, Hazel, sat on Leda's bed and admired their rings, thin bands of silver braided to- gether. They had gotten them at the abstinence fair run by their local church. They'd had to sign a pledge to keep themselves to themselves. Leda couldn't sign it fast enough. Sex everywhere she looked, even among her parents, who indulged themselves in animal coupling in bizarre get-ups. She still had nightmares from the shock.

But things were different now. She'd sold her half of the business to Susan and now walked confidently. She was whole, virginal, a beacon in the hellhole of disease and promiscuity. Sluts were everywhere she looked.

"Ginny Staler. She's, like, soooo easy."

"Oh my God, she's, like, half the football team."

They shook their heads in unison and beamed up at Leda's new poster of Miss America.

"She's soooo pretty."

"She's soooo cool."

"She's soooo . . . you know."

Hazel nodded. They gazed up at the virgin, who beamed down from her photo, wearing her chastity like a crown.

"Come on, let's practice." Leda pulled at Hazel's sleeve and they slid off the bed.

"You be the guy this time."

"Okay." Hazel put on a scowl. Leda smiled and batted her eyelids. She slipped off her ring and presented it to Hazel.

"I have waited for you."

Hazel took off her own ring and handed it to Leda, growling, "I have waited for you, too." They fell forward into an embrace, rubbing their lips together and gyrating with their pelvises. They fell back onto the bed with a long sigh.

"Sixteen will be a perfect age to get married," said Leda.

"I can't wait."

"A white wedding, awesome band, champagne fountain, and then bonk city!"

Jack parked behind the nightclub and then sat back on his cycle, listening to the loud music emerging from the small side door. He watched the crowd, mostly young girls in tight jeans teetering on high-heeled boots like fragile colts. His eyes were slits, his mouth slack. This was it. He had missed his chance. The woman he loved was taken. There was no more reason for restraint. It was time to get back in the saddle. Time to rejoin the teeming, gyrating orgy called the human race. He was a man, after all; he was going to do what a man did. He was going to screw everything in the place. He heaved himself off his cycle.

Inside was like the center of a coal fire: hot, bright, sizzling. Jack strode in and headed for the bar. It had been a long time since he'd been on the prowl. He ordered a Jack Daniel's and tossed it back in one swallow. The fire burned through his body, cleansing it of all insanity. He was back. He cased the joint like old times, eyeing what was on display. Two young girls sashayed around the pool table as if doing a pole dance. Jack sat on his stool and lapped at his beer. One in particular caught his eye. She was young, balancing on worn purple pumps, her long caramel hair skimming the tops of her jeans. She'd lean over the pool table to shoot and the whole place would hush, eyes glued to where her skimpy shirt lifted and exposed the spider tattoo on the small of her back.

The guy playing her was all smiles, hiding his hard-on behind his cue stick. He'd give her tips, which she took with a breathless air. He'd slide his arm over hers to show her how to shoot. She was a real loose cannon, but just enough on target to make Jack wonder whether perhaps she hid the heart of a hustler. When her ball dropped into the pocket, she'd hop up and down like an excited bunny, pumping her hands in the air, her breasts shaking with glee. Jack sat there with his own pitcher, palming peanuts. His eyes never left her ass as it twitched around the table.

They all watched her. Every damn man in the bar. And she knew they were all staring at her: She'd flick her eyes out to check, then hide behind a waterfall of hair. She would lean against her cue stick, cocking a hip. She looked as if she could take them all on, one after another, and not even break a sweat. She glanced over at Jack and her smile faltered. His head was jutted forward, his eyes too intense, his legs parted, his groin pointed right at her. She replaced the cue on the side of the wall. The show was over. Nature called.

Jack was ready for her when she came back out. He leaned over her.

"Wanna drink?"

She stuck her finger in her mouth and nibbled it, grinning at him from under her bangs.

"Sure."

He led her through the crowd and ordered her a fruity

margarita. She twirled her long hair around her finger while she examined her catch, her eyes leaving the equivalent of finger-prints all over his body.

"What's your name?" he asked.

She laughed, shaking her head as if he'd just asked for her social security number. A wholly unnecessary transaction. She leaned forward and licked his ear. She reeked of bottled pheromones, the kind sold in department stores. Jack handed her the margarita. She drank quickly, expertly, then licked the salt from around the rim with a tiny pink tongue. Jack throbbed. She replaced her empty glass on the bar next to him with a decided clink.

Jack let his eyes linger on the crevasse between her spherical breasts—they were too large for her rib cage, and he anticipated a steady firm handful. She let her head fall back and regarded him with half-closed eyes. He reached out and drew his hand down her arm, reveling in the smooth satiny feel. He edged closer. His back prickled with sweat. His groin purred like a Harley.

She jutted her face close. She didn't say anything, just waited, her mouth hovering in his personal space. He hesitated. He didn't want to get it wrong, not to mention that her lips were so glossy Jack feared he might slip off. But he took the plunge anyway. "Oh, yeah," he moaned before coming down on her mouth with all the accuracy and weight of a jumbo jet.

His swimming prowess came in handy, as they didn't come up for air for a long while. Her kisses were different from Heather's, which always had a tennis-y quality: your serve, then my return, and so on. And very different from Molly's; kissing Molly was like jamming in a cool Parisian café, feeling yourself into the music. This one kissed as if she were at a PlayStation, quick, impatient, intent on the kill. Jack tried to keep up.

"Jack! Don't do it!" A large hand clamped down on him and

wrenched him from the soft, warm, almost too liquid, lips. Jack wheeled around to find Gerald from the Born Again Virgin group, glaring at him with evangelical eyes. Gerald's face was red, burnished to a high sheen with sweat. His mustache dripped where it had been repeatedly dipped in beer. He hitched up his pants and stepped toward the girl as if he were going to knock her lights out.

"You bothering this man?" he growled.

Jack stepped in front of her. "Whoa, wait, it's okay."

Gerald glared at her over Jack's shoulder. "They don't give up, do they? Always at ya. Always tempting ya. But you just gotta know how to say no."

Jack put up his hands. "Hey, I'm not in that program anymore."

Gerald softened. "Look, we've all had those nights. I know where you're at. But you gotta stay firm . . ."

"No, really . . ."

Gerald suddenly grabbed Jack and enveloped him into a bear hug. "I am here for you, buddy. You can make it!"

Jack shook him off. "Get away from us."

Gerald raised his hands in placation. "Hey, I'm not here to give you a hard time, but you gotta have strength, man. She is not the solution. She is the problem."

Gerald lunged for the girl. She stumbled back with a cry and scurried away. Gerald bellowed after her "Begone, you hussy. Begone." Jack closed his eyes wearily.

Gerald returned to Jack, rubbing his hands. "What do you say, bud, no hard feelings? Why don't we go to Jerry's for a coupla subs?"

Jack glanced over to the girl. She had alerted a friend—a large, beefy, scowling friend, who was wrenching himself from his chair and heading Jack's way.

Jack made for the door. Gerald raised his hands in the air as he followed him. "Born again, man. Born again. Woowoo" he shouted as he bounded out.

Outside, Jack made a break for it, peeling out of the parking lot, leaving Gerald still looking for his car. As he barreled toward the highway, he fumbled with his cell phone. He should have thought of it sooner. Clean, professional, discreet. Tonight he was going to get back into the saddle, even if he had to pay for it. By the time he got to his front door, the girl was waiting. White-blond, dressed in a trim black leather dress and holding a black leather briefcase. She looked like a bondage executive.

"Candi?"

"That's me." She licked her lips.

"Let's go." Jack unlocked his door.

"Do you mind if my boyfriend waits outside? We want to go to dinner later." Jack peered behind him. A fat frat boy leaned against Jack's gate.

"Knock yourself out."

He grabbed Candi's hand and pulled her inside. She stood in the hallway, her hand on her hip. "So where do you want me?"

"Bedroom."

"Great. God, I am so sick of kitchen counters." She walked up the stairs, her impressive derriere swinging back and forth in its cage of leather.

"Nice house," she said.

Jack didn't answer, all brain cells intent on getting her peeled out of her dress as quickly and as efficiently as possible. In the bedroom, she placed her briefcase on the desk and clicked it open. She pulled out a small basket and placed a selection of condoms in it. She shrugged off her jacket and draped it carefully over the back of a chair, then stepped onto the bed and reached up and slid her dress over her head. Jack found himself eye to eye with an impressive set of knockers. She smiled. "Nice, huh?"

It all came back, the ache, the need, the urgent need. He stepped forward and reached out. What bliss, what a handful. He dived into her skin as if it were the warm aquamarine waters of the Caribbean. No beginning, no end. Nirvana. Still, he was a bit rusty, moving slowly, fumbling through this foreign terrain, trying to remember where he'd left everything. He must have been doing something right, though, because his ears soon filled with her ear-splitting expressions of desire. He took aim. But then hesitated. He stared down at her. So this was what all that waiting and dreaming had come down to. An efficient business exchange. He examined the merchandise: unlined skin, eyes screwed tight, gaping mouth. He noticed a slight scar under her chin and touched it softly. Candi opened her eyes, startled.

And then he heard her.

"He's a friend of mine. Will you stop grabbing me? Let go!"

It was Molly, downstairs at the door, arguing with the boyfriend. Jack put up his finger. "I'll be right back." He drew on his shorts and tore down the stairs to find Molly pushing her way in, the boyfriend behind her.

"It's okay," Jack said. "Let her through."

The boyfriend shook his head and walked out.

"Oh, Jack." Molly put her hand to her chest. She was breathing heavily, as if she had run all the way from her house. Her hair was its usual crazy self, zinging from her head. Her eyes shone like topaz. Her belly, weighty with wonder, pressed sensually against her jeans. She was life itself, capable of creating even more new life. And she, he remembered glumly, would never be his.

She rushed up to him and kissed him—fully, completely; he

floated on a cloud, the way she kissed. She pulled back and gazed deep into his eyes.

"Oh, Jack," she said again.

He continued to regard her stone-faced, knowing that she would never love him the way he loved her.

"What do you want, Molly?"

"I'm not marrying Richard."

His heart did an involuntary flip. But he stepped back and crossed his arms. What a blank canvas he must be. What an open window his broken heart must be. His face didn't move a muscle.

"Why tell me?"

"Well . . . I thought you'd be interested. You said . . ."

Jack measured his words carefully. "Of course, I'm interested. I consider you a friend and so I'm concerned for your welfare. Frankly, I didn't see Richard as your type. Which is funny, because your type is so varied. But as your friend, I want you to know you have my support. Whomever you choose."

She stood staring at him as if not quite computing what was coming out of his mouth. Jack took cold comfort in the fact that he was completely baffling her. He watched as the rejection finally washed over her. But instead of moving toward the door, she took his hands in hers.

"I love you, Jack. You are my hero. You always have been. Because you stand up for what you believe in. Don't change that. Believe in love. It takes courage."

Jack was speechless. She reached up and stroked his forehead. "You have kept your honor. You haven't let them take it away. Cheapen it. Or sell it. You say to the world, My heart is worth something. So I say yes, Jack. Yes. I will. Yes."

His heart stopped beating. Time stood still as his lips found hers and he clung to them. He crushed her to him. "You are so good," she murmured in his ear, "so principled, so . . ."

"Hey Jack, the clock's ticking!" Candi called from upstairs.

Jack blanched. Molly stepped away and looked around. "Are you with someone?"

"No!" Jack reached for her.

"Use it or lose it, Jack!" Candi cried.

Jack paused. "It all depends how you define 'someone.'"

Molly pushed his arms away and rushed out the door.

Outside, the air was still, the sky gunmetal gray. Jack lurched out the gate. The short palm trees that lined the footpath loomed over him like giant insects. He headed in the direction of the water, certain Molly would have taken that way back.

As he stepped out onto the sand, he saw her. She was standing by the edge gazing out to sea. He raced toward her. The water, blue black, billowed in big round mounds. The birds were calling madly. The waves beat like slow drums on the sand.

When he reached her side, she looked up, her eyes bright. She nodded and returned her attention to the sea. That was the great thing about Molly, he thought as he stepped up to her: she never had to have the obvious explained.

She reached up and pulled off her shirt and shimmied out of her shorts. She stretched luxuriously, sliding her hands around her body as if rubbing herself down with cold clean air. Jack stripped quickly and held out his hand. She took it like a princess and they walked toward the sea. The churning, vital sea. What better place to begin their lifelong union?

As they stepped in, they let out yells and gritted their chattering teeth. They sprang forward, tripping on the waves and collapsing with belly flops into the freezing water. Molly sprang up and jumped up and down screaming with delight and hypothermia. Jack stood immobile, the heat in his loins chilling to ice water, his gonads shrinking to the size of hazelnuts.

He reached forward and grabbed Molly by the shoulders. Their lips touched and sparked a flame that crackled and shot through their bodies. They clung to each other, breathless. Jack whispered things into her ear, things a child would say, simple, naïve, probably cringe-making, but he couldn't stop himself. It flowed from him, this love. He fingered the curled tendrils of hair stuck to her cheek. His heart swelled. Jack felt nothing now but the feel of her smooth wet skin, the perfect molding of her buttocks. The taste of her neck turned the glacial sea into a tropical paradise. He kissed his way around her sturdy body. She was Aphrodite, born of the sea. Steam rose from their bodies.

The moment had come. Finally, the moment he'd been living and sacrificing for all these years.

"Ready?" he whispered.

As she nodded her assent, he raised her body around his, weeping with the beauty of it.

Suddenly lights flashed up all around them. A megaphone called out. "Step away from that woman, your hands above your head."

Together they blinked into a glare of lights. The silhouette of a cop walked into their line of vision. Jack recognized the policeman from the Venice Beach station.

"Sergeant?" he said, trying to shield Molly from his stare.

"Come out and put your clothes on," ordered the cop, stepping back from the edge of the water to make sure his boots didn't get wet.

Jack carried Molly out of the sea and placed her gently back on the sand.

"I'm going to have to arrest you for indecent exposure," said the sergeant. "And for the illegal act of fornication in a public place."

"But we hadn't gotten there yet," Jack said.

"It was your intent."

The sergeant clicked handcuffs around Jack's wrists and led him to the police car, its blue and red lights circling the boardwalk like a lighthouse beacon. His partner escorted Molly to the other side of the car and folded her into the back next to Jack.

"Oh, Jack," Molly said, looking up at him, her eyes shining with love. He tipped her chin up with his finger and kissed her deeply. It's not easy being a virgin, Jack thought as they were driven off to be booked and fingerprinted, but then some women are worth the wait.

ACKNOWLEDGMENTS

My sincere thanks to Laurence Carter, Roger Sanderson, Leigh Greenwood, Karen Sayed, Katherine Greyle, Melissa MacNeal, Rod Casteel, and Anna Sugden for their insights into the world of romance writing; to my sister, Mandy Davis, my agent, Isobel Dixon, my writers' group, and my dear friends in Crouch End for their unwavering encouragement; to Colin Dickerman for his superb editing; and above all, to Andrew, Lara, and Ben for their love and laughter.

A NOTE ON THE TYPE

The text of this book is set in Bembo. This type was first used in 1495 by the Venetian printer Aldus Manutius for Cardinal Bembo's *De Aetna*, and was cut for Manutius by Francesco Griffo. It was one of the types used by Claude Garamond (1480–1561) as a model for his Romain de L'Université, and so it was the forerunner of what became standard European type for the following two centuries. Its modern form follows the original types and was designed for Monotype in 1929.